Chapter One

It began, as so many stories do nowadays, with a duke.

Alex, Duke of Harcastle, managed to keep his face blank despite the stale air, redolent of old cigar smoke and unwashed bodies, in the cramped upstairs room in the Nimble Rabbit. This lowly, rather dirty establishment was not among his usual haunts, but the opportunity to see Miss Evangeline Jones, spiritualist and medium, in the flesh was too tempting. This might not be the setting he'd envisioned for their first meeting, but the woman herself did not disappoint.

To her credit, his unexpected appearance at tonight's séance provoked no visible reaction. If she was angry with Mr. and Mrs. Lennox, her clients, for inviting him without her knowledge or consent, he detected no sign in her demeanor. Her hands remained steady as she positioned a pile of slates in the center of the small circular table around which they sat. Over the last ten years, he'd personally exposed countless spiritualist scams. Either the girl was ignorant of his fearsome reputation as an exposer of frauds, or she had nerves of steel. He wasn't sure which would prove more interesting.

The Lennoxes kept up a steady stream of chatter, perhaps uncomfortable with the silence that would otherwise reign. Fervent believers, they swore tonight would cure him of his famous skepticism. They were acquaintances from the Spiritualists Association but the sort who thought themselves his intimates. In truth, Alex had no intimates outside of his immediate family. His rank daunted most people; his reserve excluded the rest.

Outside of the occasional "yes" or "no" for the sake of politeness, he kept his attention fixed on Miss Jones and her precise movements as she rose from her seat and crossed the meager space to close the threadbare curtains. Tonight was the first time they'd met, though it was *not* the first time he'd seen her. He possessed two photographs of her, though she didn't greatly resemble either one.

The first image he'd obtained was the official cabinet card currently in circulation among respectable society. This showed a plain, thin-lipped woman of indeterminate age, dark hair drawn back severely just as she wore it tonight. For all he knew, the simple black gown she wore in the picture might be the very one she had on now. Despite these surface similarities, the real woman looked younger, smaller, and if not precisely pretty, intriguing to look upon. Her too pale skin, shining black hair, and dark brown eyes drew his gaze, while her prim neatness brought to mind religious icons with their inviolate but exquisite female saints.

As for the second, much rarer photograph...

Alex resisted the urge to reach for the inside pocket of his coat where he kept the crumpled picture. The keeper of the small print shop in Holywell Street claimed the image was one of a kind, and Alex had paid an embarrassingly large sum for the privilege of ownership. He'd reasoned it might be

the Ruin of
EVANGELINE JONES

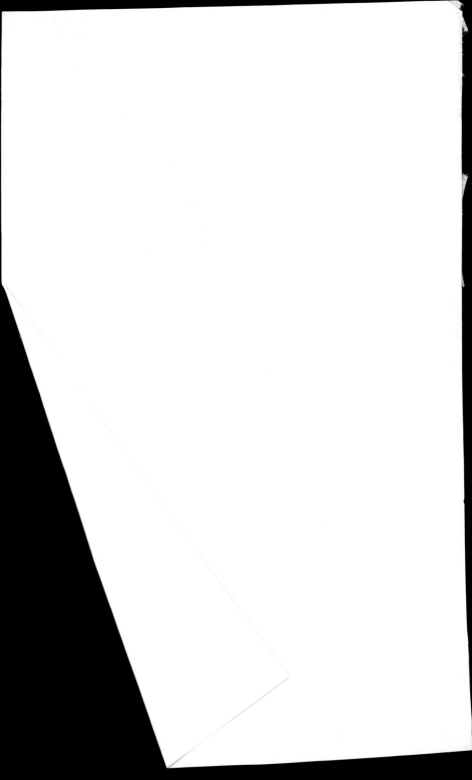

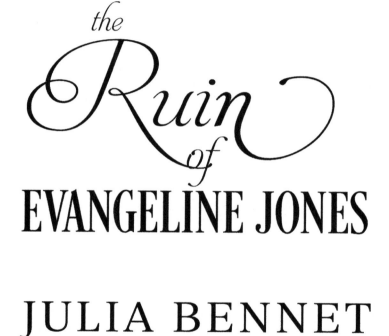

the
Ruin
of
EVANGELINE JONES

JULIA BENNET

Entangled Publishing, LLC
2614 South Timberline Road
Suite 105, PMB 159
Fort Collins, CO 80525
rights@entangledpublishing.com

Amara is an imprint of Entangled Publishing, LLC.

Edited by Alethea Spiridon
Cover design by Mayhem Cover Creations
Cover photography by The Killion Group Images
bastan/DepositPhotos

Manufactured in the United States of America

First Edition April 2020

To Sam and Oliver, the best children in the entire world and I'm not even biased.

useful if he decided to go ahead with his investigation of this new medium, but the truth was he'd *wanted* the thing with a hunger he didn't like to recall.

Why he kept it with him at all times, he didn't know. All he need do was close his eyes and he saw the image in perfect detail: Wispy tendrils of black hair framed the subject's face. Not artless but someone's deliberate attempt to make her look as though she'd recently engaged in frenetic amorous activity—a stark contrast to Miss Jones's sleek perfection this evening. Lips made full and soft-looking with the aid of cosmetics smiled invitingly, as though he might graze the photo with a fingertip and feel the warmth of her mouth. Wearing nothing but her undergarments, she sat astride a simple wooden chair, the front of her combination gaping open to reveal the slopes of small, pert breasts, and most tantalizing of all, dark nipples peeping from behind linen and lace.

Such a provocative image.

But what fascinated him most about the woman in the picture, whether her name was Evangeline Jones or "Sally Harper" as the legend printed across the bottom claimed, was her expression. Despite her soft, almost dreamy half smile, her stare pinned one to the spot. Hers were the sort of eyes one might see glaring over the barrel of a loaded pistol.

Those same eyes flashed his way now, filled with the familiar icy contempt.

Alex met the look with a determined unconcern, but he noted with almost scientific detachment the rush of blood to his groin. A natural enough reaction, he reasoned, owing to his recent, vivid recall of the Sally Harper photograph. He'd learned to associate those cruel eyes with partially unveiled breasts. Or perhaps he was simply depraved.

Either way, it was inconvenient; he needed his wits about him.

Mr. Lennox cleared his throat. "Miss Jones, how should we begin?"

"First," she replied, her speech curiously accentless, "if someone would please dim the lights."

Lennox did so. The request didn't surprise anyone. They all knew spirits preferred dim lighting and tended to be more active in the dark. Soon, the already poorly lit room was black except for the flickering orange glow of the fire, and the steadier yellowish light of a paraffin lamp turned down low and placed with the slates near the table's center. Alex noted with interest the slates were not to start off hidden in gloom as at most séances.

"Thank you." Though her lips were thin, her twist of a smile gave her an engaging, almost cheeky air at odds with her otherwise solemn demeanor. "Now we must form the circle."

Clearly, this was no one's first time. Without hesitation, the four of them joined hands, palms flat on the table, little fingers touching. Alex made sure *both* of Miss Jones's hands were visible on the surface. He'd once witnessed a medium fool those on either side of her into touching *each other's* hands, thereby freeing her own for table-rapping and the like.

In a light, slightly off-key soprano, Miss Jones began to sing. "*Abide with me/fast falls the eventide…*"

The Lennoxes joined in immediately. With a sinking heart, Alex knew he'd have to do likewise or Miss Jones might claim he'd offended the spirits with his lack of piety. Religion meant little to him but her charlatan's hypocrisy set his teeth on edge. Throughout the eight verses of the hymn, he watched Miss Jones's hands, which remained on the table. No telltale movements swapping her hand for a false one.

Vigilance at this stage could stall a séance entirely. An attentive gaze played havoc with the spirits. More often than not, if he managed to arrange things so that he sat next to the medium instead of across from her as he did now, the entire evening would pass without a single instance of paranormal activity. He'd always found it extremely telling that communication with the other side depended so greatly on the free movement of a medium's hands and feet.

No wonder he'd grown cynical.

"Such a beautiful hymn," Mrs. Lennox said, once their warbling had drawn to a merciful close. "I do hope the spirits are talkative this evening."

"Is there anyone in particular you wish to contact?" Miss Jones asked.

"Our grandson Bertie," came the naive response.

If Miss Jones had done her research as Alex had, she'd know that grandson Bertie had died of influenza several years before. Even if she hadn't studied her mark prior to this evening's meeting, poor Mrs. Lennox's candor had made Miss Jones's work a damn sight easier.

"I'll see what I can do. Let's bow our heads in prayer."

The Lennoxes obeyed but Alex *never* closed his eyes during a séance. This simple act of rebellion had undone many a fraudster over the years. Long minutes passed during which Miss Jones never once raised her head. A coal shifted in the fire. Outside, carriage wheels splashed through a puddle. Somewhere downstairs, the inn's patrons sang a rowdy rendition of "The Boy I Love Is Up in the Gallery." Otherwise, silence.

At last Miss Jones opened her eyes. "Jack is here."

Excited murmuring from the Lennoxes broke the near silence. Jack was Miss Jones's infamous spirit guide—her invisible conduit to the other side. His job was to act as intermediary between his medium and the other spirits. A sort of ghostly messenger boy.

"Can he bring Bertie to us?" Mrs. Lennox asked.

The sound of her voice, trembling with excitement, made

Alex want to smash something. The hope on her face was like a knife to his gut. Sad, silly woman. Had he ever been this credulous, even as a child? Had he ever been this good? For Mrs. Lennox was the sort of person who would never dream of doing harm, and so couldn't conceive of such behavior in others.

Miss Jones tilted her head to the left, as if cocking her ear toward a voice. She pantomimed listening for several seconds, then smiled at Mrs. Lennox in a way that seemed almost kind. "I'm sorry, Mrs. Lennox, but Jack says Bertie can't come."

"Oh." That one tremulous syllable encapsulated an ocean of disappointment. "Perhaps another time then."

"No, Mrs. Lennox, you misunderstand." Miss Jones's look was still kind or what passed for it. "Bertie can't come today or any day, but Jack says you mustn't worry. Bertie no longer dwells in the in-between place. He's moved on. He's at peace."

"Peace?" Sudden hope lit Mrs. Lennox's wizened face.

"Yes. Isn't it wonderful?" Miss Jones's face shone, a deliberate mirror for the older woman. She glowed with an almost religious zeal. "Bertie is with God now."

Ah, now *that* Alex hadn't expected.

How was a medium supposed to keep clients on the hook if she told them their dearly departed couldn't at least visit the—what had she called it?—in-between place? Either she played a long game or she had a conscience. Years of experience led him to expect the former. The apparent kindness only deepened his suspicion.

Mrs. Lennox broke the circle as she hurled herself into her husband's arms, sobbing out her relief against his chest. Miss Jones looked at Alex. *Nothing to say?* her gaze demanded.

He forced his lips into a faint smile and shook his head.

Even if he were wrong, even if Miss Jones had been trying

to do the Lennoxes a kindness by telling them a beautiful lie… Beautiful lies were still lies. When he exposed her for the fraud she was, the small comfort she'd given this grieving couple would die along with her reputation. And perhaps that was the true reason she'd done it. She'd neatly arranged things so that he would be complicit in their pain. For that alone, he could hate this woman.

"Oh, but what about His Grace?" Mr. Lennox said. "Surely the spirits have something to say to him?" To Alex, he added, "Didn't I tell you Miss Jones was the real thing, sir?"

Miss Jones lifted her eyebrows. "Shall we try for it, Your Grace?"

It was the first time she'd addressed him directly. He still couldn't place her accent—the result of elocution lessons perhaps?—but she pitched her voice low. The effect was provocative as befitted the woman in the lewd photograph. His body responded predictably but he ignored it.

"By all means," he said.

Once again, they formed the circle. At first, the spirits proved less accommodating. Owing to his skepticism, he supposed. Ten long minutes passed in silent prayer. Then, when Alex was moments away from calling a halt to her nonsense, Miss Jones's head jerked up and her gaze locked with his.

"Boy," she growled, and her voice sounded different. Deeper. Colder.

The back of his neck prickled when he saw the ice in her expression. This look made her disdainful stare at the beginning of the evening look like a lover's simper. He hadn't been the recipient of animosity like this since—

"Boy," she said again.

His stomach turned over as it always had when he was a child.

He took a deep breath. Just a trick, that's all. Calm down. It's all right.

As abruptly as she'd spoken, her head dropped forward until her forehead thudded on the tabletop. The "spirit" had departed.

"Oh my heavens!" Mrs. Lennox squealed.

No matter what, he would not break the circle. He would see this thing through and then he would figure out how she'd done this. He stared at the medium's bowed head. The center-parting stood out straight and perfect, as if she'd used a ruler and protractor on it. This tiny sparrow of a woman had turned him inside out with a single word. How? How had she done it? How had she known exactly what to say and how to say it? And how, *how*, had she dared?

A moment later, she sat upright and smiled at everyone as if nothing had happened. "Oh dear," she said. "Only one word and nothing to indicate who said it. Do you have any insight to offer, sir?"

Alex shook his head, allowing every ounce of his displeasure to show in his expression. He'd be damned if he'd sit here and pretend she hadn't executed a very low blow.

"No?" She shrugged, unconcerned. "What a shame. Perhaps we'll do better if we use the slate. What say you, sir?"

He glared at her. "Do your worst, Miss Jones."

Mrs. Lennox murmured something low and distressed to her husband, but Alex didn't catch the words, his focus narrowed on his opponent. Miss Jones returned his regard, her face devoid of emotion.

"Choose a slate," she said, in the same tone she might have said, "Choose your weapon."

He withdrew a leather-wrapped bundle from his coat. "I have one of my own. Would you mind?"

"I wouldn't mind at all." When she smiled, she exposed a row of neat, white teeth. Fangs wouldn't have surprised him. Not tonight and not on her. He didn't believe in spirits. Otherwise, he might be tempted to say this woman had the devil in her.

He withdrew the clean slate, its back discreetly marked, from its cover and handed it to Miss Jones. After a cursory examination, she placed it on the floor at her feet. If she made a switch for one concealed beneath her skirts, he'd know.

"Let's pray," she said again.

After ten minutes of silence, during which she remained motionless as far as he could tell with the table between them, she checked the slate. "Nothing, I'm afraid. Why don't we try singing? The spirits love to hear our voices raised in joyful praise."

The religious cant disgusted him. What would she do if he cast the Sally Harper photograph onto the table? The Lennoxes might not even recognize her as the same woman, but Alex knew. Those infernal eyes... Not for one moment did he believe she'd had a religious epiphany since that photo was taken. Her perfidy tonight argued against it. The spirits didn't talk to her. They didn't talk to anyone.

"The host of God!" the others sang. *"They come to us/on heavenly mission bound..."*

This time, he didn't join them. She wouldn't use his non-participation as an excuse for the simple reason that she clearly enjoyed taunting him. Though the slate remained obstinately blank despite the singing, he didn't doubt the spirits would act soon. The delay only served to heighten the suspense as Miss Jones was well aware.

"Perhaps we haven't prayed enough," Mr. Lennox suggested.

Alex used the opportunity their bowed heads provided to look beneath the table, but he couldn't see a thing in the gloom. Endless minutes passed in prayerful silence. He watched Miss Jones's hands, still linked at the fingertips to

Mrs. Lennox on her left and Mr. Lennox on her right.

"There! Do you hear it?" Mrs. Lennox cried.

Alex listened. Faint but unmistakable, he heard the scratch of chalk against slate from beneath the table.

"Shall we look again?" Miss Jones said when the writing sound ceased.

"Oh yes, please do." Mrs. Lennox bounced in her seat.

Miss Jones retrieved the slate and slid it across the table toward Alex. "Why don't you do the honors, sir?"

Even in the weak light afforded by the lamp, a single glance informed him that this was still his slate. The mark was plain to see if you knew where to look. He swallowed. She was a fraud, of that he felt sure, but she was also clever and well-prepared. He dreaded to see what she'd written.

"Don't be afraid," she told him. "The circle is a safe place. Nothing the spirits reveal will leave this room."

Damn you for being a mind reader, Miss Jones.

He reached out and flipped the slate onto its back. In an untidy scrawl, the spirits had written a single phrase:

Boy, stop wasting time.

Bile rose in Alex's throat. He stood, overturning his chair.

"Your Grace?" Miss Jones rose too, her eyes wide with shock.

He couldn't deal with her duplicity now. "Excuse me," he said, and all but fled.

He left the door gaping behind him and shoved his way downstairs and through the crowded taproom. The smoke, the stench of ale, and the din of slurred voices raised in conversation and, in parts of the room, song, were all unbearable. No one got in his way and finally he erupted onto the dark and dirty Soho street. One deep breath and the city smells of coal smoke and rubbish assailed him. He gulped the fetid air greedily as he waited for his heart to cease racing. It pounded so hard inside his chest that he half expected to see his shirtfront jump with each pulse.

Christ, he'd forgotten what terror felt like.

As the fear faded, he doubled over laughing. Not because there was anything remotely funny about the situation. God, no. He laughed with relief; his father was still dead and Miss Jones was still a fraud. A better class of fraud than he'd grown used to perhaps. For now at least, she'd got the better of him.

With the thought, his mirth subsided as quickly as it had begun.

No one had witnessed his outburst except a lone drunkard standing under a streetlamp. The man swayed on his feet and went on smoking his cigarette. If he registered Alex's presence at all through his obvious alcoholic daze, he saw nothing and no one. A fellow drunk. A swell out slumming. The theater around the corner wouldn't disgorge its audience for at least another hour. As for the only witnesses to what had occurred in that little room, the Lennoxes were good people who would never dream of repeating what they'd seen. They were irrelevant.

Only Miss Jones mattered.

Her dirty tactics had won the preliminary round, but he wouldn't underestimate her again. The thrill of the chase had grown stale after so many years but this one would be different from the others. Miss Jones was different. And when all this was over, he was going to crush her for tonight's work.

Alex straightened his coat and turned in the direction of home.

Chapter Two

A moment after she'd closed the door on Mr. and Mrs. Lennox, Evie leaned against the scuffed oak panels and sighed wearily. Séances always exhausted her and this one had been the most challenging yet.

She couldn't stop thinking about the look Harcastle had given her in that final moment, as if he wanted to overturn the table and grab her by the throat. If that had been all, she could have shrugged it off—she'd endured violence at male hands before—but she'd seen something else too. A vulnerability that had stolen her breath. Her lucky guess, calling him "boy" in that gruff, raspy voice, didn't seem lucky anymore. His reaction told her she'd stumbled into highly sensitive territory—territory he would guard with all the fierceness of which he was capable.

Put on a nice, safe show, she'd thought. No pyrotechnics. Nothing that can give the game away. Get him in, get him out, and refuse any further sittings. One did not poke a sleeping beast.

So much for that.

It sickened her to remember that momentary glimpse of naked anguish before she'd seen murder in his eyes. Now he had her in his sights, and she was terrified. So terrified that she jumped a clear foot when someone knocked at the door on which she was still leaning.

"Yes?" she called, her voice little more than a croak.

"It's me," came the muffled response.

Jack! Thank heavens. If Harcastle had returned, she didn't know what she'd have done. Barricaded herself in, probably.

Jack leaned against the doorjamb, his head cocked to look up at her as she opened the door. He'd never told her his true age but she guessed he was much older than his diminutive height suggested. Beneath his shock of red hair, slanted blue eyes gazed at her steadily. Her so-called spirit guide might be more corporeal than her clients would like, but he still unnerved her at times with his little boy face and ancient stare.

"Well?" he said.

"Hello to you, too."

His plump Cupid's bow lips curled into a wry smile. "My apologies, ma'am," he said, with a low bow. His overdone courtesy reminded her of Captain, their common benefactor. Jack idolized him.

She curtseyed and beckoned him in.

"You must have heard the uproar," she said, once she'd closed the door behind them. The Lennoxes had been extremely distressed.

"'Course," he said, his eyes lighting on the still overturned chair. "But I couldn't tell what it was about. Was the row because I sent the right message or the wrong one?"

"Right, so far as it goes. Perhaps a little too effective. You took your time, though. I thought we'd have to sing those bloody hymns forever."

Jack winced. "And no one wants that. You're a rotten

singer, Evie."

She swatted at him but he ducked away, laughing.

"Anyway, I had to fetch Captain," he explained. "'Boy' ain't much to go on, is it? I didn't know what to write. Then Captain had to find paper because I didn't know 'ow to spell 'wasting.' It'd look a bit rum if the old duke forgot how to spell since he died, wouldn't it?"

"All right, all right. Don't nag." But they were both smiling. "Is he still here?"

"Who, Captain? Yeah. He's waiting to walk you 'ome."

"I should think so."

At this time of night, the denizens of Soho tended to get rowdy and, these days, she had a reputation to protect. Evangeline Jones wasn't her real name but it would do as well as any. Miss Jones didn't stand for wandering hands. She sang hymns, said her prayers, and kept her ankles decently covered. The prissy, touch-me-not air suited her fine. If she sacrificed any warmth or pleasure as a result, she also escaped a world of pain. She'd seen enough of men and women together to realize that heartbreak, degradation, and penury were the most common outcomes of love and lust.

Still, she felt the usual twist in her gut whenever she had to spend time alone with Captain. Or time with him in any capacity, really. There'd been a time when she'd felt absolutely safe with him, but now… Now she knew what lived beneath the jolly, hail-fellow-well-met exterior.

"Mind you don't leave anything behind when you clear up," she said, gathering her outdoor things. If the duke didn't return in the next day or two to examine the room, she'd dance naked at her next séance.

"Do I ever?" he asked, without looking up from his work of rolling back the carpet.

She left the room and went downstairs to the taproom.

Despite the crush, she spotted Captain easily, seated at

the best table as usual. He liked to splash his money around as ostentatiously as possible. *How else*, he always said, *will people know to respect me?* She used to wonder why no one took advantage of him when he was so friendly and generous. But that was before she saw firsthand how vicious he could be. Even with that deceptive twinkle in his eye, no one dared ask precisely what he was Captain of and he never volunteered the information.

Evie knew more about him than most. She knew he'd trodden the boards and, prior to that, had traveled with a circus, but who or what he'd been before remained a mystery.

He rose when she approached, his gaze warming. Despite everything, a small part of her softened in response.

"There you are, my dear." He inclined his head in greeting.

As always, he was immaculate, his suit made of good-quality wool in dark green, his moustache waxed to a flawless handlebar. Last month it had been an imperial. He liked to experiment with different styles; the showier the better. Personally, she preferred Harcastle's simple, close-cut beard. She didn't know Captain's age. He might have been anything between thirty-five and fifty. But he was handsome. Women, young and old, flirted with him wherever he went.

Unlike Jack's cordial yet overdone courtesy, when Captain bowed over her hand, he did so with every appearance of sincerity. Though they were not related, he had never once tried to take liberties. Without him, she'd probably be dead.

"Well?" he said. "How did it go?"

"I think the Lennoxes were pleased."

He raised his brows. "You know that's not what I mean, but now that you mention it, they're not likely to be good for much after what Jack told me."

She returned his gaze without flinching and waited for him to continue.

"'*Found peace?*'" he said, a note of exasperation creeping in. "I ask you, is that any way to do business?"

This wasn't the first time they'd had this argument. Evie reasoned that people who fell for cheap tricks had problems bigger than the loss of the pittance they paid her. Besides, her punters enjoyed the show. She entertained them, like a magician, and she was perfectly willing to levitate tables, rap out yes and no to their questions, and scratch nonsense on slates. But she drew the line when it came to bilking the bereaved long-term. When people like the Lennoxes came to her, she'd do what she had to do, lie as much as needed, to keep her reputation intact. But she refused to keep them on the line indefinitely so that Captain could milk them for every penny.

To Captain, her scruples were a useless sop to her conscience, but he let her have her way. She suspected he had his own reasons for doing so. One day, he would want something in return. Her victories over Captain were never permanent. His generosity always had a cost.

He offered his arm. "Are you ready to leave?"

She nodded and allowed him to guide her through the noisy patrons and out into the night. The theater crowd would be out soon, so she was glad of the escort. A woman alone was considered fair game.

Together they made the walk to Brewer Street in silence. Evie hadn't noticed how suffocating the loud, smoky, ale-drenched inn had been. The cool breeze soothed her tired eyes. *Blowing the cobwebs away*, her roommate would call it.

"What about Harcastle?" Captain asked. "Did Jack get the message right?"

"Yes. Thank you for helping him." Though, with the force of the duke's displeasure focused on her as the figurehead of their joint enterprise, she didn't feel particularly grateful.

Perhaps some of that ingratitude showed in her tone because Captain lowered his voice. "Harcastle flew out of the

Nimble Rabbit like a rat with a terrier on his tail. How did you know what note to strike?"

Even his obvious admiration failed to cheer her. "We knew the father's reputation. When the son walked in tonight, he looked so..." She struggled for a way to describe it in a manner Captain would understand. Harcastle had walked in, tall and broad-shouldered, dressed in black from head to toe and, for a second, she'd thought him handsome, even beautiful, with his chiseled features. Then she'd seen his cold, dead eyes—shark eyes—and shivered. Yes, he was handsome, but as hard and joyless as granite.

Captain waited.

"He looks like he doesn't know how to be happy. I couldn't imagine that he and his father had an easy relationship. A man like the late duke couldn't have that with anyone and Harcastle seems cast from the same mold."

"Well done, girl."

She shook her head. Captain saw tonight as a triumph rather than the mistake it truly was. Harcastle would be back. If she began to doubt that, she only had to recall his parting look. Retribution, that's what that look had promised. Yes, she had avoided exposure for the length of a single sitting with Harcastle, a distinction few, if any, other mediums could claim, but she wouldn't risk a second meeting, assuming she had a choice.

She glanced at Captain's profile in the glow of the streetlamps. To say he'd been pleased by the duke's interest in tonight's proceedings was a ridiculous understatement. He saw attracting his notice as the pinnacle of their achievements to date. Aristocratic patronage, though obviously not from Harcastle himself, would almost certainly follow. From that point of view, this was a coup, but they were in danger as long as Captain failed to comprehend the magnitude of the threat the duke posed.

"So that's it now, right?" she said. "We've got through tonight unscathed, but we need to keep clear of Harcastle. Now is as good a time as any to try the continent, at least for a few months."

Captain was already shaking his head before she was halfway through speaking. "What, turn tail like cowards when we've got him on the run? No fear!" His jovial tone didn't fool her. If she wanted to flee, she'd have a fight on her hands. "Onward and upward," he said, in the same hearty tone. "We must capitalize on tonight's success."

"I don't…"

Shame made her dig her hands into her pockets and stare at the ground. Even now, after everything that had happened, she hated to refuse Captain anything. She knew him now for the stone-cold villain he was, but he was still the man who had fed and clothed her for years, the man who taught her to read and to speak properly, who'd taught her every trick she knew. It was his contacts and capital that had launched this enterprise. Even though she knew he'd done none of it for her, that self-interest governed every move he made, she still felt beholden.

"I can't," she gritted out.

He said nothing further as they turned onto Dean Street. Two minutes of uneasy silence later, they reached the little print shop beneath her lodgings. Captain never came up to her room, but now he drew her into the recessed entryway. One of the brass buttons of his coat glinted as it caught the light from a nearby streetlamp.

"Evangeline, look at me."

Instead, she clenched her teeth and focused on that button, on the tiny glimmer of reflected light. Sometimes she hated this life. It had brought her a measure of independence and a strange sort of respectability. In many ways, she was fortunate. But the lies got easier and easier. One day she would look in the mirror and see a stranger, someone hard and empty. Captain had taken her choices from her. Having invested his time and money, he didn't intend to let her go. Not ever. Like it or not, she was his.

"All right," he said, on a sigh. "Close your eyes."

She sighed, too. After years of knowing him, most of his tricks were familiar, this one included. She obeyed anyway because it was easier. Because she was tired. But she had no intention of allowing Captain to change her mind. Perhaps he was right. Perhaps a healthy fear of Harcastle's investigative powers made her a coward. So be it. She'd rather be a coward than a fool.

"Tell me your earliest memory," he said, once her eyes were shut.

"Captain—"

"Do as you're told for once."

"I don't know what you want me to say."

"Think back, that's all. What do you remember from when you were small?"

"I…" The question loomed in her mind, so simple yet somehow unanswerable.

Her time with Captain was vivid, full of warmth and small comforts. Before that, she remembered Miss Rose who'd employed Evie as a drudge at her 'Home of Introduction,' a polite euphemism for a brothel. They'd worked her hard there, but she hadn't minded the fetching and carrying or even cleaning up after the girls and their gentlemen. Miss Rose had taken her in when she was three or four, but before that…

"Do you remember your parents?"

"You know I don't."

"Someone must've taken care of you, though."

"No, there's only me." Other children came and went, but no one whose name she recalled. She hadn't lived anywhere permanent, of that she was sure. All her memories—flashes really—were of cold, dirt, misery, and...

"Hunger," she said, a decisive note creeping into her tone. "I remember I was always hungry." Sometimes with great, gnawing pangs, and sometimes with a dull emptiness that left her literally asleep on her feet, and eventually, too weak to lift a hand.

"What did you do when you were hungry?"

She flinched as his breath brushed her cheek. Lost in the past, she'd almost forgotten him.

"I..." She didn't want to talk about this.

"Go on."

"I begged." Even now, saying the words aloud caused a hot surge of shame. "I..."

"All right. You're all right." Captain's voice had turned soothing. "Now think about that duke. Think about Harcastle. Do you think he's ever known true hunger?"

An image of Harcastle formed in her mind. When he'd risen from the table, he'd overturned his chair, his movements fluid and powerful even in his moment of panic. He'd towered over her, his lips pressed into a grim line, his eyes no longer cold but burning with fury. Whatever his distress in that moment, he reeked of money. It wasn't only the black silk waistcoat or the sparkly gold pocket watch hanging from its chain, but the man himself. His shining black hair, the elegant hands with long pianist's fingers, his strong body, and the way he held his head erect as if he'd never known a moment's shame.

"Think of the pampered life he's led," Captain urged. "Think about his clothes and his carriages, his fine estates, and enormous townhouse, then open your eyes."

She did, and this time she met Captain's gaze squarely.

"Are you, Miss Evangeline Jones, going to let that spoilt dilettante chase you away from your city? From your career and your only defense against starvation?"

"No," she said, and lifted her chin. Fear had given way to a seething resentment. Resentment against Harcastle for being rich, well-fed, and invulnerable. But perhaps even more against Captain who manipulated her so blatantly.

"That's my girl."

"No, I won't run away, but I'm not going to poke a stick into a wasp's nest, either," she snapped, wiping the smile off his face. "We've come this far because we've been careful. We're not going to do anything reckless."

He smiled again and swept her one of his low bows. "It will be exactly as you command."

But she saw the hard glint in his eye.

"You're right about one thing. I've survived things that duke couldn't imagine, so no, I won't leave when my career's about to take off, but if you think I'm one of your pigeons ripe for the plucking, you're losing your touch. We can fool Harcastle for an evening but not a second beyond."

They exchanged a strained good night, and as Evie climbed the rickety stairs to her lodgings, she wondered what price she would have to pay for her defiance.

A light shone from underneath the door. Inside, Mags stood by the double bed, in the middle of pulling her nightgown on over her head. They'd been rooming together for the last year, though Captain had begun to talk about finding Evie somewhere better, more respectable, now that things had started to go so well. Mags, who was an actress at one of the lesser Soho theaters, was no longer a fitting companion for the irreproachable Miss Jones. Evie's resentment against Captain redoubled at the unwelcome thought.

"You're back early," Mags said, tugging the white cotton into place. Physically, she was Evie's opposite, tall and buxom, with a mass of untamable blonde curls. "What's wrong? Your jaw has that militant set."

"Oh, nothing worth worrying over," Evie said, removing

her coat. Having finally got rid of Captain for the evening, she didn't want to think about him, much less discuss him. "Tell me about your night."

"Hall says I can play Olivia."

"Oh, that's wonderful."

Mags had been vying for the role for months. Next to Viola, Olivia was the best part in *Twelfth Night*, but Viola required a boyish figure. Evie would have been perfect had she possessed any talent for acting. What she did every day wasn't acting because Evangeline Jones was real, anything else Evie had ever been long suppressed.

"There's a cost, though. I have to be *kind* to Mr. Chase. At least he's handsome." Mags's tone was matter-of-fact. This wouldn't be the first nor the last time she'd kept company with a gentleman for the sake of a role, nor something she would ever *choose* to do. She wasn't even attracted to men.

She watched Evie's face closely, perhaps trying to detect some hint of disapproval.

Evie shrugged. "You do what you have to do."

You're not alluring enough to make a decent courtesan, Miss Rose had said when Evie was all of seven years old, *but when you're old enough, you'll have to start receiving gentlemen of the poorer sort.* Captain had saved her from all that. When he'd come to Miss Rose's looking for a girl to run scams with, she'd leapt at the chance. Though she didn't have the stomach to sell her body to strangers, especially strangers who sometimes treated the girls roughly, she would never condemn Mags for the choices she made to survive and prosper. It was a man's world and sometimes it proved impossible for a woman to get anywhere unless she was willing to make certain compromises. Evie wished she could give them both a fairer world.

Mags shrugged too and rolled her eyes. "At least I'm honest, even if I *am* a whore."

"I wish I could say the same. Everyone's heard of the honest whore, but there's no such thing as an honest medium."

"No?" Mags teased. "No spirits? No life after death?"

"Oh, I *believe* in life after death," she said, as she began to undress, "but spirits hanging around down here? Even if they did, why would they need me to talk to the living? And why spend their time rapping on tables and blowing invisible bugles?"

Mags sat on her side of the bed and tilted her head to one side, apparently lost in thought. Evie slipped her nightgown on and pulled back the covers. After a long night, she wanted nothing more than to curl up. The evenings were drawing in, and she was glad of Mags's warmth. Strange how she'd got used to the other woman's presence in their bed. Once she would've had to sleep with a knife under the pillow.

Mags turned out the lamp. "Don't worry, Evie. You'll find a way out. Maybe one of your patrons will fall in love with you and make an honest offer."

"Ha!"

"And then you can tell Captain to bugger off."

Evie smiled in the darkness. "I couldn't abandon Captain," she murmured. "I owe him my training, my education—"

"He's had plenty in return for his trouble."

Evie shook her head but remained silent.

"Night, love," Mags said, as she settled on her side.

But the moment Evie closed her eyes, she saw the anger and pain in Harcastle's expression. Whatever she'd said to Captain, she couldn't lie to herself. Things between her and the duke weren't finished. There would be a reckoning; her puny tricks against his power and rank. It wasn't a fair fight. She had no hope of victory.

All she could do now was pray she survived.

Chapter Three

Even six months after his father's death, Alex could sense the old duke's presence everywhere in Harcastle House.

Though grand with its graceful renaissance symmetry, stone facing, and tall windows overlooking the Thames, the sight of the building lurking on the riverbank, a monster lying in wait, always filled him with anxiety.

He was the Duke of Harcastle now, yet his sire's twisted soul lingered in every room, as though the flesh-and-blood man might shamble in at any moment to abuse and terrify.

Alex found the study particularly oppressive. He couldn't bring himself to sit at the immense ducal desk, which was why he was sitting in an armchair by the fire. As to why he had removed his shoe and sock from his right foot, the reason was more complicated.

On the floor by his chair, he'd placed a slate similar to the one he'd taken to last night's séance. With a small piece of chalk clamped between his first and second toe, he scratched at the surface. He'd been practicing for almost an hour. The scrape of the chalk sounded about right, but he couldn't make the words *stop wasting time* small enough to fit on a single line, let alone legible. Of course Evangeline Jones had been practicing her arts for years, so he couldn't expect to duplicate her abilities in a single morning.

"Blast!" he muttered, as the chalk slipped from between his toes. He slumped back in his chair, momentarily defeated.

Without his intending it, his gaze wandered to the small side table to his right, where he'd leaned the Sally Harper photograph upright against a vase. Her rouged nipples peeped enticingly, but what really got to him was her eyes and their piercing gaze.

"Don't give me that look, you saucy minx," he said fondly. Though he hadn't entirely forgiven her for last night's dirty work, a few hours' sleep had placed events in their proper perspective and cooled his temper significantly. His love of the chase had reasserted itself, any desire he'd had for vengeance converted into a sharpening of his determination to strip her lies bare. "I'll find you out soon enough, just you wait."

Sally Harper regarded him coolly. Nothing moved her, would ever move her. No doubt the real woman would watch him with the same detachment if she were here. Last night, she'd met his gaze only when necessary, but she hadn't appeared shy or cowed by his social standing. *I am too great a professional*, her manner said, *to permit the presence of a mere duke to affect my composure.* Whereas her tricks had kept *him* awake for hours before he finally achieved those few hours of rest. In fact, he'd lost far too many nights of sleep to Miss Jones, first to her provoking nipples and then to her even more provoking eyes.

"What are you doing?"

Alex jolted upright in his seat at the sound of Jude Ellis's voice. How long had his cousin been standing in the doorway? The man moved like a pickpocket.

"Research," Alex said, and flipped the photograph facedown on the table.

"I see." Ellis observed him gravely. "I won't ask what sort of research requires one shoe on and one shoe off. Clearly, it's none of my business."

Alex bent to put his sock and shoe back on.

Ellis went to the desk. Under his arm, he carried several sheaves of paper, each tied with string. Alex couldn't remember the last time he'd seen him *without* paperwork of some sort. Despite the fact that, as cousins many times removed, they were distant blood relations, they'd only known each other a few years. The old duke had summoned Ellis from Jamaica to learn about the dukedom. His sire had made clear his hope that Alex would relapse into old habits and drink himself to death, leaving Ellis to inherit everything.

Though he and Ellis had developed a friendship of sorts, there was a reserve to the other man that prevented him developing close ties with anyone. Even with his wife, he was stiff and formal. Alex was grateful for him. The financial mess the old duke had left was beyond his power to disentangle, let alone rectify, on his own.

"Does that bundle of papers you're carrying mean you've unraveled my affairs enough to explain them to me?"

Ellis nodded. "Do you have time to go over some things?"

Alex indicated a chair on the other side of the fire.

The monstrous desk with its green leather surface loomed large in the room. A more imposing piece of furniture he couldn't imagine. A quartet of carved mahogany deities—Apollo, Ares, Hades, and Poseidon—formed its legs. How like his father to choose a desk held up by gods. The servants carefully dusted around everything as if they feared he might return and demand to know why the inkwell had been moved two inches to the left. No doubt the leather chair still bore the imprint of the ducal backside.

Worse even than the desk itself was his father's picture looming on the wall behind. Winterhalter had painted it in the sixties during what turned out to be the famous artist's final visit to London. Despite Winterhalter's romantic, almost wistful style, the duke managed to look nearly as sinister and forbidding as he had in life.

"If it bothers you that much," Ellis said, apparently reading his mind, "throw it all out. Move your own things in. You're the duke now, after all."

Alex wasn't so sure. He hadn't assumed the full mantle yet. The idea of doing so—of finally, irrevocably, becoming Harcastle and all that entailed—made him sick inside. He'd always known he'd rather die than turn into his father.

A shame that he looked so like him.

The portrait had been painted before the duke grew frail. Like Alex, he'd been tall and dark, with an olive complexion. Both men had dark brown eyes, which Alex's half sister Helen had also inherited, and the same ferocious scowl. Looking at the painting was like looking at his doppelgänger.

"Fine." Alex stood and rounded the desk. Gingerly, he lowered himself into the chair but it felt wrong. Like sitting on his father's ghost.

While Ellis busied himself arranging the papers in the right order across the desktop, Alex put on gold-rimmed spectacles. "So," he said, "how bad is it?"

As it turned out, very.

Alex listened to Ellis explain the figures and the knock-on effects of agricultural decline. As the piles of paper began to make sense, one fact fought its way past the morass of information until it eclipsed all else. Alex had always known his father was a cruel, bloody-minded despot, but until this moment he hadn't understood how negligent he'd been. The debt he'd accrued was staggering. And for a man who hadn't gambled, who'd had no public vices, the accumulation of debt looked almost deliberate.

"Your father must have suspected how bad things had got, yet he did nothing," Ellis said, echoing Alex's thoughts.

In the last few years of his life, the duke had been unwell both in body and mind, but the problems were of much longer standing. This neglect had been going on for decades and had slowly escalated. Had he deliberately run the estates into the ground? He'd certainly resented Alex's attempts to learn more about the dukedom, as if he believed his son longed for dead men's shoes.

Eventually, Alex had learned to show less interest, and then none. He didn't remember precisely when he'd ceased to care for the dukedom and the duke himself. He only knew that he had. And, if he were honest, didn't he feel a healthy contempt for both to this day?

"Your personal fortune, everything that was yours before you inherited, is a drop in the ocean," Ellis continued. "In real terms, you're worse off than you were because the estates cost far more to maintain than they bring in."

"I don't suppose you have any bright ideas as to how we might fix things?"

Generations of dukes had gone before Alex. Despite his scorn for the role he must now inhabit, he had no wish to go down in history as the man who lost it all.

"I have three." Ellis took a deep breath. "More or less."

"Frankly, more or less is better than I'd hoped for."

Ellis ignored him. "First, you could sell off some antiques."

Alex felt himself begin to smile. "Like the desk."

"For a start. But it's only a short-term solution. The deficit isn't going anywhere and eventually you'll run out of things to sell. We'd have to be discreet because nothing alerts a creditor to the fact that you're struggling like a sudden selling-off of assets."

"That's something to consider." His poor relationship with his father was widely known, so perhaps if they concentrated on the old duke's furniture, the creditors wouldn't take fright. Selling his dead father's things? At long last, a ducal task Alex was happy to contemplate. "What else?"

"You could marry." Ellis rushed on before Alex could interject. "I've looked into it and there are some eligible ladies. In particular, there are some American girls with enormous fortunes. I'm sure one of them would be honored by an offer from the Duke of Harcastle."

Alex shuddered theatrically. He wasn't a romantic—far from it—but the idea of a marriage on purely mercenary terms chilled him. It was something his father would have done.

"It might not be so bad," Ellis said. "I'm sure many of the heiresses are pretty and even-tempered. As long as you and whoever you choose *like* each other, I'm sure marriage wouldn't be so terrible." He didn't sound certain and, not for the first time, Alex wondered about his relationship with Mrs. Ellis. The old duke had arranged the match shortly after Ellis's arrival in England and thus far the couple had spent most of their married life apart. On the few occasions Alex had seen them together, they'd seemed like acquaintances rather than intimates.

"Not tempting," Alex muttered. "And the third option?"

Ellis shifted in his seat. "Well, that's where the *more or less* part comes in. Your father didn't believe in life insurance, but if we insure you—"

"I think I see where this is going. We insure me, I die, and the duchy is saved, is that right?"

"I admit, the plan has its faults."

For the first time since they'd sat down, Alex felt an urge to laugh. "You cheeky bastard. Still, at least *you* stand to benefit from it."

He had meant the remark as a joke but he immediately regretted it when Ellis's face turned ashen.

"I will never inherit," Ellis said, a muscle ticking at his jaw. "Because you're going to marry and have sons. Lots of them."

If any other man had spoken those words, they might have sounded resentful. When Ellis said them, they sounded like an order. When he'd arrived in England, Alex and another cousin had stood between him and the position of heir apparent. He'd been content with that state of affairs. Then the duke had died and, a few months later, the cousin had been carried off by a bilious attack. The word *appalled* didn't do adequate justice to Ellis's reaction. He was terrified by the idea of inheriting. Alex had learned not to refer to such a possibility. Not even in jest.

He opened his mouth, intending to change the subject, when an idea came like a thunderbolt. "My God, I've got it!"

Ellis blinked. "Really?"

"How can I have been so stupid?" Alex leaped up and lunged for the discarded slate and chalk where they still lay on the floor by the fire. "Do you have any string?"

"What—?"

"String, man, string!" Alex cried, snapping his fingers six times in rapid succession.

"Oh, for the love of..." Ellis tore the string from one of the bundles of paper on the desk, then handed it over.

Alex tied the slate to his left leg. "Hand me another piece."

Ellis grumbled but did as requested.

Alex secured the chalk to his right leg at roughly the same height as the slate. "Now listen."

With tiny, barely perceptible movements of his legs, he rubbed the chalk against the slate.

"It sounds like someone writing," Ellis said, unimpressed.

"Exactly!" In the space of a minute, Alex had gone from frustrated and depressed to exultant. Solving a problem always lifted his spirits.

"Is this about the séance you attended last night?"

Alex barely heard the question. Untying the strings, he let the slate and chalk fall to the floor. "Now all that remains is to ascertain how she got the message onto my slate." He picked up Miss Jones from the end table and tucked her away in his pocket where she belonged. "I'll see you later, Ellis."

"Where are you going?"

Alex kept moving. "The Nimble Rabbit."

"And our discussion?"

"Sell some antiques. Buy us some time. Start with *that* painting," he said, jabbing a finger at the old duke. "I'm sick of him breathing over my shoulder."

Maybe he'd commission a painting of Miss Jones exactly as she looked in the photograph and hang her in the vacant spot. Her glare boring into him from the wall of the study seemed a curiously appealing prospect.

• • •

The Nimble Rabbit appeared even more dilapidated by the light of day.

Mud and hay fouled the yard. Once-cheerful blue paint peeled from rotting window frames. Even the sign, with the eponymous rabbit leaping to avoid the snapping jaws of a sinister fox, had seen better days and creaked alarmingly as Alex passed beneath. The next good wind might well bring the thing crashing down.

Inside, someone pounded the keys of an out-of-tune piano while rough male voices roared out a barely intelligible version of "Where Did You Get That Hat?" Alex strode past the afternoon revelers to where the innkeeper sat by the fire, poring over a heavy-looking ledger. He rose the moment he saw Alex approaching, his eyes wide. A duke turning up once in his humble establishment was shock enough to last him a lifetime. This unlooked-for second visitation rendered him speechless.

"I need to see the room from last night," Alex said.

The man frowned and glanced around to see who might be observing, but Alex had spoken quietly and the clientele had clearly been drinking for some time, despite the hour. No one but the keeper knew who Alex was, so no one much cared what he was doing there.

The man found his tongue. "This…this way, sir."

Upstairs, outside the now-vacant room, Alex impatiently tapped his cane on the floor as the man fumbled with the key. "Does Miss Jones always use the same room when she holds meetings here?"

A quick nod was the only response.

"Often?"

The key turned in the lock with a loud clunk. "At least once a month, sometimes more. No regular date."

The interior appeared larger with the curtains open and daylight struggling through the grimy window.

"What condition was the room left in after the séance?"

"Miss Jones always leaves things the way she found 'em."

And yet something bothered Alex. What was it?

The small, circular table stood in almost the same spot near the fire. Someone had shoved it half a foot to the left, clearing a path to a door which led into a small sleeping chamber. Alex hadn't noticed the opening last night because of a screen that had been positioned in front of it. None of that was what troubled him, but the presence of an adjoining room certainly provided additional opportunities for trickery.

"Was Miss Jones alone up here? No one in *there*, for instance?"

"So far as I know, she was on 'er own. A gentleman waited downstairs and the little lad, 'is servant, cleared up for 'em, same as always, but neither one of 'em was up 'ere when you was."

"What gentleman?"

"I don't know 'is name." There was something about the way the man said the words. They were the truth but not entirely.

"Young, old, fat, thin?"

The innkeeper stroked his whiskers, apparently deep in thought. "About my age or a little older. Forty maybe. Flash suit. Always has lots of cash to splash about. Likes the best table in the taproom."

So Miss Jones had accomplices. He wasn't surprised—most mediums did—but he couldn't help feeling irritated. He enjoyed chasing *her*. Whoever these helpers were, he had no interest in them.

"Were they downstairs the entire time?"

"Well, no, the boy weren't. He made the odd appearance but mostly he was elsewhere."

"Where did he go?"

The man shook his head. "I don't know, sir."

"Is this the only room Miss Jones rented last night?"

"Yes, sir."

When people lied, Alex could usually tell. Liars made too much eye contact or not enough. They fidgeted. Their stories sounded rehearsed. The innkeeper betrayed none of these symptoms. Either he was a virtuoso of deceit, or he was telling the truth.

"Very well. Wait downstairs."

The man bowed and withdrew.

As soon as he was alone, Alex set to work. First, he walked the room, including the tiny bedroom annex, trailing his fingertips over everything, examining every nook and cranny by touch as well as sight. Then, even though it belonged to the inn, he inspected the table in minute detail. Miss Jones was unusual in not insisting on the use of her own furniture. The table was unlikely to be the key to understanding her technique, unless she carried out modifications in every venue in which she performed—a risky proposition if she didn't remove the alterations again afterward. Was that what the boy did when he cleaned up?

When his scrutiny produced no clues, he sat down in her place at the table, identified as such because it was opposite his where there had been a small *Y*-shaped chip in the surface.

"How did you do it?" he asked her.

He didn't normally talk to the mediums he investigated when they weren't even in the room but it was becoming something of a habit with Miss Jones. The photograph in his pocket created a strange sense of intimacy. He *knew* her. He'd seen a glimpse of Miss Evangeline Jones no one else had seen.

Except for the photographer.

And the print seller.

And whoever else had managed to get a copy of the print.

He laughed softly under his breath and nudged the rug with the toe of his shoe. It needed pulling up.

Once he'd shoved the table out of the way, it took him only a few moments to roll the carpet back. Was it his imagination or did one of those floorboards look a touch newer than the others? If the rest of the floor hadn't been so uniformly grubby, he wouldn't have noticed. It mightn't mean anything, yet…was this even the same rug? He had no idea because he hadn't noted the pattern last night. An irritating oversight.

The innkeeper was hovering in the vicinity of the stairs when Alex descended. How interesting. Was this nervous attention because he had a duke in his inn or did it originate from some other cause?

"Who booked the room underneath Miss Jones's last night?"

"A lady." The man's gaze flicked to Alex's left. Looking for an escape? "She's one of my regulars."

"Is she still here?"

"No, sir."

"But she was inside the room while the séance was going on?"

When the innkeeper hesitated, Alex took a step forward; a deliberate, yet he hoped subtle, intimidation tactic.

"Well, no. She's an actress, see? At that hour, she was performing."

"I'd like to see that room as well."

The room had a new occupant but, once given a small financial incentive, the man was easily persuaded to step out for a moment. Alex only needed one look at the ceiling beneath the séance table. The paint looked...convincing. Not too white. Tinged with yellow as if exposed to tobacco smoke over the years. Yet the small patch of newly applied paint didn't quite match the rest of the ceiling. Miss Jones might not insist on her own table, but she'd apparently brought her own rug. Under the cover of all that hymn singing, the slate had been removed, through the floor, to *this* room via a ready-made opening in both rug and ceiling.

"Got you," he whispered.

"Sir?" The keeper stood waiting on the threshold.

"Who is this actress?" Alex asked, without taking his eyes from the discolored patch above him.

"Miss Margaret Carmichael. She's on at the Dovecote."

Alex nodded. It was high time he and Miss Carmichael became acquainted.

• • •

Evie experienced no presentiment as she rose to answer the door. There was nothing remarkable about the soft *tap, tap, tap*. Which was a shame. A warning might have been nice because, when she saw the Duke of Harcastle standing in the hallway, arms folded, leaning one shoulder against the flimsy partition wall, her heart lurched in her chest.

A man of his exalted status really ought to employ a more portentous knock.

If her mouth hung open, the aberration lasted a moment at most before she schooled her features into their usual emotionless mask. She knew very well how convincing her mask was. Captain had made her practice in front of her looking-glass over and over again, until bland inscrutability came as naturally as breathing.

"Miss Jones," Harcastle said, and she could have sworn he sounded surprised.

"Your Grace." To her irritation, her voice sounded breathy, like one of the prostitutes at Miss Rose's after a particularly energetic encounter.

"Won't you invite me in?" His voice shook with suppressed laughter. Had *she* amused him or did he amuse himself?

"I'm not sure." His eyebrows rose but she pressed on. "I'm a woman alone. You might do anything to me. You seemed fit to wring my neck last night."

Added to which, she didn't even own a chair on which to offer him a seat. This room was by far the best lodging she'd had since she ceased sharing with Captain, but she couldn't help seeing the place as Harcastle would probably see it; bed taking up most of the space, faded curtains, rag rug, chipped plaster, and peeling paint. Even the colorful scarves Mags had hung to brighten up the place would seem quaint and shabby to him.

She smothered the spark of shame. After all, why should

she care what he thought? Who was he to her? A threat, that was all. And he demonstrated how much of a threat he was by stepping past her into the room. For a duke, it was simple. He wanted to enter and so he did.

Apparently, he also wanted to sit on her bed.

A duke on her saggy, second-hand mattress, the superfine wool of his black coat, the silk and velvet of his waistcoat, and the impossible whiteness of his shirt all a stark contrast to the faded cotton of her poor bedspread. The incongruity of the sight almost startled a laugh from her. Good Lord, had this room always been so small? With him inside, the walls seemed to close in.

Oh, she'd known she would see him again soon, but not here. Never here.

"Do sit down," he said. "I'm not going to devour you."

She left the door wide open and stood on the threshold, as far as possible from her unwanted guest.

"You left precipitously last night, sir. Did you wish to discuss the messages we received from the spirits?"

"No, Miss Jones, we can't begin that way. There must be no lies between us. You are a fraud, a fact we both know to be true. I must insist, at least when we are alone together, you refrain from speaking to me as if this weren't so."

A fine speech and spoken in the masterful tone of a man accustomed to obedience from the likes of her. It woke a devil within her.

"Your skepticism is notorious," she said sweetly.

"Does Miss Carmichael often aid and abet you?" he asked. "I came here looking for her, not you." Then he smiled, if such a knowing smirk could rightly be called a smile. *I'm here to play*, it said.

Evie couldn't afford to indulge him. The stakes were too high.

"Leave her alone." She spoke from pure instinct, the urge

to protect Mags momentarily overriding her common sense. He smiled again. Why not? She had revealed a weakness. "Miss Carmichael only booked the room. She has nothing whatever to do with my…business. If you harm her—"

"Harm her? Come, Miss Jones, I don't harm people. That's your talent, not mine."

Oh, she didn't believe that for a minute. He was enjoying himself too much, like a cat playing with a canary. Except that she resembled a crow more than a canary and he was something more like a tiger. Was all this because she'd raised his father's ghost? Or did he toy with all the mediums he investigated?

"I don't hurt people," she said. At least she *tried* not to.

With his head on one side, he considered her words. "Are you really so deluded?"

"Who have you seen me hurt? Not the Lennoxes, that's for certain. My spirits float tables and bring people flowers. When someone comes to me looking for a lost loved one, I talk about eternal rest. What harm is there in that?"

"Lies are always harmful."

The words stung, perhaps because there was truth in them. "Such integrity. You're fortunate your wealth and privilege shield you from ever needing to compromise your scruples."

"Wealth and privilege have nothing to do with this."

Now it was her turn to smile. For an intelligent man, he was being remarkably obtuse. How very typical of his class. Sudden anger revived her flagging courage. "Let's cut to the heart of things, shall we? You've made serious allegations against me, but do you have any evidence to support them?"

A shrug. "None whatsoever."

"I see." With effort, she managed to suppress a sigh of relief. "Well, you're welcome to search for it." *Just not at one of my séances.* "Now, if you'll excuse me…"

She stood aside and gestured to the open door.

He didn't move. "Am I?"

"Are you what?"

"Welcome to look." He rose and stepped closer. "You seemed so confident a moment ago. Do you really think I won't succeed?"

His dark-eyed gaze burned into her and too late she realized her mistake. As she'd noted, he was used to people complying with his demands. Paltry though her resistance today had been, to him it held all the appeal of novelty.

He took another step forward. "A week. That's all I'd need."

Too close. His breath ghosted across her cheek, and she shivered in response. Stupid body. Didn't it realize the threat he posed? *Wait, wait,* she wanted to protest, *you've got it all wrong. I don't feel confident in the least.* If she said the words aloud, would he lose interest?

"One week in your company," he went on, "and I'll have unearthed all your secrets."

Slow and deliberate, his gaze traveled the length of her body, lingering at her breasts. Such a crude perusal would appall the God-fearing spiritualist she pretended to be, so she tried to manufacture a modicum of disgust, but something in him called to her. The haughty stare, the icy contempt, even the way he challenged and threatened her. In short, the attributes that should have sent her running stirred her deeply. Perhaps her years at Miss Rose's had turned her depraved.

"What are you thinking?" he asked. "Why can't I read your expression? What are you hiding? Who are you really?"

"Why are you so interested?"

"One week," he repeated. "For one week, I go where you go. If I haven't obtained any evidence by then, I'll leave you be."

His expression, so intent in its scrutiny a moment ago, cleared abruptly. Had he realized how mad he sounded? But perhaps not mad at all. He must guess she'd never willingly perform another séance in his presence, unless he offered inducement. And she was tempted. One week and she'd never have to see him again. It might be safer in the short-term to refuse to sit with him, but what about her public displays? She could hardly bar him from those. At least this put a time limit on his investigation.

"Why would you do that?" she asked.

"Perhaps I enjoy a wager."

"And what if you win? What then?"

"You must agree to explain the tricks of your trade before the Society for Psychical Research."

The SPR was an organization of believers and skeptics all devoted to the scientific investigation of spiritualism. Some of her existing clients were members. If she confessed to fraud, naturally she would lose all of them.

"The risk is all on one side."

"Yes," he admitted. Clearly, to his mind, the wager didn't require balance.

She wanted to take a step back but that would take her out into the hall. Instead, she forced her shoulders to relax. Her appraisal last night had been accurate. His was a handsome face devoid of warmth, his lips set in a grim line which his beard did nothing to disguise. She couldn't imagine that mouth softening in tenderness. Couldn't imagine him kissing anyone.

"Let's speak hypothetically. If I were to lose this wager and carry out the forfeit, what would I do then? Have you ever stopped to consider what would become of me if you remove my only source of income?"

"I suppose," he said, with a bored sigh, "you'd have to find honest employment."

"As a shop girl?"

He shrugged negligently. "Or a seamstress, perhaps."

"And what do you know of the lives of shop girls and seamstresses, Your Grace?" Before he could respond, she went on. "Let me tell you a few things about life for ordinary women in this great metropolis of ours. Most of them don't make enough money to afford both food and lodgings. How do you suppose they survive? Wait, don't tell me," she said, when he opened his mouth to respond. "You suppose their husbands make up the shortfall, or their fathers, or their brothers or sons. And perhaps in some cases that's true. But what of those women unfortunate enough to be all alone in the world? How do you think they supplement their earnings?"

His sudden frown sent triumph flooding through her. Finally he was catching on, but just in case, she decided to make things explicit. "They prostitute themselves, Your Grace. Thousands of them. Every day."

He might as well have been made of stone for all the emotion her words produced. Inexplicably, she was disappointed, and she gestured again at the door. "So forgive me if I choose not to take the risk."

"Very well," he said, remaining where he was. "I'll compensate you."

"Excuse me? Did you offer me money if I lose? Because that's not how wagers usually work."

"The wager can work any way we choose. When you deliver your confession to the SPR, I'll give you…shall we say five hundred pounds? You have the wit to make good use of it. If you have to resort to prostitution after that, it won't be my doing."

So close.

She'd been so close to getting rid of him, but he offered a way to end his interest in her once and for all, and if she failed, she had a five-hundred-pound safety net. Quite frankly, if it weren't for Captain, she'd aim for the money. This wasn't a life she'd choose for herself if she saw other opportunities.

"And if *you* lose, you'll leave me to carry on as I am?"

He nodded. "On one condition. You continue your present policy with regard to the bereaved." He seized her arm, his fingers encircling her wrist like a manacle. She waited for terror—the only sensible response—and instead experienced a rush of heat, a tingling excitement as if her entire body had been poised for this moment. *The first touch.* "If I hear of you fleecing some poor, grieving widow, I'll bring you down so fast you won't have time to blink."

That's when she knew.

Win or lose this wager, she would never be free of him. As she went about her work, his eyes would always be on her, and she would know. It didn't matter that she had no intention of breaking her self-imposed rule. She would always be aware of his gaze.

These were not helpful thoughts, so she pushed them away. All he meant was that he would keep track of her career. In all probability, when she didn't step out of line, he would get bored and she would be free. It never occurred to her that he might not fulfill his end of the bargain.

Despite her prejudice against his class, she'd imbibed the general belief in aristocratic honor and assumed such behavior beneath him. She assumed this despite the fact he clearly didn't think consorting with thieves and charlatans beneath him.

In spite of this small blind spot, she understood the expression in his eyes when he looked at her. She recognized lust when she saw it. "Do we have a bargain?" he asked, and she could even hear it in his voice.

Reckless now, she offered her hand. "Why not?"

He didn't take it. Instead he smiled. "Now, Miss Jones, let's talk terms."

Chapter Four

Alex ordered his coachman to halt the carriage a little further down Brewer Street, where it wouldn't be visible from Miss Jones's window. A persistent drizzle misted the air, slowly turning the fallen autumn leaves into brown mulch. Pedestrians trudged past, shoulders hunched, heads down, uniformly damp and miserable.

He flipped open the blue enamel case of his pocket watch. Ten minutes until their first appointment. Patience had always been one of his strengths, yet the short wait would not be easy. Ever since the séance—no, even before that. Ever since he'd first seen that photograph, his behavior had been unsatisfactory—Yes, that seemed the best word—but he observed his own rash conduct as if hovering outside himself. Even so, he couldn't repent the foolhardy wager. Miss Jones affected him strangely.

When he'd still been a small child, his nurse had smuggled him out one night to see a fireworks display. His father would never have allowed Alex to take part in anything so frivolous, so she'd waited until he was at his club and bundled

Alex into his warmest things. It was one of the few happy memories from his childhood and for that reason alone, he would always remember it. But then, as they'd huddled on the common, *ooh*ing and *aah*ing at the Roman candles and fountains, a Catherine wheel had slipped its post, flying into the crowd. Fortunately, no one had been seriously injured and the firework quickly burned itself out.

Since he'd first seen the medium, his spirits hissed and fizzed like that firework about to fall. He could only hope for a similarly benign outcome. The investigation—

But could he truthfully call what he was doing an investigation?

No, he wouldn't lie to himself. An investigation was dispassionate. What he was engaged in now was pursuit. The pursuit of Miss Jones. And there was nothing dispassionate about it. He was awake for what felt like the first time in years. He wanted to expose her lies. He wanted to take her to bed. Those two desires could not coexist.

If he was honest, lust had driven him since he'd set eyes on that damn photograph. The séance and, even more, the lecture she'd read him yesterday at her lodgings—no woman had *ever* had the temerity to rebuke him—had intensified his feelings so that he could no longer deny their force.

Who was she really? Who would she be when he bedded her?

He shifted in his seat, uncomfortable with the crude turn his thoughts had taken. He didn't fixate on women this way. His few lovers had all been women of his own class. His desire had been moderate. An *appropriate* amount, not this peculiar hunger. He did not trust these feelings, and more importantly, he did not trust himself in their grip.

The door next to the print shop opened. He glanced down at his pocket watch again; still five minutes to go but it was definitely her. Not only hadn't she waited for his knock but she descended early, forestalling any chance of his reentering her inner sanctum. He'd caught that glimmer of dismay on her face as she'd opened the door to him yesterday.

She hadn't seen the carriage yet. Neat and precise as always in a black coat and hat, she fiddled with her gloves as she neared the curb. A young maple tree drooped in the rain, its remaining few leaves golden and on the brink of falling. One drifted down, coming to rest on the veil of her hat. Apparently satisfied with the state of her gloves, she lifted her head and gazed along the street, probably trying to decide which direction he was likely to approach by. Her only reaction when she saw his carriage was to walk quickly toward it. No betraying flicker in her composure today.

"Good day," he called as she approached.

She stopped at the carriage door. "Your Grace." As she inclined her head, eyes lowered modestly, the leaf fell from her veil and wafted out of sight. An insignificant thing, yet he noticed it as he noticed everything about her, and not because he was a good investigator; his scrutiny of this woman had nothing to do with professional interest and bore no resemblance to anything he'd felt in what he now realized was his tepid sexual history. Meanwhile, he'd left her standing in the drizzle for several seconds while he stared.

Belatedly remembering his manners, he climbed down and assisted her in. The weight of her hand in his was almost imperceptible through their gloves. She was dressed so decorously, every hair in place, every button done up, and he wanted to untidy her. To unpin her hair and unfasten each button. To lift her skirts and pull her shirtwaist aside to expose—

She tugged her hand from his grasp. He'd retained it far longer than necessary or appropriate, but he didn't apologize. It would have drawn even more attention to his lapse. Besides, he wasn't sorry.

When she settled herself in the forward-facing seat, he ordered the coachman to drive on. Their journey lasted no more than ten minutes, during which neither of them spoke. Her lips formed a tight line as she gazed out at the passing streets. Their agreed destination was a dilapidated Georgian, once a sizeable townhouse but long since converted into separate apartments. A spirit photographer by the name of Nightingale rented the top floor as his studio.

When Alex handed Miss Jones down from the carriage, he made sure to release her hand in a timely fashion. She muttered her thanks and walked ahead of him toward the building. Inside she led the way up rickety stairs, past walls with crumbling plaster. Four flights they climbed, until they reached a door painted a flamboyant red. She rapped sharply with her knuckles.

"Mr. Nightingale doesn't advertise," she said. "I bring my clients to him if they request the sort of services he provides." Her gaze dropped to his empty hands. "I thought you would bring your own photographic plates as you brought your own slate."

He'd considered it, but in the end he'd decided not to bother. Several years ago, he'd exposed the great spirit photographer Michael Eliot by insisting on the use of his own plates. Alex didn't care to repeat himself. Besides, he wasn't interested in Mr. Nightingale.

She knocked once more a moment before the door swung open to reveal a middle-aged man with a handlebar moustache. "Evangeline, my dear!" he cried, wringing her hand heartily. "A pleasure as always. Come in, come in. Introduce me to your friend."

The large attic they now entered had rows of smallish windows. Though the drizzle outside continued, the sun had emerged from behind the clouds so that dust motes danced in the light. Unseen wings flapped somewhere up in the rafters.

Pigeons, he realized, when he heard them cooing. The room was bare except for an upholstered sofa, varnish peeling from its spindly legs, and a camera atop a wooden tripod.

Miss Jones performed the introductions, but after a perfunctory exchange with Nightingale for the sake of politeness, Alex turned his attention to the camera. It was a beautiful piece of equipment, all rich cherry wood and brass fittings. It didn't look new, which made sense, considering the Spartan appearance of the premises. It might even be second hand. If Nightingale had purchased it recently and Alex found it necessary to find out more about the man, he might be able to locate the merchant and see what he knew.

"Just an ordinary machine, I'm afraid, sir," Nightingale said. "No magic in it. The spirits appear in the images because of Miss Jones's gift, not because of anything I do."

"So you're nothing but a humble photographer?"

"Exactly, sir."

The man seemed extraordinarily pleased with himself for some reason. He also fit the innkeeper's description of the older of the two accomplices; dark hair, moustache, forty or thereabouts. His light gray trousers, black superfine coat, and gold and blue striped waistcoat certainly met Alex's definition of "flashy." Clearly, a degree of intimacy existed between him and Miss Jones—Evangeline—judging by the tiresome way he made free with her Christian name. This might well be the man.

"Did you bring your own plates, sir?" Nightingale asked.

"No." At this second mention of them, Alex almost wished he had so that he could witness what Miss Jones and her associate had intended to do with them. "That's not a problem, I take it?"

"Indeed, no. I have a plentiful supply in the dark room, if you'll excuse me."

Alex nodded his assent and waited while Nightingale

walked to a door at the far end of the attic and passed through.

Evangeline stood at the edge of the room near the exit, her arms crossed over her middle. A curiously defensive pose for the woman who'd upbraided him so magnificently not twenty-four hours before.

"You've hardly said a word since entering my carriage. Not getting cold feet, I hope."

Instead of responding immediately, she went to the sofa and sat.

"Well?" he persisted. "Are you regretting our bargain?"

A quick lift of her brows showed her utter contempt. "Hardly."

"This is why I like you. Those occasional flashes of spirit. Underneath that meek exterior, there's a firebrand struggling to the surface."

"A firebrand? How patronizing. I suppose you do it on purpose."

He suppressed a smile because she was right on both counts.

"Here we are," Nightingale said, bustling back into the studio. He deposited a cardboard box onto the floor beside the camera. On top was printed the words *Eastman's Dry Plates*. Nightingale removed a small knife from his coat pocket and worked the blade around all four sides of the box, creating a lid, which he then removed. "Would you like to choose one?"

"I'm sure whichever Miss Jones selects will suffice."

Evangeline rose and went to kneel beside the open box. The plates inside were wrapped in brown paper, two to each parcel. She removed the topmost and placed her hand flat against the wrapping.

"Come and place your hand over Miss Jones's, if you please, sir."

At these words of Nightingale's, she glanced up quickly,

but her face gave no clue to what she thought or felt.

Alex was only too happy to comply. He knelt beside her, so close that he could feel faint warmth emanating from her. She smelt of lavender water, which he knew was to be had for pennies. The ladies of his acquaintance favored expensive perfumes, and the simpler fragrance pleased him, perhaps because it was novel. She kept her head bowed over the plate, supposedly praying, but he felt the tension in her hand beneath his. For good or ill, she wasn't unmoved by his touch. Just this once, he allowed himself to close his eyes and bask in her nearness.

Nightingale cleared his throat and Alex wished him a thousand miles away.

"Amen," she whispered and pulled her hand free.

Alex opened his eyes to find them both watching him, Nightingale with a certain smug satisfaction, Evangeline with wide-eyed consternation. What had they seen in his expression to make them stare so?

"Well, that's that," Nightingale said. "Now if you'll take a seat on the settee, we'll see if the camera can detect any spirits."

"His Grace is a skeptic, Mr. Nightingale. We mustn't speak to him as though he were a believer. We'll only irritate him."

"A skeptic?" Nightingale shook his head sadly. "Oh, now that *is* a shame."

"He may even be one of those unfortunates who refuses to admit the truth regardless of the evidence. He doesn't wish to believe." Her expression remained solemn throughout this little speech, but her voice had a teasing lilt to it, a faint echo of that mocking tone she'd used when she challenged Alex to flip the slate.

Did Nightingale know her well enough to detect these subtle nuances? His face was grave as if he took her words at face value, but Alex knew enough about the company he was in not to believe everything he saw. Which, ironically, chimed perfectly with Evangeline's assessment of him.

The sagging upholstery sank even further under Alex's weight as he sat. "Now there you are wrong, Miss Jones. I may be a skeptic, but I would like nothing better than if you proved me wrong."

"Indeed?" Her lips twitched. She was trying not to laugh, he was almost certain. "Never tell me that underneath that cynical exterior, there's a man in search of something to believe in."

He placed a hand over his heart. "You wound me. After all, am I not a man like any other?"

"Is not a duke a breed apart? Isn't your supposed superiority the reason you feel you've the right to lord it over the rest of us?"

She glanced at Nightingale and whatever she saw in his expression checked her. Alex hadn't noticed how animated she'd become until the light in her eyes dimmed. She seemed to retreat into herself, the woman who teased and challenged subsumed once more into the role she played.

"I had no idea—" A spring prodded Alex through the faded brocade, so he shifted to the right. "I had no idea you were a radical, Miss Jones." But it was no use. She refused to meet his eyes. Irritated, he turned his attention to Nightingale. "Were you at the Nimble Rabbit two nights ago, sir?"

"As it happens, yes, I was. A right friendly establishment, the Rabbit. Very popular with the theatrical set. Always good for a sing-along."

Yes, this must be the same man. Alex was almost sure.

"The sun's gone in again," Nightingale said. "I'll have to use extra flash powder."

"Oh no." Evangeline took several steps back, and Alex's confidence in Nightingale's capabilities as a photographer decreased accordingly. Flash powder was a newish invention and notoriously hazardous. If the photographer used too much or if the powder was damp, someone might lose a limb or even their life.

Nightingale ignored Evangeline's retreat and peered at Alex through a square he formed with his thumbs and index fingers. "Would you like to employ the headrest, sir?"

"Thank you." If Nightingale was going to detonate a loud and potentially dangerous explosion, Alex would need the headrest to help him remain still. Nightingale's methods would be easier to decipher if the image he began with was free from blurring.

While Nightingale retreated to the darkroom to prepare his powder, Evangeline retrieved a wooden stand from behind the sofa, unfolded it, and adjusted the headrest to the correct height. Alex leaned back before she'd quite finished, and her hand brushed his neck as she withdrew, setting off a thousand tiny sparks. He'd never been this sensitive to a woman's touch before.

"Is that comfortable?" she asked. Her voice sounded different. Low and hoarse. A bedroom voice.

He looked into her face but as usual it gave nothing away. He couldn't be certain she'd felt the same frisson he had from that brief moment of accidental contact, but he hoped.

"Yes," he said, and somehow his voice matched hers. "Thank you."

She nodded, then retreated to her earlier position, well away from the forthcoming explosion.

"Won't you come nearer?"

"Not bloody likely," she muttered. He loved it when she dropped character like that. There was no need for pretense between them after yesterday. Their cards were on the table. Which was one of the many places where he'd like to—

Nightingale returned with a small dish of flash powder.

He set it on a small stand which jutted out from the tripod. When he was in the darkroom, he must also have loaded the plate into its holder, a wooden box with sliding panels on either side. There was no way for Alex to ascertain whether a switch had been made but, frankly, he didn't much care. The man vanished under the black drapery of the camera's hood. Wood scraped against wood as he slid the holder open. Now all that protected the plate from exposure was the shutter. "Are you ready, sir?"

Evangeline sighed. "Let's get this over with."

Nightingale lit the powder but for two seconds nothing happened. Then blinding white light, followed by an anticlimactic *bang* so muffled it was barely a pop. Nevertheless, a thick plume of smoke shot up and then outward.

Nightingale doubled over, coughing at the floorboards.

"For heaven's sake!" Evangeline rushed to the nearest window and raised the sash.

Alex had taken care not to look directly at the light but even so the room had taken on a sepia glow. Nightingale straightened, still coughing, and tried to speak. The only word Alex understood was *Grace*.

"He said, '*Thank you, Your Grace. You may relax your pose now.*' Oh, let's get out of here before we suffocate." Without a word more to Nightingale, Evangeline strode to the door and yanked it open. Alex followed.

Their occasional coughs and the creak of the stairs under their feet were the only sounds until they emerged onto the street.

"Thank—" A series of dry coughs halted her words. Despite her hasty retreat at the first mention of extra powder, she'd actually run into the smoke to open the window. Consequently, she was more seriously affected than Alex. "Botheration," she groaned, once she'd caught her breath.

Despite her near-asphyxiation, spirit photography had

been an astute choice of activity on her part. No results until tomorrow or later today at the earliest, and little risk to her if Alex detected a fraud. Which he would. Nightingale had taken the picture, so she'd simply declaim all knowledge and place the blame squarely on the photographer. He'd known before they started he wouldn't obtain any evidence against her today, and that was fine because he didn't want their time together to end too quickly. What he hadn't considered was that the entire appointment had taken—he glanced at his pocket watch—less than a quarter of an hour.

"Are you ready to leave or would you like to take the air a while?" he asked.

"No, thank you. I'd rather go home."

"Mr. Nightingale seems an interesting man," he remarked, once they were again seated in the carriage. "How long have you known him?"

Before she had a chance to respond, the carriage lurched into motion. For some reason, that set her off coughing again. *Or perhaps she doesn't want to answer the question.* He felt his pockets. Yes, he had his hipflask.

"Would you like some water?"

She snatched the silver flask eagerly and drank deep, head tilted back. It was a good job he'd been telling the truth about its contents. He watched her throat work with each gulp, an oddly intimate experience. Until that moment, he'd seen her only as his opponent or an object of perverse desire, but now he was struck by how fragile and human she was. Despite her rather dishonorable profession, he also knew her to be brave and clever. He *admired* her.

"Thank you," she said, holding the flask out toward him.

"Keep hold of it until we reach your lodgings."

"You know, you're the first gentleman I've come across who keeps water in his hipflask instead of something more... medicinal."

And, just like that, he remembered other things about her. That she was cunning and conniving, that he couldn't trust her with any personal information about himself.

"I like water," he said.

The truth was he never drank spirits because he found them addictive. For a time, the loss of inhibition— No, more than that. The loss of *himself* in drink had been his only escape from the old duke. Ironic then that his father had been the one to save him.

"Wretched sot!" the old man had snarled from behind his ridiculous desk. "You've fulfilled your early potential, as I knew you would. Worthless. Useless. Would that you had never been born!"

As inspirational speechmakers went, his father had broken the mold.

Alex had stopped drinking the very next day out of spite.

"What's this?" Evangeline leaned forward and plucked something from the floor at Alex's feet. Her face, always pale, turned ashen. In her hand, she held a small crumpled black square. For a moment, he didn't know what it was, then he recognized the white creases as something he'd seen many times in reverse.

The photograph.

He must have dislodged it from his pocket when he removed the hipflask.

His first reaction was irritation because she'd found him out before he was ready. He hadn't wanted his attraction to get in the way of this week's activities. After the wager concluded, he would have waited for the right moment to declare his dishonorable intentions.

Then her gaze shifted from the image of her scantily-clad alter ego to his face, and he realized he hadn't considered how she might feel about his possession of that particular image. Had he thought she had duelist's eyes before? Nothing had prepared him for the hate filling them now.

"What kind of man are you? What were you going to do, throw this onto the séance table at the end of the week once you'd had your fun?"

The worst of it was that a similar thought had crossed his mind that first night when he was furious with her. He never would have done it but she couldn't know that. Belatedly, he realized the photograph would seem like a whip to be held over her.

"Evangeline—"

"Don't you dare presume to call me by my Christian name. Tell the coachman to stop."

Immediately, he rapped on the ceiling and the carriage began to slow. She reached for the door, and without thinking, without making a decision, he seized her arm. All he wanted was a moment to explain himself, but her gaze riveted on his hand encircling her wrist. She didn't pull away, but her entire demeanor transformed. The anger and panic of a moment ago vanished, replaced by an eerie calm.

"What now, Your Grace?"

The ice in her tone horrified him. What did she think he was going to do? What kind of men was she accustomed to dealing with?

The sort who restrained her against her will, obviously.

Releasing her, he jerked back so suddenly that he banged his elbow. "I would never have shown that photograph to anyone."

Her eyebrows rose in lofty disbelief. "Why should I believe you?"

"Even if I were capable of so deplorable an act as publicizing a photograph of that nature when you clearly wish it to remain private…" He searched for a way to convince her. "It would make no logical sense."

He wouldn't have thought it possible for her frown to

deepen further, yet it did.

"The photograph proves that you...have a past. But it doesn't prove that your spiritualist gifts aren't real."

"It would end my career all the same. Isn't that what you want?"

"That's not..." God, the way she looked at him, the set of her jaw rigid, her arms wrapped around her waist. He couldn't imagine that she'd ever teased him or allowed him to tease her. That she'd ever let him close enough to detect the scent of lavender. "That isn't how I work or how I want to win."

"Then why did you have it on your person in the first place?"

The true answer to that question was mortifying, but in the circumstances, how could he offer her anything but complete honesty?

"I keep it with me..." He took a deep breath, then released it slowly. "I keep it with me because I like it."

Chapter Five

Once the words were spoken, everything changed.

I keep it with me because I like it, Harcastle had said, as if confessing a deep, dark secret. And perhaps that was exactly how he felt.

She couldn't think about what his words might mean. She needed to focus on the photograph and what its continued existence meant. She looked at the image, at the stranger gazing back at her; a foolish girl, with a willful, sulky expression, straddling a chair in nothing but her undergarments.

The photographer had been an old crony of Captain's, a portraitist with a sideline in dirty pictures. The money he'd offered her to pose had been more than she'd ever earned before from a single afternoon's work, and she'd been tempted by the prospect of earnings of her own. Every other penny she'd ever made had been quite rightly shared with Captain.

How naive she'd been when she'd told herself that Captain wouldn't care.

Even now, she felt sick when she remembered his anger as he stormed into the studio a moment after the image was taken. Anger wasn't even the word—he'd been incandescent with rage. He'd halted in the doorway for a moment, his eyes sweeping the scene, then he'd yanked her from the chair and backhanded her, the first and only time he'd ever hit her.

"You stupid girl! You'll ruin everything!" he'd snarled, and while she watched in frozen horror, he'd smashed every plate.

Or so they'd thought.

A few weeks later, his former friend had tried to extort money from him in exchange for the finished photograph. She didn't know what transpired after that, but Captain must have done something because the photographer packed his bags and fled in the middle of the night.

"I've sorted it out," was all he would say when she'd asked him about it. He'd had a great deal more to say about her stupidity and he'd made certain she understood the true terms of their partnership. Despite his avuncular manner, she was an investment and she'd better pay out or he'd throw her back into the gutter where he found her.

That was the last time they'd discussed the matter.

She clutched the photograph. What were the chances that this was the last surviving copy? Perhaps there were dozens of them waiting to be discovered in print shops all over London. Captain was going to kill her. It wouldn't matter that he was partly to blame.

"I'll take you home," Harcastle said, and rapped on the ceiling.

A moment later, they began to move.

Harcastle stared out the window, and she knew somehow that he wouldn't speak again unless she spoke first. She sensed no displeasure in his silence. If anything, he seemed embarrassed, an emotion of which she hadn't believed him capable an hour ago.

"Do you have other copies?" she asked.

"No." He regarded her with those empty eyes. "The print seller in Holywell Street told me it was one of a kind."

Her relief was short-lived. He might be lying or the print seller might have lied to make the sale. But God, she wanted to believe him.

"Holywell Street?" The narrow street off the Strand, full of bookshops, printmakers, and pamphleteers all jumbled together, was a byword both for political radicalism and obscenity. In the mood for a socialist pamphlet? You'd find dozens in Holywell Street, and while you were there you could pick up some top-notch pornography, perhaps even from the same shop. She couldn't imagine Harcastle there. "Do you frequent such places often?"

He shook his head. "I went there looking for your photograph. I'd had agents investigating your past and one of them found the printmaker."

"Agents? How sinister."

He gazed past her. He ought to be more than embarrassed—he ought to be ashamed. Prying into her past. Keeping that photograph. Carrying the thing around with him.

I had it because I liked it.

"What did you mean before?" she asked.

"What did I mean about what?"

"When you said you liked the photograph. What does that mean?"

He glanced away.

It was such a small thing, the way he averted his gaze, but it told her everything. He knew it too, she could tell. Her own shame and humiliation were still fresh. It was only fair that he share in them. The balance of power was shifting.

"Did you like the way I looked?"

"Yes," he said, the word soft as silk.

"I would never have believed it of you." He seemed too

cold and untouchable to fall prey to idle lust. There had been that moment in her room when she'd sensed his interest but compared to this, that seemed a perfunctory thing, the desire of any man who'd been without a woman for a day or two. But to keep the photograph in his pocket, to take it out into the world like an infatuated boy with his sweetheart's picture in a locket...

"Did you look at it often?"

Jaw clenched, he looked away again.

"Did you?" she pressed.

"Yes, damn you." Ah, he was recovering, channeling his shame into anger.

"Did you..." He didn't like this line of questioning. She really ought to stop, but a devil had her in its grip. Part of her wanted to humiliate him further, but other desires rose within her. Illogical though it might be, she *liked* the idea of him alone with her photograph. "Did you touch yourself while you looked?"

He froze. What a hackneyed phrase. Evie had used it before to describe someone's shocked reaction, but until now she'd never actually witnessed true motionlessness in another person. He ceased even to breathe.

"Yes." He hissed the word through gritted teeth.

Stop now, a small voice said. *You've pushed far enough.*

"And you imagined...doing things to me." Her clumsiness of expression frustrated her. Lord knows she'd spent enough time around the prostitutes at Miss Rose's to acquire the requisite vocabulary. Why couldn't she use the words? "What did you imagine doing, Harcastle?"

The air crackled around them, and her body woke heavy and aching.

"Tell me." She sounded nothing like Evangeline Jones.

He shook his head and turned away toward the window. In that moment, she would have done anything to have his gaze scorch her again. Her hand reached out as if of its own volition.

What are you thinking? said the little voice. *You know what he'll do if you touch him.*

Yes. Yes, I know exactly.

He was on her the moment her fingertips touched his shoulder. No man had ever kissed her before but he didn't appear to notice her momentary flinch as his tongue touched hers. The moment passed and she kissed him with equal fervor, matching his thrusts with her own. His hands tugged at her skirt, pulling it up and up.

He pushed her legs apart and the hard weight of that part of him, the part the brothel girls had called a cock, pressed through his trousers. He groaned in what sounded like relief as he pushed against her. She knew what he wanted, but the risks were far too high, the consequences too serious. Fortunately, that didn't mean she had to deny them *every* pleasure.

"Show me," she whispered into his ear. "Show me what you did to yourself while you looked at my picture."

He eased slightly away, his breaths ragged. "What? I don't—"

"Do it before it's too late." They'd be at her lodgings in a few short minutes. "Do it now. For me."

With a shiver, she watched lust overcome propriety, his aristocratic reserve, and his sense of self-preservation. Violating all three, he unbuttoned the fall of his trousers with shaking hands and looked into her eyes. What he hoped to find in them she couldn't imagine. Her feelings were such a strange brew of fury and longing, and for once she didn't care if he knew.

"Show me," she said again. A dare. A challenge. "Show me now."

In this man, anger and desire looked the same. As

he grasped his cock, she thought of that moment when he overturned his chair at her séance. The look on his face now was the same, his brow low, his jaw set, as he stroked himself hard and fast.

"Help me," he said.

"No. I want to see exactly what you did. You have to do it yourself."

He stopped and his hands slid up to the buttons of her coat. "Then obey the rules you set. Your clothes were undone in the picture. I want to see you."

He had her coat open before he'd finished speaking, but she wasn't ready to relinquish control of their encounter. She pushed his hands away and reached for her shirtwaist. Several buttons went flying as she tore the front open. Seizing the front of her combination, she met his gaze. "You can't touch me, understand?"

At his brief nod, she yanked the fabric down until her breasts were bared to him like in the cabinet card.

"Evangeline…"

"No," she reminded him. "Now, show me."

He did, his grip firm as he pumped his fist up and down. She'd seen partially exposed men before, but she'd never cared to look until now. Until him. And he was beautiful. She watched the almost violent motion of his hand, her breath quickening. A pulse beat between her legs. Her breasts ached. She wanted more. Her entire body throbbed with the need to be filled.

His gaze traveled over her exposed nipples, then up to her face. Their eyes met and he must have seen something of what she felt in her expression because he moaned. He began to move his hips in counterpoint to the frenzied stroking of his hand until his gaze lost its focus.

"Is that what you like?" she whispered.

"I…" He looked like a man in agony or about to die of

pleasure. "Yes."

"Harder. I want to see you do it harder."

He did, and she knew he was about to lose himself.

"Now, Your Grace. Come now."

The noise he made, this powerful man, a small gasping sound as he spilled hot and wet over her breasts, made her lip curl in satisfaction. He slumped against her, helpless in that final moment. Helpless and so very beautiful.

The carriage halted outside her lodgings before they'd even had time to straighten their clothes. Harcastle's hand shook again as he reached for the door, but Evie had never felt more powerful than she did at that moment.

"I'll see you tomorrow," she said, jumping down before he had a chance to move. "I'm holding a séance at Lord Stein's tomorrow night. Ten o'clock."

She walked to her front door without looking back.

Chapter Six

By six o'clock that evening, Alex was still in shock.

Show me. The utter unexpectedness of those softly spoken words. The challenge in Evangeline's eyes. Her solemn expression as he'd given her what she'd demanded. The light kindling in her eyes as she'd watched.

Two versions of her, prim facade and lewd fantasy, blurred together and became something that unmanned him utterly. From the neck up, not a hair out of place, but lower, those pert breasts exposed as she writhed beneath him.

But you can't touch me.

The patter of rain against the windowpanes of the study startled him from a reverie he hadn't known he'd entered. Countless times throughout the afternoon, he'd given a similar jolt and realized he'd been in a daze, whatever activity he'd been engaged in forgotten, obliterated by thoughts of her.

He adjusted his reading glasses and returned his attention to the papers spread across his father's desk: several inventories of old furniture and God knew what else scattered across the many Harcastle estates. His task was to place a mark by things he wanted to sell. Dull work but necessary. Judging by the number of pages in each list, it was high time they had a purge. Afterward, he'd consider selling one of the minor properties to free up more capital.

The old duke's painted eyes bore into his back from the Winterhalter portrait.

Don't blame me, Your Grace. You're the one who mismanaged everything.

The sooner they found a buyer for that monstrosity the better. If it took much longer, he might donate the blasted thing to the National Gallery. He'd already placed a cross next to several other family portraits. Strange that he wouldn't miss seeing their faces every day when he already missed the photograph Evangeline had confiscated.

Why? Why did this raging lust continue to plague him? This afternoon's activities ought to have assuaged his hunger, if only for the day. If anything, their peculiar encounter had only served to whet his appetite.

A knock on the door brought him back to the here and now. "For Heaven's sake," he muttered, realizing he'd drifted off yet again. Where was his self-discipline? The small losses of control reminded him of when he'd still been drinking. He glanced at the portrait. He wasn't sure but he suspected it was the only Winterhalter to depict a sneering subject. Perhaps that might add to its value.

"Come in," he called.

FitzHerbert, the butler, entered and placed a thick envelope on the desk. Nightingale's spirit photograph, no doubt.

"Who brought this?"

"A young lad, sir."

Probably an ordinary errand boy, but just in case… "Tell me what he looked like."

FitzHerbert sighed. He'd worked for the old duke for almost thirty years, and Alex's requests often made him shake his head, as if to say, "*Your father would never ask me to do this.*" Never mind that the old duke had slowly lost his mind, necessitating the permanent presence of a mad doctor in the house for the final six years of his life.

"The boy was perhaps seven or eight years old. Red hair—an appalling color—and he wore a gray velvet suit."

Clearly, FitzHerbert had forgotten that Alex's own sister had bright red hair, but Alex decided to let the remark pass. "Velvet?"

"Yes, sir."

Unusual for an errand boy, but with second-hand clothes shops springing up all over London, not impossible. Still, it gave one pause. Ordinarily, if a lower-class boy somehow obtained a quality suit of clothes, he'd save them for Sunday best.

"Was the velvet shabby?"

Another sigh. "A little worn along the seams, perhaps, but no, not particularly shabby."

"Thank you, FitzHerbert."

Alone again, Alex slid open one of the desk drawers, searching for the letter opener. The contents were organized meticulously, his father's stationery in neat stacks, the writing utensils evenly aligned. He hadn't yet moved all of his things from his old lodgings. If he went there now and opened the drawer of his desk, he'd find things in a similar orderly state. The realization that he and his father shared this trifling affinity made him want to rush across town and untidy everything. Instead, he seized the sterling-silver letter opener and got on with his task.

Inside the main package, he found two further envelopes marked *1* and *2* respectively. He simply wasn't capable of opening *2* before *1*. The existence of those numbers written in the corners forced him to follow the suggested viewing sequence whether it had been designed by Nightingale or by Evangeline herself. Number sequences were like maps; if one ignored them, one risked missing an important detail.

And that was how one ended up at the arse-end of nowhere.

The first envelope contained this afternoon's photograph as he'd expected. It showed himself sitting stiff, upright, and unsmiling in the attic studio. Was this the person Evangeline saw when she looked at him? Was that why seeing him figuratively at her feet this afternoon had afforded her so much satisfaction? He'd seen the proof of her feelings in her eyes. The look of triumph as he'd spilled over her tits.

Naturally, he was not the only figure depicted. Nightingale had worked his magic. Next to the sofa there stood a tall, shadowy figure dressed in black. The image was faint and blurry, rendering the apparent ghost's facial features impossible to decipher, but...yes, if Alex were the gullible sort, he might easily mistake that vague face for his father's.

But he wasn't the gullible sort and he'd expected to see something of this nature. He was able to view the image without emotion. Undoubtedly, a double exposure. Nightingale had simply used an enlarger to transfer the image from a second plate over the image from Alex's plate. Two photographs on the same paper. Child's play, yet people fell for it every day.

He reached for the second envelope. Hopefully, it wasn't only the bill.

Inside he found a second photograph. Surely not a mere copy? Why bother with a separate envelope? But no, when he flipped it over, he saw immediately that they'd exceeded his wildest expectations.

He recognized Nightingale's studio again, but the light had a different quality. If he had to guess, Alex would have said it was taken on a bright summer's day, but he couldn't be sure. Evangeline lay on the same sofa on which Alex had posed, her eyes closed. Instead of her usual black, she wore a plain white day dress. She looked sweet, almost girlish, like the virginal heroine of a Gothic romance, but her feet were bare. He'd never considered feet particularly erotic, though for several moments he stared at hers.

The image was another double exposure, but far superior to the one of Alex. A second, ghostly Evangeline was emerging from the inert body of the first. Only her head and torso were visible as though her spirit were in the act of rising from her body, her back arched, her head thrown back in ecstasy. Astral projection caught by the camera, but in its own way, this photograph was as sensual as the cabinet card. What he wouldn't give to see the flesh-and-blood woman this way.

Why had Nightingale sent this to him? Or had Evangeline done the sending?

He wondered about that old photograph. She'd seemed genuinely distressed when she saw it, but perhaps that was all a part of the game they were playing. He'd never experienced anything like their interlude in the carriage. He'd had lovers over the years, but he'd never touched himself in front of any of them. The thought never even occurred to him. If it had, he'd have dismissed the idea as vulgar. What woman would want to see such a thing?

Even now the remembrance of what he'd done made him hot with something close to embarrassment. The entire exchange had been depraved and he wanted to do it again as soon as possible.

Was this seduction?

He wanted her now more than ever. More than he'd wanted anyone before.

Tomorrow night, he would see her again.

A séance at a private residence was a vastly different affair to one held at a public inn. She would find it impossible to hide her techniques from him, yet now they'd reached the probable end of their wager, he found he wasn't ready. He didn't *want* to win yet, and he couldn't help but think he was falling neatly, willingly, into a trap.

· · ·

On the evening of the séance, Evie was reaching for her coat when someone knocked. She wasn't looking forward to facing Harcastle after yesterday. What did a woman say to a man after she'd watched him toss himself off? Nicely done, sir?

Comments like that, the irrational way she sometimes lowered her guard in his presence, were precisely the sort of thing that had got her into this situation. She didn't trust herself not to say something inappropriate when she saw him. It was she who'd started things in the carriage. All he'd done was comply. Enthusiastically. When they were surrounded by people at Lord Stein's, it would be easier, but Harcastle had a nasty habit of turning up where she didn't want him.

She braced herself as she opened the door—*you will hold your tongue, you will be polite and formal*, she told herself— only to feel a perverse disappointment when it was Captain on the other side. He didn't usually come to her rooms, so she wondered what his appearance might mean. She hadn't told him about the photograph and a tiny part of her was afraid he'd found out somehow. He looked particularly fine this evening in a burgundy red waistcoat with a new pocket watch suspended by a golden chain. He'd been at the pawn shop again.

"Good evening, my dear," he said. "Since I can't accompany you tonight, I thought I'd pay you a visit. Have you decided what games are afoot?"

The trouble with conducting a séance in someone's home was that you couldn't go sawing holes in the ceiling or hiding accomplices in neighboring rooms. Not without the connivance of your host. She hardly knew Lord Stein, though he had been to see her at the Nimble Rabbit. He'd struck her as an ill-mannered boor, but money was money.

"Oh, the usual." Instead of inviting him in, she joined him in the narrow hallway. "You don't mind, do you? I was about to leave."

If he was offended, he didn't show it. "The duke's going to be there, isn't he? If he's only given himself a week to rumble you, he's going to be watching like a hawk. You'd better pull out all the stops."

That was exactly what she mustn't do. The more she did, the easier Harcastle's job became. Which might make for a lackluster séance, but it couldn't be helped. This was a matter of survival.

"Don't worry. I know what I'm doing."

He opened his mouth to argue, then changed his mind. "Is Jack walking you?"

She nodded. "He's not coming in, though."

"Good. We must look after your good name."

Her cheeks warmed as she remembered how little care she'd taken of her reputation yesterday. Forget the photograph. Harcastle could ruin her with a few well-chosen words, but if he were dishonorable enough to tell tales, he'd be dishonorable enough to invent slanders. Perhaps she was naive, but she didn't think him capable of either.

Captain watched her face. "Is everything all right? Do you have something you want to tell me, my dear?"

He knew her too well.

"It's about the picture. The Sally Harper one."

His expression darkened. "What about it?"

It was even harder than she'd imagined to say the words

with Captain looking at her so coldly. The harsh set of his mouth reminded her viscerally of that day when he'd blacked her eye. "Harcastle had a copy."

"Had?"

"I took it from him. He *says* he has no others and I think I believe him."

His lips quirked in an expression she found difficult to read. He almost seemed amused. "And how did you discover this?"

"He offered me his hipflask—I was coughing, thanks to your flash powder—and the card fell out of his pocket."

"He was carrying it with him?" His strange smile widened. "Well, well, well. I wonder why he'd do a thing like that."

Her cheeks grew hot but she didn't allow embarrassment to distract her from the sheer wrongness of Captain's reaction. He was taking this far too calmly.

"I hate to point this out, but if Harcastle found a copy, there may be others out there."

He shook his head. "When I paid Darrow off, I made sure I destroyed everything else too. The extra plates and the pictures themselves."

"Yet, clearly, you missed at least one."

"Now there's no point upsetting yourself. You've work to do. Let me worry about everything else. Good luck tonight, my dear."

She would get nothing else from him tonight, so she let him go.

She didn't want to follow him out immediately, so she went back inside and sat on the bed. Really, she ought to be glad Captain had taken the news so well, but though relieved to have escaped an ugly scene, her instincts screamed that something was wrong.

Just get through the night.

It was what she'd been telling herself all day long. Do a no-frills séance and blame the uncooperative spirits. Harcastle couldn't prove a fraud if she didn't actually *do* anything.

Or she could let him catch her.

This wasn't the first time the thought had crossed her mind. Five hundred pounds, even if she had to give Captain half, was more money than she'd ever thought she'd possess at one time. And this would all be over. No more séances. No more Captain.

Would he consider two hundred and fifty pounds enough of a return on his investment? She remembered the eager look on his face a moment ago when they'd discussed Harcastle, and she knew he wouldn't. Captain was after bigger game.

A shower of gravel hit the windowpane; Jack saving her from her wayward thoughts. She buttoned her coat and ran downstairs to find him.

"Can't you knock like a normal person?" she asked, giving his arm a playful shove.

"You know I don't like goin' up there. Mags always pinches me cheeks."

"She's at the theater anyway—"

Out of nowhere the thought hit her. Captain had kept one of the cabinet cards. That was why he wasn't upset. He knew exactly where Harcastle's copy had come from because somehow he'd arranged the entire thing. It was the only explanation for the way he'd taken her news.

But why would he do such a thing? What possible purpose would giving Harcastle that photograph serve?

The only reason she could think of was to focus Harcastle's attention onto attributes of hers that he might not otherwise have noticed. Had Captain meant to distract him from his investigation?

"Evie? You all right?" Jack's forehead creased with concern.

"What? Oh. Yes. It's…" Why had Captain kept it at all? He couldn't have been planning this for three years. "You can't trust anyone, can you?"

"You just working that out?" He shook his head sagely. "Is it that duke? Don't you be putting up wiv any of 'is nonsense. If he gives you any trouble, kick 'im in the tallywags and run like the clappers."

She couldn't help but smile. "You're wise beyond your years, Jack."

He offered his arm. "Come on or we'll be late."

Her thoughts still whirling, she allowed him to escort her into the night.

• • •

Lord Stein owned a corner mansion on Belgrave Square. A beautiful Palladian with rows of tall, multi-paned windows, and walls rendered in clean, white stucco.

It was by far the grandest residence Evie had ever entered. Her neat little room was a hovel compared to this opulence. Even so, she didn't envy Lady Stein, a great beauty, who had apparently risen from shabby genteel roots to her current lofty station. *What a brilliant match she's made*, the gossips crowed, while dismissing as irrelevant the fact that Lord Stein was a cad. Worse than a cad.

What a pity Evie had to sit next to him.

"Excuse me," she said, and rose abruptly from her seat, thereby dislodging his hand from her knee. They were in a room with several other people, but with the séance table to mask his activities, he didn't care. "I need to turn that lamp down. The spirits are easily daunted by harsh lighting."

"Is there anything else you need, Miss Jones?" Their hostess had a quiet, tremulous voice. Rumor had it she'd been the toast of the season the year she made her debut, renowned as much for high spirits as for beauty. Now only her beauty remained. What had stolen the sparkle from her eyes? According to Jack, the servants whispered of the husband's many infidelities and his cold treatment of his wife.

Evie finished adjusting the lamp, which hadn't really needed turning down in the first place. "Thank you, Lady Stein, but everything is perfect now."

As she walked across the luxurious Persian rug to her seat, her eyes locked with Harcastle's, the first time she'd looked at him directly since he'd entered with the others a few minutes ago. Until now, she'd treated him like the sun. One didn't stare straight at that, either.

Another séance with Harcastle. She must have lost her mind.

Naturally, he'd positioned himself to her left at the table, all the better to keep a close watch on her. She took her place between him and Stein, between the devil and the deep blue sea, and tried to appear unconcerned.

The moment she sat down she felt Stein's long, aristocratic fingers graze her thigh. She shuddered. The man was a pig. To men of his ilk, it didn't matter what a woman looked like or how she dressed. He viewed all females alike as his opponents in a game, the object of which was to leer and abuse until he got a reaction. Any reaction. If she were his social equal, she'd slap him so hard he'd see stars. Sadly, her lowly position in the hierarchy made direct retaliation impossible. If she made a fuss, *she'd* be the pariah, not him.

Apart from herself, the Steins, and Harcastle, three other guests filled the table. Lady Stein's sister Miss Hale was the only other lady. She didn't say much and what little she did say was directed at her sibling. The remaining two, Lord Esher and Mr. Smythe, were Stein's cronies. The latter was the least objectionable of the trio of gentlemen but too weak-willed to do anything but follow where they led.

"Well, let's get on with it," Stein said, giving her thigh a squeeze. "And none of your hymns and prayers. Straight to the main event, if you please."

"Here, here!" Lord Esher cried.

Needless to say, this was not a spiritualist crowd. This lot wanted parlor tricks, nothing more.

The weight of Harcastle's scrutiny was heavy upon her. Would that she could mistake his stare for the hot gaze of a lover. Handling that sort of attention was second nature. She'd been doing it since she was too young to understand what it meant. Unfortunately she recognized his look as the investigator's measured regard.

"Form the circle, please," she said, in the sort of firm voice she imagined a school mistress might use. "Palms flat on the table, little fingers touching the fingertips of the people on either side of you."

A great deal of sniggering ensued between Lord Esher and Mr. Smythe, the only two gentlemen seated without a lady between them, as they positioned their hands. Evie ignored them but, judging by what she'd heard about what went on between boys at schools like Eton and Rugby, she was surprised at their silliness. She risked a quick glance at Harcastle and caught him shaking his head at them.

At least with everyone's hands on the table, she didn't need to worry about Stein's creeping tentacles. He kept rubbing her finger with his, but she could put up with that.

Harcastle placed his right hand on the table next to her left. Unlike Stein, he kept still, touching her no more than was necessary to make the circle, but a tiny shock bolted through her as his fingertip brushed hers. His hand was large, with long, graceful fingers, neatly trimmed nails, and a light sprinkling of dark hair.

Only yesterday, that same hand had torn open the fall of his trousers as she watched. She could recall every second in vivid detail. How his hand had fisted around his cock. The strong, sure strokes. Such a wicked hand.

She forced the image from her mind. "Close your eyes and bow your heads. Think of anyone you might wish to contact."

Esher laughed, the sound high and irritating. "I haven't heard from my uncle Stephen in a while. Of course, he's not actually dead."

Smythe sniggered but no one else made a sound.

Silently, she counted to ten, using the silence to create a sense of anticipation. Then, very carefully, she extended her left foot and flexed. Her ankle gave an impressive crack.

Miss Hale squealed. "Did you hear that? I heard a rap!"

Under the table, a booted heel clamped down on Evie's foot.

Harcastle, you tricky bastard. For a moment, she wanted to laugh, but she mustn't allow herself to treat this as a game because he did. He was a threat to everything she'd worked for. Though she ought to hate him, she found she admired him precisely *because* she couldn't fool him.

"I didn't hear anything," Smythe said.

Miss Hale frowned in response. "I assure you, it was quite distinct."

If Evie was honest, she felt nothing but contempt for the people who fell for her tricks. Harcastle would never be so stupid. It was difficult to respect someone who heard the crack of an ankle joint and mistook it for messages from beyond the grave.

"Jack?" Evie gave her voice a deliberate quaver. A pity the real Jack wasn't here to play the part. Evie would have to make do. "Jack?" She straightened her spine and squared her shoulders, making herself rigid. "Jack?"

Miss Hale gasped. The nervous ones like her were worth their weight in gold. Their fear heightened the tension more effectively than the most talented medium, infecting the others with the same contagion. Unease, the beginnings of genuine fear, rippled through the room.

"Jack has a message for someone at this table."

Harcastle's foot pressed down a little more firmly on hers, a reminder, in case one were needed, that she was not to take advantage of people's bereavements.

"This is so exciting." Lady Stein's eyes were closed, but for the first time this evening, her smile seemed genuine.

"Show some dignity," her husband snapped. "Ridiculous woman."

Esher smothered a laugh, and the light drained from Lady Stein's countenance until she appeared almost gray. And Stein had done it deliberately. There had been nothing undignified about his wife's enjoyment, but he had taken the wind from her sails because he preferred she remain cowed.

He opened his eyes—despite the fact that doing so was forbidden during this part of a séance—and caught Evie watching him. Without a sound, he lifted his hand from hers, breaking the circle, and made a *V* with his second and third fingers, which he then held to his lips. He stuck his tongue through the opening and waggled it suggestively.

Her stomach turned.

God knows she hadn't led a sheltered life. She was used to rough language and she'd seen a great deal during her time at Miss Rose's, including this particular rude gesture. But there was something about Stein. A predatoriness that terrified her.

Harcastle's hand shifted and covered hers. She wasn't surprised to find his eyes open. A shrewd investigator, he would never close them during a séance. But had he caught the obscene gesture? Usually, whenever she knew he was looking at her, she kept her face carefully blank. This time she let him see every ounce of what she felt. Violated by a powerful man's insults and assaults on her person. Impotent to retaliate.

Harcastle took it all in, and for her pains, he returned a single, slow nod.

A bob of the head wasn't much to go on with so much at stake, but she was angry and anger always made her reckless. What had he said about why he wouldn't use the photograph to discredit her? Something about wanting to win the right way. He cared about fairness, didn't he? In that case, he shouldn't hold her to the terms of their agreement, not in these circumstances.

Right, Lord Stein, you disgusting lecher, this is for every woman you've ever hurt.

"You may all open your eyes now," she announced.

. . .

Evangeline took a deep breath, then allowed her head to sink heavily onto her chest.

As far as Alex was concerned, Stein deserved what was coming. Something had been bothering her all night, which suggested that what he'd witnessed was only a small part of what Stein had put her through. Even if it were all, Alex wouldn't lift a finger to stop whatever punishment she decided to mete out.

Stein had always been a thug. Alex knew his reputation and now he'd seen firsthand how he treated women. Evie's position here was amorphous, neither guest nor employee, but either way, Stein owed her his protection while she was under his roof. Those were the rules society set. Seeing them disregarded so egregiously was to blame for this anger roiling in Alex's gut. Or so he told himself, but he knew there was more to it.

He had never been a possessive lover and he was

fascinated by the primitive outrage he'd felt when he'd seen Stein's filthy gesture. Scratch the surface and humankind were little better than animals. Even the aristocrats. Even cold-blooded specimens like Alex.

But his retrogressive sexual instincts weren't all. That look on her face... He'd never seen anything like it. A tumult of anger, hurt, and, worst of all, helplessness. He never wanted to see that look again, and he knew he'd do anything to keep her from feeling that way. Anything.

Ten, nine, eight, seven, he counted silently. Six, five, four, three, two...

Just as the gentlemen began to grow restless, her head swung up again.

"Good heavens!" Miss Hale cried.

Evangeline's eyes were rolled back so that no pupil or iris showed. With a painful-looking twist of her neck, she faced Stein, the expression on her face pure malevolence. "Johnny boy," she growled.

Stein's smug smile vanished.

Compared to this, what she'd done to Alex at the last séance had been almost kind. Despite the threat he'd posed, she'd put hardly any effort into scaring him. It hadn't been personal, he realized. This was.

"Johnny boy, what have you been doing?"

Smythe chuckled. "Lord, that made me jump. A look like that should have killed you on the spot, Stein."

Lady Stein watched Evangeline, her eyes wide. "Who is she, John? Who's talking to you?"

"Who is she?" Stein mimicked. "Don't be ridiculous, woman. It's only the medium putting on a show." But his bravado rang false. Alex had never seen a living man turn so pale, like every drop of blood had drained from his face.

Evangeline's voice turned pleading. "Don't you recognize me, sweet Johnny? Remember how I used to sing to you."

A look of pure horror contorted his face. "What is this? How are you doing it?"

She went in for the kill. In her high, wobbly soprano, she sang:

"Oh, don't deceive me
Oh never leave me
How could you use
A poor maiden so?"

Stein was hooked. That was obvious even before his eyes filled with tears.

"Mama?" he whispered.

"How could you slight so pretty a girl who loves you?
A pretty girl who loves you so dearly and warm?"

Stein broke the circle, burying his face in his hands as he began to weep. Esher and Smythe watched, aghast. This gossip would spread like wildfire through London's gentlemen's clubs tomorrow. Alex was almost relieved when Evangeline bowed her head again, her way of signifying the spirit's supposed departure.

Unfortunately, Stein didn't take the hint. "Mama?" he said, between great, gulping sobs. "Mama?" With shaking hands, he reached out.

Alex half rose from his seat, determined to intercept Stein before he could manhandle Evangeline again, but the moment Stein's hand closed on her shoulder, her head jerked up. Everyone present, Alex included, jumped about a foot.

"I'm very, *very* cross with you, Johnny."

Stein yelped. Miss Hale screamed and fled the room. The two other gentlemen leaped back from the table, overturning their chairs. It was chaos. Slowly Lady Stein rose from her place, caught Evangeline's hand, and kissed it.

"Thank you," she said simply.

Chapter Seven

Alex almost missed the moment Evangeline slipped from the room.

He strode past his host, now weeping in his wife's arms, and out into the cavernous entrance hall after her. No footman lingered by the door but she heaved it open herself and slid out into the night.

If he waited for his hat and coat, he'd lose her.

"Miss Jones," he called as he closed the door behind him. "Miss Jones, wait."

She stood on the bottom step, about to step onto the street. "Did you see what Lord Stein did?" she asked without turning.

"I saw."

"Then you understand why I'd rather be alone. I'm afraid I've had enough of aristocrats for one evening."

"I can't allow you to walk home at this hour. We don't have to talk if you don't want but please permit me to see you home safe."

She leaned ever-so-slightly forward and, for a moment,

he thought she was going to bolt. Instead, she turned to face him. "Do you have any idea how many times I've walked home alone at night? And in places a million times rougher than Belgravia."

"You're obviously upset."

"Am I?" Sparing him a final defiant glare, she walked away.

He followed three paces behind, making no effort to conceal his pursuit. After all, the object was to keep her safe, not scare her to death. She skirted Green Park as she made her way to Piccadilly. A chill lingered in the air, a reminder that summer was long over. Mist gathered, a prelude to what would no doubt be a thick fog. As highhanded as he'd been, he was glad he'd followed her. London's fogs were unpredictable and sometimes fell with miraculous-seeming suddenness. He would have worried.

"Well, you win," she called back over her shoulder. "When is my humiliation at the SPR to be?"

"You don't think I'd let you off so easily, do you? The wager stands, tonight notwithstanding."

She slowed, permitting him to catch up. "What are you talking about? I summoned the spirit of Lord Stein's dead mother, something you expressly forbade."

"Stein doesn't count. He's an animal, not a person."

"Careful. I could take that logic and run wild with it."

Somehow he didn't think she would.

"Why 'Early One Morning'?" he asked, referring to the song she'd sung.

"According to—" She stopped short of naming an accomplice. "According to certain sources, his mother used to sing it to him when he was a boy."

"Only that song?"

"Of course not. There were a few. Why?"

Her choice of song told him volumes about who she was.

"Early One Morning," despite its sprightly tune, was about an unfaithful man. Stein's treatment of his wife bothered her because it outraged her sense of justice. Of fairness. She had her own peculiar moral code, and he admired that about her.

"What's the matter?" he asked, ignoring her question completely. "You don't seem pleased. Do you tire of our wager already?"

She kept walking, her head down so that he couldn't see her face.

"You could always forfeit. Take the money. A clever, resourceful woman like you could do so much with five hundred pounds." He couldn't really spare that much, but he could lay his hands on it easily. It wasn't enough to save the dukedom on its own. Whether he kept it or gave it to Evangeline, he was still going to have to marry one of Ellis's heiresses.

His gut twisted at the thought, but it was the only viable long-term solution.

He couldn't think about that now. There was still time before he'd need to bite that particular bullet, and he knew how he wanted to spend it and with whom. Evangeline still hadn't said anything, which was concerning.

"Is something the matter? Something other than Stein's behavior, I mean."

She stopped walking and peered into his face. "Harcastle, are you being kind?"

"I'm being fair. I assure you, I am never kind."

She studied him through the gloom. "No, this definitely feels like kindness. But since you tell me that's impossible, I suppose you have an ulterior motive."

"For asking after your wellbeing? Why shouldn't I feel an interest in you after—?"

Before he could finish, she pivoted on her heels and marched away across the street.

"Evangeline, wait!"

"Not unless you promise not to say what I think you were going to say. And stop calling me Evangeline."

"If you're worried I'm being kind because I want to sleep with you—"

She stopped again so abruptly that he nearly careened into her back. "Kindly lower your voice."

"It's true, if you must know. I *do* want to take you to bed."

Her eyes widened. "Then I'm sorry, but you're going to be very disappointed."

"That's not all, though. I realized tonight that I also happen to *like* you. Although, to be honest, I'm not sure why."

"Is that supposed to be charming?"

"You lie for a living, you take people's money under false pretenses, you rarely smile, and you have all the warmth of the Thames in midwinter. Yet I'm fond of you."

"Oh really?" She lifted her chin, rising to the bait magnificently as always. "Well, you're arrogant, you have no understanding of the real world or how real people live. And you have the *gall* to call me cold? I've seen hotter stalagmites."

He wanted to kiss her. No woman had ever inspired even a tenth of the lust that she did. He didn't care that they were on the edge of Soho or that it was closing time and they were about to be surrounded by drunks. He wanted to hold her hard against him until all her spikes and sharp edges melted away and she was consumed by desire the way he was.

The combative light faded from her eyes and her expression turned soft.

She knew what he was thinking.

"It's late," she said, and he knew that she wouldn't take things further. At least not tonight.

Several minutes later, they turned into her street. The shop beneath her lodgings had seen better days, but the building must have been handsome back in Soho's glory days.

As they reached the front door, she turned, about to bid him good night.

"Before I go, I need to know if I owe you an apology for yesterday."

In the shadows he couldn't be sure, but he thought she might be blushing. "No, of course not, but we mustn't let it happen again. I'm sure you agree."

He nodded even though he most emphatically did *not* agree. She might not be ready to admit it but they were on a collision course. It was only a matter of time before the sparks between them burst into flames.

"I'm glad you feel the same way."

"Good night, Evangeline."

He'd taken perhaps two steps when her hand caught his arm. "Harcastle, wait. After tonight, we mustn't talk about this again. The subject must remain completely out of bounds."

He bowed. "Of course."

"But, just so you know, so that there are no misunderstandings, what you did yesterday, what *we* did... well, you looked beautiful, that's all."

Without a word more, she fled upstairs. Confounded and unspeakably aroused, he began the long walk home.

• • •

Evie woke at dawn after a restless night. Pale light filtered through the threadbare cotton curtains. Soon the knocker-upper would be round, tapping on downstairs windows and shooting dried peas at the upper stories to wake those who had paid her sixpence for the alarm. Mags was already awake, staring at the ceiling.

Twelfth Night opened at the Dovecote in two days' time and she was nervous.

"Are you all right?" Evie asked.

Mags sighed and pushed a flaxen curl away from her face. "I've never played such a large role before."

"You'll be wonderful."

Together they'd practiced Mags's lines countless times. She made a beautifully coy Olivia as she catalogued her beauty for Viola: "*Item, two lips, indifferent red. Item, two gray eyes with lids to them.*" The audience were going to fall in love with her right along with Count Orsino. Evie had butchered all the responses. Her attempt at the famous willow cabin speech must have had Shakespeare spinning in his grave like a mouse stuck in the mangle.

"It's not only about speaking the lines," Mags said. "It's about charisma. A great actress possesses a certain something that captures an audience. I won't know if I have it until after the performance." She turned over and shuffled closer. "Let's not talk about me anymore. How was last night?"

Evie pulled a face. "Not good."

"Did Stein heckle you again?"

"I wish that were all. Turns out he has wandering hands. His wife was sitting a few feet away."

"Dirty old git."

"I put him in his place." Evie smiled at the memory. "With the help of his dead mother." Her work might be disreputable and dishonest, but it also allowed her to rob Stein of a little power. How often could a girl of her class say that about an aristocrat?

Mags crowed with laughter. "I'd give anything to have seen that. I never get to see you work anymore."

"You can tonight if you like. Captain's having one of his get-togethers. I know you don't like him but you'll come, won't you?"

Mags nodded. "With Chase."

The wealthy Mr. Chase had first noticed Mags when she

appeared in the chorus of *Medea*. All it had taken was a quick word from him to the Dovecote's owner Mr. Hall and Mags had been told the part of Olivia was hers *if* she entertained Mr. Chase in her spare time. She'd fulfilled her part of the bargain but she rarely talked about how doing so made her feel.

Chase was young and handsome, which Evie imagined must make it easier to bed him than if he were eighty with bad breath and hair sticking out of his ears, but the decision had been imposed upon Mags. If she wanted to progress in her chosen career, she had no choice at all. An actress was always racing against time.

Evie thought about the photograph hidden in the bottom of her dresser drawer. Until the day she'd posed, no man had seen her naked breasts. Captain had guarded her virtue like a miser hoarding gold, then he'd put that picture in Harcastle's way. Wild and impulsive as her actions in the carriage had been, she now wondered if she'd been manipulated and not by Harcastle.

"Is the duke attending?" Mags knew about the wager.

"Of course. It's his big chance to expose me in front of an audience."

"You *are* being careful, aren't you?"

How to respond when the simple answer was no? *No, I'm not being careful. I'm deliberately walking into danger and I don't know why.*

"As careful as ever," she replied, but she'd hesitated too long and her words rang false.

Mags drew her into the crook of her arm. They'd only known each other a year but since they'd moved into this little room, they'd grown close. Evie worried what would happen if she had to run. She'd warned Mags more than once that she might need to disappear without a word one day if one of her scams went wrong.

"I worry about you," Mags said. "When I first met you I thought what a perfect little prude you were, but I know better now. There's a recklessness in you. Don't let that duke hurt you just because you've got some silly idea you deserve it."

Evie murmured a response, feigning a return of sleepiness. She couldn't promise to be careful. In her mind, she was on the edge of a cliff as waves crashed against jagged rocks beneath. Spellbound by the sea's beauty, she couldn't make herself take the necessary step back to safety.

All she wanted was to leap forward and revel in the exhilaration of her fall.

Chapter Eight

This couldn't be the right address.

From the comfort of his carriage, Alex eyed the crumbling old theater in one of the rougher parts of Soho. An informal party, Evangeline had said. But the theater looked like it had been abandoned for years, its walls smog-blackened and the windows boarded up.

An ancient poster, faded and barely legible, depicted a ballerina *en pointe* with what appeared to be two clowns flanking her. Clearly, this had never been a first-rate theatrical establishment.

A young couple approached the main entrance. The man, well-dressed and tall with fair hair, looked familiar. The woman on his arm wore a serviceable yet plain coat which contrasted with the luxurious fur draped stylishly about her neck. A gift from the gentleman who was almost certainly not her husband.

Once the couple had disappeared inside, Alex rapped on the ceiling. A footman opened the door and lowered the steps. Alex descended and dismissed the coachman. He had no idea how long this would take.

By the time he pushed through the dilapidated double doors and entered the dimly-lit lobby, the young couple had vanished. All was quiet, except somewhere in the distance a fiddle played. A faint odor of damp assailed him as he followed the sound through another set of doors. Beyond was a narrow hallway lit by a single candle set in a dish on the floor. The air reeked of blended dust, mildew, and old smoke. Now he could discern not only fiddles but an accordion and, if he was not mistaken, a tin whistle, all mingled with the hum of voices.

Yet another set of double doors waited at the end of the passage, their glass windows so thick with grime that no light penetrated. He stepped through and found himself in what had once been the stalls. The sight that greeted him was unlike anything he'd ever seen before.

The cavernous space blazed with the light of hundreds of candles covering every surface from the ledges of the balconies on the levels above to each and every wall-sconce. The old boxes, where the most expensive seats had once been, were empty. Indeed, they hardly appeared safe with their obviously rotting wood and faded gilding. The once-ornate molding was crumbling so that plaster dust caused motes in the flickering candlelight.

The mural that once graced the ceiling had faded, its naked and fornicating gods and goddesses now grotesquely distorted by water damage. Every seat in the groundlings had been torn out, leaving a space as big as a ballroom between where he stood and the orchestra pit from which a jig floated.

There were people everywhere. Almost everyone danced, some in couples but others alone, as if they couldn't keep their feet still long enough to find a partner. The setting was strange, but the people were stranger still. Everywhere he looked, the eccentric mingled with the mundane.

Around the edges of the room, small tables had been set up, each with its own cluster of chairs. At one, identical twin sisters sat with a pack of tarot cards laid out between them. To his left, Alex spotted a white terrier tottering on hind legs as its owner weaved circles around it.

Elsewhere, someone had suspended a tightrope between two chairs. While a man weighted each seat, a group of young men and women took turns wobbling across the rope. Like the man and his dog, this didn't seem to be a deliberate attempt to entertain anyone but more as if they'd seen an opportunity for a spot of practice and didn't much care whether people watched or not. Most peculiar of all was a man dressed all in black, a top hat on the table in front of him. On catching Alex's eye, he reached into the depths of the hat and withdrew a gray pigeon. The bird took wing and soared up into the gods.

An old woman with a careworn face watched its ascent. "Bloody 'ell, Jim. Couldn't you leave 'im at 'ome? We'll all be covered in bird shit."

Alex nodded to the pair politely, then continued searching the crowd. Evangeline must be here somewhere.

At last, he spotted her near the stage. As always, she wore a plain black dress buttoned up to her chin and the same severe hairstyle. She was untouchable. Sexless. But he knew better, and one day, sooner or later, she would be his to touch. He knew it in his bones.

The crowd parted slightly and he noticed Nightingale beside her. They stood close together, clearly deep in conversation. She shook her head in vehement denial of something he was saying. Nightingale placed a placating hand on her arm, and everything in Alex tensed. True, the man was old enough to be her father, but the murky nature of their connection worried him. He couldn't help but resent it.

As if she felt the weight of Alex's stare, she glanced his

way. Their gazes clashed and she stepped forward, dislodging Nightingale's hand. Without bothering to excuse herself, she strode through the throng, ignoring a juggler who tried to get her attention.

"Your Grace," she said when she reached his side.

"Who *are* all these people?"

"Friends of Mr. Nightingale." She gave a thin smile. Yet even that slight tilt of her lips transformed her face. Whenever she smiled, he felt gifted with a glimpse behind the facade. For a moment, she showed him the true woman. All she need do was smile and he was her slave. He prayed she never realized.

"Are *all* Mr. Nightingale's acquaintances performers?" Alex liked actors. His half sister Helen had grown up in the theater and spoke fondly of her life there. Evangeline didn't fit with all these carefree theatrical folk but perhaps the woman underneath did. He wished he knew one way or the other. He wished he knew *her*.

"Not at all," she said. "You needn't look at me like that. A medium may have theater friends without being a performer herself, may she not?"

"That wasn't what I was thinking." Besides which, many respected mediums booked theater engagements. There had always been an uneasy correlation between the two worlds, suggestive perhaps of fraud among spiritualists but not evidence.

"What then?"

"I was wondering where you came from."

He didn't expect her to enlighten him, which was why he wasn't too irritated when a cavorting couple careened into them, ending their *tête-à-tête*. Alex recognized them as the couple he'd followed inside.

Evangeline smiled at the woman with genuine pleasure. "My goodness, Mags. How many have you had?"

"Sorry, Evie," Mags said, breathless from dancing. "I'm giddy as a fish." Her well-dressed escort whispered something in her ear. "Certainly. Miss Evangeline Jones, may I present Mr. Chase?"

Ah, that was why the man looked familiar. They moved in similar circles. They'd even met once or twice. Evangeline—or was it Evie?—allowed Chase to bow over her hand. As he did so, his fair hair flopped into his eyes. He was Alex's opposite, golden and cheerful. Somehow he doubted Chase would be of much interest to Evie. His angel liked the shadows. So did Alex for that matter. All these years of polite, even-tempered paramours, only to discover now that he truly longed for something dark and deep.

"Your Grace." Chase nodded. "Are you here to see Miss Jones's display? I hear you take an interest in such things."

"Of course, but what brings you here?" Chase didn't strike Alex as a likely spiritualist.

Chase slid an arm around his companion's shoulder. "I follow wherever Miss Carmichael leads...or try to. The collision this evening was entirely down to my clumsiness."

Alex looked with renewed interest at the tall blonde. This was the same woman who'd rented the first floor room at the Nimble Rabbit. Evie stiffened and he remembered how she'd defended Miss Carmichael. He wished there was something he could say to put her mind at rest. This was his fault for taunting her with the possibility that he might harm her friend that day they'd made their wager. He'd hoped they'd moved beyond that inauspicious beginning.

Didn't she realize he would never hurt anyone she cared for?

He caught Miss Carmichael's eye and smiled while Chase looked from face to face, no doubt trying to trace the source of the sudden tension. "Oh, I love this tune," she said, tapping her toe in time with the music.

Chase took the hint and, excusing themselves, they returned to the dance.

"Do you know Mr. Chase well?" Evie asked. He liked this new name. It suited her better than the staid Evangeline.

"Only a little, but he seems pleasant."

She nodded, her eyes on her friend as Chase whirled her about. "You should find a table. I need to prepare."

Alex watched her walk away, back straight, head held high, with a pang of disappointment. No more smiles. Her mask was firmly back in place.

He found himself a vacant seat with a good view of the dancers. Earlier, he'd used the word *carefree* to describe these people but, whatever Evie thought, he'd seen enough of the world to suspect they drank and danced jigs to forget lives much harder than his own.

The light gradually dimmed as a young boy flitted from candle to candle, extinguishing flames with a snuffer atop a long pole. He had the reddest hair Alex had ever seen and wore a gray velvet suit. Good quality but slightly worn about the seams.

Was this the errand boy who'd delivered the photographs for Nightingale?

As the room grew darker and darker, the musicians ceased playing. When most of the lights were out, a spotlight illuminated the stage. Evie walked calmly into its circle. The boy reappeared, this time without the snuffer, and made his way to the front of the gathering spectators. Positioned to the side and front of the room, Alex had almost as good a view of the front row spectators as he did of the stage. His was the perfect position from which to spot instances of collusion. An expectant hush fell, rippling back from the stage until the entire room was quiet.

Evie stepped forward, her face ghostly white above her black clothes. "Ladies and gentlemen, with so many people here tonight, it's my belief we can work together to bring forth a manifestation."

Someone gasped. Evie rarely performed manifestations, perhaps because they were difficult to execute convincingly. To his knowledge, she'd never attempted one in a venue as large as this.

"Will someone lead us in prayer?" She looked to the boy in velvet. "You, child. Do you know your prayers?"

The boy frowned at his feet, shuffling as if embarrassed to be singled out. "Yes, Miss. I know the Lord's Prayer."

"Then pray and don't stop, no matter what happens. When you reach the end, start again at the beginning and do that until I tell you to stop."

The lad began, softly at first but with steadily increasing confidence. His voice had yet to break and the simple, powerful words spoken in his clear treble cast a spell over the room. It was an exceptional performance.

Alex fixed his gaze on Evie.

The spotlight went out. The only illumination now was a single, feeble limelight shining from stage level. Eyes closed, head thrown back, she began to moan. One or two people near Alex smiled knowingly but most of the crowd appeared transfixed. Even these people, with their knowledge of stagecraft, longed to believe the lies she pedaled.

Another moan, longer and louder. She must know how she sounded. Like a woman overwhelmed by passion. He wanted to pull her from the stage and away from all these prying eyes. He wanted to be on stage with her, kissing her, touching her, making love until she screamed. He wanted those sounds to be for him.

A last agonized moan and she held her left arm aloft. All the while, the boy continued to chant. The crowd gasped as her hand began to glow. Barely perceptible at first, then bright yellow and undeniable.

"Ectoplasm," someone cried.

Oil of phosphorous, the cold, rational part of Alex's mind corrected.

And she stood not one foot from a burning Drummond light. How could she be so stupid? He was going to kill her if she didn't go up in flames before he had the chance.

The boy's praying grew louder, reaching a crescendo as she gave a last low, keening cry. A stream of glowing green vomit gushed from her open mouth and the boy faltered and fell silent, his face stricken with horror. If Alex hadn't been secure in his skepticism, he might have believed something had gone terribly wrong. That he was in the presence of some powerful evil. A terrible silence fell and Evie collapsed like a marionette whose strings had been cut.

Uproar.

Alex shot to his feet as a woman screamed, sparking a mad stampede for the double doors. In the midst of the heaving crowd, Nightingale swept the redheaded boy up and carried him, slung over his shoulder, toward the exit. Alex pushed through the panicked mass, traveling against the stream to the stage. He saw no steps, so he vaulted onto the now darkened proscenium.

Evie was gone.

• • •

As the first scream sent everyone scattering, Evie raced backstage.

The mixture of soap, gelatin, and egg white tasted vile and she needed to get rid of it. She found the washing things Captain had left for her and cleaned her phosphorous-stained hands. Then she filled a tin cup with water and carefully rinsed her mouth. Finally, she removed the black apron she'd worn to protect her dress and let it fall to the dust-covered floor.

A curious depression had settled over her when she ought to be feeling triumph over a successful performance. Was this to be her life now? Lies and pretense until someone exposed her?

Let it be Harcastle, then. Let it be now.

The back of her neck prickled with awareness. Someone had followed her. As she started to turn, strong hands clamped down on her shoulders.

"Stay still," Harcastle ordered.

The prickling intensified, dancing up and down her spine. "Your Grace—"

"Shut up."

Trapped between the wash table and his body, she felt no urge to escape. He could do anything to her and she wouldn't care. His hands warmed her through the fabric of her sleeves and she closed her eyes as they glided down, curiously gentle despite his obvious anger, and circled her wrists. With her hands held captive and unable to see his face, she ought to have been afraid, yet no fear came. She waited to see what he would do.

"Do you have any idea how dangerous oil of phosphorous can be?" he said as he thrust her hands back into the water. His touch rough now, he scrubbed the left, then the right with the bar of lye soap. "Mediums have set their clothes on fire. You were standing in front of a naked flame, for heaven's sake. You could have gone up like a torch."

She didn't deny it. Oil of phosphorous was highly flammable. She and Captain had argued all the way to the party, but he'd insisted she use it.

"What do you think I trained you for all them years?" he'd said, his accent slipping worse than usual. "Do as you're told or I'll be looking for an immediate return on my investment."

Harcastle spun her to face him. "Answer, damn you!"

He hurled the soap across the room, sending it ricocheting off the wall. His anger pressed in on her, yet she sensed something else beneath, something that made her almost pity him. Tears clogged her throat but crying was a weakness she didn't have time to indulge. She couldn't look at him, so she stared at his chest, at his tie-pin, its ample diamond glinting in the candlelight.

"Say something!"

"I don't know what you mean. I don't even know what oil of phosphorous is."

His grip on her arm tightened painfully but only for a moment before he released her entirely. His hand shook as he raked his fingers through his hair. When he spoke again, his tone had gentled. "Look at me." He tilted her chin up, his touch so soft that she found herself leaning into it. "Tell me what the matter is."

Sometimes he seemed so cold, but the hardness in him only made these moments of tenderness more devastating. And she was weary, so weary of holding him at a distance. Tired of being Evangeline Jones.

Out front, the musicians struck up again. The fright she'd given the crowd hadn't been enough to end tonight's festivities completely. As the autumn evenings lengthened, people naturally gravitated toward light and music. Anything to brighten the end of a hard day's work.

"I'm tired, that's all."

"Then I'll escort you home." The anger seemed to have drained out of him, replaced by an aching tenderness.

That wasn't all, of course. His eyes had that heavy-lidded look. The carriage. He wanted it again, that loss of control. His or perhaps hers this time. Revenge or a repeat performance. Either way, she didn't think she could refuse him. She was weak and the temptation he presented too powerful.

"Yes," she said, though she was uncertain exactly what

she'd agreed to. "The back and side doors have been bricked up. The only way out is through the front."

He nodded and followed her through the dark hallways back to the stage. Not everyone had returned to the party but many had. She didn't want to speak with anyone, so she weaved through the crowd swiftly, twisting and turning as the fiddles played. Harcastle dogged her steps, his hand sometimes grazing her shoulder or brushing her arm before she slipped away again. Her heart drummed in her chest as he pursued her all the way to the double doors. A strange giddiness rose in her as she slipped out ahead of him. She was through the next set of doors before he'd breached the first.

In the lobby she stopped dead.

He emerged and collided with her back, sliding an arm around her waist to steady her or perhaps himself. Then, like her, he went absolutely still.

A man and woman writhed together in the shadows. Even in near-darkness, the panting and groaning, the rapid rock of the man's hips amid the woman's rucked-up skirts, were unmistakable.

Evie had glimpsed scenes like this at Miss Rose's but never with a man pressed against her back. The warmth of Harcastle's hand burned through her clothes down to the softness of her belly. Her breasts felt swollen and far too sensitive. She wanted to cover his hand with her own and guide him down to the sudden ache between her thighs.

If she turned her head, she knew she'd find his gaze riveted on the fornicating couple, but she remained still. His breath stirred the hair at the nape of her neck as he pulled her tight against him. She shivered and pressed back, sighing as his thick hardness pressed against her bottom.

"I want that with you," he whispered. "I want to fuck you like that. I wouldn't care who saw us."

It was a shocking thing to say, and perhaps there was

something wrong with her because she wanted to let him. More than that, she wanted to pull him into the dark right here and now, the other couple thrashing beside them, and urge him to take her whatever way he wanted.

She didn't know what she might have done next if not for the doors crashing open behind them. Three laughing women burst through, all singing loudly, as they made for the exit. None of them noticed the couple in the shadows.

Harcastle took Evie's arm and steered her out after them. It was past closing time and a steady stream of people poured from the nearby taverns, homeward bound or off in search of other amusements. Rain pelted down and, in seconds, her hair was soaked and plastered to her scalp. The sensual daze she'd fallen into dissipated with the first stirrings of discomfort. Her coat was back at the theater but she'd rather drown than return to the lobby and the amorous couple. What had seemed enticing, seemed terrifying now the moment had passed.

As if he too was desperate to escape what they'd witnessed, Harcastle propelled her forward. "We need to find a cab."

When she didn't respond, he looked back at her and, just like that, the rain soaking through the fabric of her dress meant nothing. The rapid rise and fall of his chest, the rigid set of his jaw, the light in his eyes. All exactly like that day in the carriage when she'd known she only need touch him and he would snap.

"Evie?"

She watched his mouth and willed it to descend on hers. Her heart leaped as he paced toward her, his intent plain on his face. There was no fear in her heart as he dragged her into the nearest side alley and shoved her back against the wall. As he leaned in and pressed a hot, open-mouthed kiss to the hollow at the base of her throat, her fingers tangled in his hair, holding him firmly in place.

"Do you feel how hard I am?" His lips brushed the shell of her ear. "I've wanted you all evening. I want you here. Now."

She urged him closer as he nipped her neck with his teeth. It wasn't enough and she moaned with relief as he yanked her skirts up around her thighs, his fingers grazing the tops of her stockings. She pushed against his chest, thinking only of getting a hand free so that she could touch him.

"No?" he said, mistaking her.

Yes! her body cried and pushed against his seeking fingers.

He leaned his forehead against hers, the mists of their breath mingling in the air. "Tell me what you want."

Fuck me, she wanted to say. *Take me. Overpower me. Don't make me choose.* But she couldn't speak the words. She was still on that cliff's edge, but she couldn't make herself let go. She couldn't allow herself to fall. Not yet.

"Evie?"

When she still didn't answer, he stepped back. She almost cried out at the loss, and his hands shook as he lowered her skirt back into place. He straightened his clothes, withdrawing into himself as she watched, the fire in his eyes banked to almost nothing.

"We need to find a cab," he said again.

She followed him back to the main street.

The reflected light of streetlamps sparkled in the puddles. She waited by the curb while he searched for a vacant hack. Even now, she knew all she had to do was go to him and take his hand. He would lead her back into darkness. They'd rut against the wall and when he finished...

He'd be finished.

A man like him—rich, handsome, and dissatisfied— wouldn't stay interested long. She was a novelty, she understood that. What else could she be when they weren't even of the same class? For him, the thrill was in the chase. Wasn't that why he did what he did? Safety, security, and caution had to be the watchwords of a woman like her, a woman who came from the streets. Desire meant nothing in the grand scheme of things, the affection she'd begun to feel even less. Walking away was the wise course.

Yet she wanted him. She was twenty-four years old, but this was the first time her desire for a man had outstripped her common sense. If she was going to do something this foolish, she wasn't going to settle for a tuppeny upright in some dank alleyway. She wanted the whole night. A single, glorious evening when she was his and she would do anything he asked. She wanted this even though she knew it would devastate her. Her fondness for him had come on gradually, growing in such imperceptible increments that she hadn't known she'd begun until now when she was already in too deep. God help her, she *liked* this man. Difficult as he was, she'd come to care about him.

"Miss Jones." Harcastle gestured to a waiting hansom cab, the driver hunched under a thick oilskin, whip poised.

They didn't touch on the way home. The cab offered protection from the rain but the front was open to the air. She shivered in her wet things while Harcastle stared ahead at the sea of bobbing umbrellas moving from pub to home or, knowing Soho, from pub to brothel.

"Tell me what you want," he said again. The fever had gone from his voice, replaced by calm detachment. "Whatever you want, I'll give it to you if it's mine to give."

This was the part when she was supposed to name her price. He wanted her badly, but enough to make her his long-term mistress? What if he did? A kept woman enjoyed a certain respectability and, when their affair ended, she might have saved enough to make herself financially secure.

Being his, even for a little while…

"I hope I haven't offended you." Nothing of the nature of their conversation showed on his face. He was as polite as if his proposal had been the honorable kind.

"I'm not offended."

"It wouldn't have to be sordid. I want you and I think you want me. I could take care of you." His low, silky voice made the words decadent.

Captain would be furious.

The cab halted outside her lodging before she'd even begun to sort through her chaotic thoughts. The rain had slowed to a drizzle, though somewhere nearby water rushed into a gutter. The mundane sound grounded her, made her realize how insane all this dreaming was. Harcastle would tire of her in a few short weeks or months, and what would happen to her then? With her reputation gone, she'd be no use to Captain. Living in Soho all these years, she'd seen what too often became of discarded mistresses.

"The answer's no, isn't it?"

"I'm afraid so."

She searched for her key—she could never remember which pocket she'd left it in—painfully conscious of Harcastle's silence. Was he disappointed? Had his offer meant even a fraction to him of what it meant to her? As usual, his face told her little.

"Found it," she said, withdrawing the key.

The ghost of a smile lit his face as he helped her down from the carriage. "I think I'll walk home from here. Good evening, Miss Jones."

It was difficult to make herself turn and walk away. The few yards to the front door seemed like miles. If she didn't get inside quickly, there was a chance she might run after him. *Of course* the key wouldn't turn. Blasted thing. Always getting stuck. She jiggled it in the lock to no avail. Again.

Once, twice, then at last the key turned.

Her heart seized in her chest as someone spun her round.

Harcastle, his hair still disheveled from the rain and her fingers, with a wildness in his expression she'd never seen before. He looked nothing like himself. The duke was just a man as his mouth covered hers in a kiss as wild as he was. Hot and demanding at first, then gentling until his lips were whisper-soft against hers.

"Change your mind," he said, his mouth drifting to her throat.

She sighed and buried her face against his chest.

"Change your mind."

"I…" She couldn't. She couldn't say yes, no matter how much she longed to. "I'll think about it."

"Yes," he said. "Think about it and, when you're sure, send for me."

She turned her face away before he could kiss her again. "Good night, Harcastle."

That ghost of a smile was back. "Good night, Evie."

Chapter Nine

By the time Evie arrived at the abandoned theater the next morning, most of the detritus—the burned-out candles, empty tumblers, discarded cigarette ends and the like—had already been carted away.

Only a few of Captain's helpers remained. The venue was one he returned to again and again, so he took care of it like he owned it.

He sat at one of the tables, sleeves rolled up as if he'd only recently stopped work, a newspaper spread out before him. As she drew near, he glanced up. "Evangeline, my dear! Congratulations on a truly superlative performance last night. I hope the duke was suitably impressed."

"Impressed is one word for it." Though the phrase "apoplectic with rage" was even better. After spending the morning so far refusing to think of Harcastle, it irritated her that his name was almost the first word Captain had said to her. "He's no fool. He knows oil of phosphorous when he sees it. There isn't a trick we can pull that he hasn't seen a hundred times before." Then, because she was finished pretending, she added. "As you know very well."

"What about the ectoplasm? That's a showstopper!"

"That nonsense wouldn't fool anyone of any sense, let alone a man like the duke, but you knew that too."

"You're particularly churlish this morning, my dear." He smirked. "Rough night?"

There it was; the sign she'd been looking for. His knowing tone suggested he knew what had been going on between her and Harcastle. He knew because he'd orchestrated the entire thing by somehow gifting the duke her photograph before she'd even met him. Either he didn't know she was onto him or he didn't care.

Whichever it was, she'd had enough, so she sat down facing him and folded her arms on the tabletop. "I need to know what's going on. What are you up to?"

"Up to? Me? I don't know what you mean."

This was the point in the conversation where she'd usually retreat. How convenient for him that she preferred to stay on good terms. Worst of all, he knew she was afraid of him now. He knew and he *enjoyed* her fear. It *amused* him.

Something snapped within her. The last thread of her gratitude. Captain might not have given her life, but he'd been a father in other ways. Like a child with an unsatisfactory parent, she'd finally run out of thanks. If she ceased to care whether she displeased him, she had no more use for her long-standing policy of appeasement. Her fear was neither here nor there, a useless emotion she must learn to ignore. And of late she'd had plenty of practice. She'd been terrified of Harcastle, yet she'd faced him down.

If she could dare a duke's wrath, she could dare anything.

"Harcastle has exposed countless mediums. Why would you risk a second, let alone a third and fourth meeting? It makes no sense, unless there's more to it."

He smiled and leaned back in his chair. "Clever girl."

She wanted to slap the smug look from his face. Instead, she lowered her voice, drawing him in. "Why did you give Harcastle my photograph?"

"Which photograph?" he asked with an enigmatic twitch of his lips. He was laughing at her.

"Don't play games with me. I know you arranged for him to have it. What I want to know is why. Why would you want him to see through a lie you helped create?"

For the first time, he looked almost impressed. "I must say, you surprise me. I didn't realize you were so perceptive. As to *why*, I think a girl clever enough to guess my gambit with the photograph would know the answer already. You tell me."

"It isn't because you want to distract him. This isn't about the spiritualist scam."

"Are you sure? You get the duke on our side and no one can touch us."

She shook her head.

"Use your head, girl. A man like that has a dozen secrets. You find them out and you'll have him in our pockets for the rest of his life."

She almost believed him. She *did* believe him as far as that went, but she was sure there was more. They were supposed to be partners. They were going to help each other make a living, that's what he'd said when he took her from Miss Rose's years ago. What a fool she'd been to imagine she knew the limit of Captain's ambition.

"Why Harcastle? Why not someone else, someone easier?"

"The bigger the risk, the bigger the payout."

"But it could still be anyone with a lot of money."

"No, it has to be him." With this admission, his false geniality fled and his tone was icy.

Even as her stomach knotted, she felt triumphant. At last,

she was getting somewhere. "Why?"

"Because he has to pay, that's why!" he shouted. "Did you let him bed you yet?"

Mind your own damn business. She wasn't silly enough to say the words out loud. The last time she'd seen him this angry was the day he'd caught her posing for the photograph and he'd ended up blacking her eye.

She thought fast. His anger that day had been real which meant the photograph hadn't been part of his original plan for her. Clearly, he'd improvised, turned a liability into an asset. He had reacted to events, which meant he didn't know everything.

"No," she said.

"Good. No sense letting him have you too easy. Men like that want what's denied them. Play your cards right and he'll offer to keep you. When he does, you say yes, understand?"

"He won't ask me."

He regarded her in silence, his expression calculating. She kept her face blank, the way he'd taught her. He knew what her poker face looked like, but if she was lucky, he wouldn't know what it concealed.

"This is what we've been waiting for. This is our chance. The big one."

"What *you've* been waiting for."

"Don't give me that. Why do you think I took you from Miss Rose? Why do you think I kept you safe from all the men who offered me money for a tumble with you? When it comes to that, why do you think I didn't bed you myself?"

Evie struggled against a sudden surge of nausea. She wanted to scream the obvious answers at him: *Because I was a child! Because you raised me!* Every muscle in her body strained to get away from him, but she couldn't let him see the effect of his words.

Once again her image of who he was transformed.

Everything he'd done for her had been part of a larger calculation. She had always known this to some extent but she hadn't realized until this moment that he didn't care for her at all. She was a means to an end. Nothing more.

"This is why I took you from the brothel. This is why I fed and clothed you and kept you safe. If not for me, you'd be a used-up whore by now. Your loyalty is to me and you'll do as I say. Harcastle will offer for you, if he hasn't already, and you'll say yes. Eventually he'll tire of you, but long before he does, you'll bleed him for every secret, every sin. Understood?"

"Yes," she whispered, her skin crawling. "I understand."

And I will never let you hurt him.

• • •

Alex gazed grimly into the ornate mirror while his valet fussed at his clothes, checking for lint and stray wrinkles. He looked without seeing, his thoughts as always focused on *her.* It troubled him, this single-mindedness where she was concerned.

He'd always been monomaniacal about his work. His fascination with the occult had begun early, perhaps as a reaction to his father's extreme empiricism. At first, he'd been determined to find a genuine medium, but the more he investigated the spiritualist movement, the less he believed in its merit. Each time he'd uncovered a new fraud, his anger had grown until exposing fakes and charlatans had become the entire point, both his reason for living and why he was the best in his field. He was obsessive by nature. Prone to *idée fixe.* But this obsession with Evie had no practical purpose and needed conquering, much like his addiction to alcohol.

Doing so would be even more difficult now that his affections were engaged. When he'd walked her home from Lord Stein's, he'd admitted he liked her, but the fury he'd felt when he realized she was using oil of phosphorous forced him to acknowledge a deeper truth. He cared about her, a fact he found especially disturbing when he considered that the addition of Evie's name to the list of people he cared about brought the grand total to three. His sister and her husband were the other two.

The people who called him a cold fish—never to his face of course—were right, but he made no apologies. So why, instead of striving to overcome his feelings, had he asked her to become his mistress? Gone were the days when he deluded himself into thinking he'd tire of her quickly. Such a connection would only make things worse. Even so, he couldn't bring himself to fully repent his actions.

He couldn't afford a mistress; that alone was reason enough to retract his offer. Yet he wouldn't, and that was the true source of his regret. That he couldn't bring himself to take the logical, practical course. On the contrary, he fully intended to persist in an action he knew to be folly.

There would be pain too. One day, perhaps a year from now or perhaps less, he would have to choose one of Ellis's heiresses. He couldn't in good conscience continue to keep a mistress when he had a wife whose money he'd be spending to rescue the Harcastle holdings. Giving Evie up would hurt him and perhaps her too. But harder to contemplate was the idea of never having her at all.

Farrell, his valet, disappeared into the dressing room and returned with a top hat under his arm. Alex took it automatically and pretended to consider its fitness since that was what Farrell expected. Before he'd had time to murmur his assent, a knock came at the door.

"Come in."

A footman entered, bearing a silver tray. Placed carefully in its center was Evie's card, a single white rectangle with *Miss Evangeline Jones – spiritualist* printed neatly in the middle.

"The person insisted on waiting, sir."

Strange how the world turned on a moment. She was here in his father's house. Come to deliver a verdict. Her answer would change everything, one way or another. Alex deposited the hat onto the nearest surface. "Where is she?"

A slight pause was the footman's only betrayal of surprise. "In the main entry, sir."

Alex dismissed the servants and strode briskly to the top of the stairs. There he stopped and took a deep breath. Anticipation knotted his stomach. He couldn't predict what she would say, but his heart lifted because she was here. The very air felt different, crackling with delicious tension.

He was halfway down the grand staircase when he saw her, a small black-clad figure standing amid all the austere grandeur of Harcastle House, dwarfed by the vast expanse of black and white marble flooring, the statue of Aries, and the Doric columns. She looked impossibly vulnerable with her head down, but then as he neared the bottom step, she glanced up and he saw those duelist's eyes.

"Your Grace."

He bowed. "Miss Jones."

"Might we talk?"

"Please." He gestured in the direction of the study. "Allow me." He picked up the small carpetbag at her feet, trying not to think about what its presence might signify, and held the door open for her. She strode inside without looking at him.

Instead of waiting to be offered a seat, she sat before the desk, obviously expecting him to sit in his father's chair. He did so and found that he minded less now that the portrait had been taken down. It stood with its face to the wall, and soon it would be sold.

"I'd like to concede our wager," she said.

He felt his eyebrows inch upward. For once, he hadn't

been able to school his features in time. "Unexpected," he said. "I confess, I didn't think you capable of it."

"And ordinarily you'd be right, but these are special circumstances. The fact is, I need your help."

For the second time in as many minutes, she'd surprised him. "Go on."

"I don't like my work. I never have, though I do take pride in being good at what I do. Giving it up has never been an option. Even if my finances weren't entangled with Mr. Nightingale's, I felt bound to him by gratitude."

Alex nodded noncommittally but inwardly he seethed. He didn't like the idea of her bound to anyone but himself. Then, too, the nature of her relationship with Nightingale was nebulous. But he had no right to question her. Not yet anyway.

"In recent weeks, my feelings on this matter have changed." She rose and began to pace. "You've investigated a great many mediums, but what made you take such particular notice of me?"

He shrugged. "You started to become popular. I make it my business to stay informed."

"But you went far beyond that." She stilled in front of him and pinned him with a look. "Be honest. Was it the photograph?"

He held her gaze. "Yes."

"You told me your agents located it for you in Holywell Street. Led there by an anonymous source, I suppose?"

He began to see what she was suggesting. "You think it was Nightingale?"

"I know so. I confronted him this morning."

He retrieved an envelope from the drawer and placed it on the desk before her. "I've been meaning to show you this."

She slid the contents—a single photograph—free of the envelope and studied it in silence for a few minutes. "At least

I have most of my clothes on in this one."

"It arrived a few days ago along with the photograph I posed for. I wasn't sure if you knew."

"I didn't." She continued to gaze at the image, her brow furrowed.

"He couldn't have known how I would react to the first photograph. Not the extent of it anyway."

"No, but he's adaptable. He hoped it would distract you but I think this particular ploy worked beyond his wildest dreams. Had you seen Captain—Mr. Nightingale, I mean—before I introduced you?"

"No. What makes you ask?"

"Isn't it obvious?" She frowned in confusion. "He's fixated on you."

"You said yourself he's adaptable. Scams like this are commonplace, though I'll grant you've been ambitious in your choice of target."

"*I've* been ambitious? No. I knew nothing of this until that day in the carriage."

Her words jibed so perfectly with his wishes that he immediately became suspicious. The fact that he wanted to believe her—longed to believe her, actually—meant he shouldn't trust his own judgment. All along he'd been absorbed by her, so obsessed that he failed to notice he was being manipulated by Nightingale. She claimed she was only a pawn but he couldn't be sure. Instinct urged him to trust her but he'd be a fool to heed it.

"Anyway, that doesn't matter." She waved away his distrust as if it were nothing. "The point is that it's you in particular he wishes to hurt. He even said so. 'He's got to pay.' That's what he told me this morning."

"Pay for what? I tell you, I'd never seen the man before you introduced us. And pay how?"

"He wants me to become your mistress so I can spy for

him. He plans to use what I find out to bleed you dry."

A shrug was all he could muster. The anger he ought to feel was truant. In its place, he found only emptiness.

Evie must have sensed it because she snapped at him. "For goodness sake, Harcastle!"

He couldn't remember the last time anyone had scolded him the way she did. He suspected his sister was often exasperated by him but she rarely allowed it to show. He tried and failed to repress a smile.

Evie rolled her eyes inelegantly and took a deep breath. "Well, I've told you. It's up to you what you do with the information. Forewarned is forearmed and now there's no way he can force me to help him."

"Force you?" Ah, there it was. Anger breaking through the emptiness. "What exactly do you mean by that?"

Her eyes widened. "That's not important."

"Like hell it isn't." He didn't care that she was a deceitful baggage who might or might not be aiding Nightingale even now. If that bastard laid a hand on her in *any* way, Alex was going to tear his throat out.

"Look, I want to get as far away from Captain as I can, but he thinks he owns me. I can't take five hundred pounds from you, even if you're still willing to give it to me, because he won't accept that. I need to become useless to him, which means you need to win our wager. Publicly. Where Captain can witness it. If you help me, you could keep the money—"

"No, you need the money." He hadn't forgotten her lecture on that score.

"I can't be your mistress, Harcastle."

"No, you can't." Nightingale had made that impossible. If she was telling the truth, he needed to help her, and he wouldn't take her to bed if she was only willing because of gratitude. If she was lying, if this was all part of the plot...

"You can't stay here," he told her. "But I still have my old lodgings. I'll give you the key and escort you there. I'll call on you tomorrow and we'll decide what to do next."

"Harcastle..." Her eyes searched his face. Whatever she'd been hoping to see, it clearly wasn't there. Without conscious thought, he'd shuttered his expression. It was his first instinct whenever he felt threatened. At the beginning of their acquaintance, he'd done it as a matter of course, and he didn't know when he'd stopped. Only now, with his defenses back in place, did he realize he'd abandoned them. *Careless, Alex.*

Evie gave a sad smile and he felt as though he'd failed her. "It doesn't matter," she said.

Logic told him he'd be a fool to trust her in these circumstances, but a deeper intuition warred against it. Distrusting her felt like a betrayal. His heart against his head. The urge to reassure her was almost overpowering, yet what good would it do? He couldn't change what he was. He doubted her and that was all there was to it.

Nothing either one of them said now would make a difference.

Nothing could be done.

No words would recover what had been stolen.

Nightingale had spoilt what was between them before they'd even met.

Chapter Ten

They didn't speak as the carriage crawled through the fog to Curzon Street. Their earlier interview had gone about as well as Evie had expected.

Better, since he hadn't thrown her out onto the street. Distrust rolled off him in waves but she didn't blame him. She understood. Yet something had died in her when he'd looked at her with such coldness. A foolish hope she hadn't known she harbored.

Jaw set, he gazed into the night, his expression impenetrable. He'd shut her out, and instead of last night's burning looks, the illicit touches, or the wicked things he'd whispered, she remembered his hands over hers in the washbowl, rough and not at all loverlike as he'd scrubbed the last remnants of oil of phosphorus from her skin. In that one moment, he had truly cared about her.

No wonder lying had become a way of life for her. No wonder he wouldn't look at her now. The truth was squalid and so very tawdry.

"My rooms are on the top floor," he told her when the

carriage halted outside a large townhouse. "Go up while I speak with the coachman."

She suspected he wanted a few minutes' respite from her company. Since she had no intention of allowing him to see how much that thought saddened her, she nodded and climbed down from the carriage without waiting for assistance.

The front door opened into a large lobby. A wide, sweeping staircase led her up past floor after floor. Her steps echoed as she climbed. She was panting lightly by the time she reached the top. He hadn't told her the number of his particular flat and now she saw why. There was only one door, which she supposed meant his rooms ranged over the entire floor. What must he have thought when he saw her tiny box of a room?

She fitted the key to the lock but, before she had a chance to turn it, the door swung open. The woman who stood on the threshold, eyebrows arched haughtily, was clearly not a servant. Tall and elegant, she had hair almost as red as Jack's. "Yes?" she said.

Evie couldn't speak. She could only think of one reason for the presence of this woman in Harcastle's bachelor apartment. He had a mistress. *Oh God.* Was this his idea of revenge? To show her how little she mattered? If so, message received.

If possible, the woman's eyebrows arched even higher. "What do you want?"

Evie made the mistake of lowering her gaze. The woman was dressed for dinner and the low neck of her gown displayed her ample bosom to perfection. Those generous curves made Evie feel small and plain. Not that it mattered now. What foolish ideas she'd allowed herself to entertain simply because Harcastle wanted to bed her. In her time at Miss Rose's, she'd seen how unimportant attentions of that sort from a man were, but despite all she'd learned there, she'd let herself believe she mattered to Harcastle.

That some sort of special bond had developed between them.

Stupid, stupid Evie.

"Helen?" Harcastle said from the top of the stairs. Evie had been so distracted by the woman's bountiful cleavage and her own wounded feelings that she hadn't heard him ascend. "What on earth are you doing here?"

"A fine welcome, brother."

Brother? Something loosened in Evie's chest at the word. Helen, he'd said. Evie recalled the name from Captain's research into Harcastle's private life. This must be Helen Carter, the illegitimate half sister who, rumor had it, had spent a decade locked in an insane asylum.

"You knew I was coming, Alex," Mrs. Carter was saying. "I wrote to you weeks ago informing you. What's more, I wrote to Jude only last week to confirm the arrangements. I take it you forgot?"

Harcastle frowned. "It's been an eventful week."

Mrs. Carter rolled her eyes. "Well, come in then."

Evie followed Harcastle inside and gaped at her new surroundings. Although Harcastle House had been magnificent, more so even than Lord Stein's, it was much like the house of any rich mark. Its austere grandeur had everything to do with the Harcastle title and nothing with Alex as a man. Though she usually strove never to use his Christian name even in the privacy of her thoughts, she couldn't help herself now. The room in which she stood was modest compared to what she had seen in his other home, but completely him.

An entire wall of the vast, high-ceilinged room was covered by bookshelves absolutely crammed with books. Not only the expected tomes on spiritualism and the occult. Even a cursory glance revealed novels, travel books, and scientific treatises all jumbled together.

A large desk stood before a tall bay window, the surface almost entirely obscured by scientific instruments. She spotted a microscope, camera equipment, an electric lightbulb coated with dust, and various wood and metal contraptions she couldn't even name. Suspended above it all was a large spherical astrolabe of gleaming brass. She felt Harcastle's eyes on her as she drifted from object to object, touching nothing but taking everything in.

"Who's the waif?" Helen Carter asked.

"Helen..." The reproachful voice didn't belong to Harcastle.

Evie turned to see a huge bear of a man emerging from an inner door.

"Yes, dearest?" Mrs. Carter said in a tone of exaggerated innocence.

The bear's lips twitched as he repressed a smile. This had to be William Carter, Harcastle's brother-in-law. She knew little about him beyond the fact that he was a skilled physician.

Harcastle performed brusque introductions but Mrs. Carter barely waited for him to complete them. "Yes," she said, "but what's she *doing* here?" Her gaze flitted back and forth between them. "Oh!" She covered her mouth with her hand, her eyes lighting with something like excitement. "Is she your mistress?"

Evie's cheeks warmed. She wasn't usually the blushing sort, but Mrs. Carter was peculiarly blunt. Her obvious glee at the possibility that she'd been formally introduced to her brother's inamorata amused Evie and she felt herself actually starting to like this strange, rather tactless woman.

As for Dr. Carter, he offered his wife no reproach this time, perhaps because he was interested to hear the answer to her question.

Harcastle gave his sister a stern look to no visible effect. "No."

"There's no shame in it, Alex. I've always said an affair would do you good." She smiled at Evie and added cryptically, "He lives too much inside his own head."

"Miss Jones is a spiritualist who wishes to leave her profession. I intend to assist her, and I brought her here because she needs somewhere to stay."

"Did you indeed?" Mrs. Carter tilted her head to one side as she regarded Evie again. "Well, we're leaving in a day or two anyway. You're welcome to stay tonight if you like. You can sleep on the sofa if you don't mind cat hair."

Harcastle owned a cat? How unlikely. Impossible to imagine him as an animal lover. Perhaps it was a good mouser and he tolerated its company for that reason. Although this theory didn't explain the profusion of long, tawny hairs she saw on the sofa cushions, which suggested a more pampered pet.

Harcastle started to speak. "I'm not sure that's—"

Mrs. Carter spoke over him to Evie. "You mustn't mind my manner. I'm like that with everyone. You'll soon get used to me."

"Why must you say aloud every thought that enters your head?" her brother muttered.

"Because I spent a decade repressing them."

Presumably, the decade Mrs. Carter referred to was the one she'd spent in the asylum. Evie had never met a former lunatic before, though she'd met plenty of people on the London streets whose wits had gone a'begging. So far, she detected no obvious signs of derangement in this woman unless outspokenness counted and, from what little she knew of mad doctors and their draconian methods, it probably did.

Harcastle shook his head but the expression in his eyes was warm. He was a kind brother, and the realization caused a pang in Evie's heart. To distract herself or perhaps everyone else, she gestured to a side table on which stood a large wooden box from which a brass horn protruded. "What's that?"

"A phonograph. I use it for dictation."

"It records your voice? Can it play music?"

"I suppose so."

"Too frivolous a use for the likes of you, I take it?"

Mrs. Carter, who'd watched this brief exchange with obvious interest, laughed softly. "Did you just insult Alex? How wonderful." Then, yawning, "Well, I'm done in. We keep country hours, you know. Good night, Miss Jones. Good night, brother."

Dr. Carter looked a trifle surprised but he followed his wife out of the room.

Alex shook his head. "Subtle."

Something had changed during the brief interview with his relatives. The tension had lifted and she no longer felt his suspicion like a weight on her heart. For that alone, she was glad of their presence.

"Shall we sit down?" He gestured to the somewhat dilapidated sofa. It wasn't merely the cat hair. The seat sagged, though the piles of fat cushions probably compensated. She got the feeling the cat sat here more than he ever had.

She did as he suggested and found the seat pleasantly comfortable despite its appearance. "How much time do you spend here?"

"These days, not as much as I'd like."

"Why don't you move all this into Harcastle House?"

"Earlier today," he said, "you called Nightingale 'Captain.'"

Clearly he didn't intend to answer her question. "Yes. As far as I know, it's only a nickname. I don't know how he came by it. He was Captain when I met him. And Nightingale. Also

Mr. Higgins, and sometimes he went by Ebert."

"What else do you know about him?"

"He used to be an actor. He tells stories about his days on the stage all the time. He's a photographer and a painter. He grew up here in London but he traveled with a circus for a brief time." Was that really all she knew? "He talks and talks but hardly *says* anything. It's all funny stories about people he used to know."

"If you think of anything else…"

"Of course."

He sat on the opposite end of the sofa. But, no, that wasn't an accurate description of what he did. Rather he sprawled, his head back, eyes closed, and legs stretched out before him. It should have been a relaxed pose but instead he looked exhausted.

"Why did you come to me tonight?" he asked.

I don't want you hurt. That was the simple truth but she doubted he'd believe it. When she didn't answer, he opened his eyes, and despite his weariness, they sparked with intelligence. Once she had thought them empty, but now she could actually *see* him thinking, analyzing. His renewed scrutiny was a tangible thing as she groped for words that were true but not too revealing.

"I didn't know this was his plan. I was going to be a successful medium, that's all. *The* most successful. To me, your investigation was an obstacle and I wanted to stay as far from you and your deductive powers as I could. Captain… I see now that Captain invited you in. I don't know why except that he wants you to pay. I want no part of that."

He nodded but she couldn't tell if he believed her. "Was he your lover?"

"It was never like that," she snapped. Captain's words— *Why do you think I didn't bed you?*—had played on her mind all day. Thinking of them now made her queasy. "He was my mentor. In a way, he made me."

His expression darkened and she knew she'd said too much. Far too much.

"Made you? There must have been a 'you' before."

She shook her head. "I was twelve when he found me. He saved me from a life you can't imagine." But she didn't want to talk about that. If he thought her involvement with Captain was sordid, what would he make of her life before?

"You sound grateful."

"I was. I am." God, this was difficult. Her feelings about Captain could not be summed up in a few brief sentences. "I always knew he didn't take me in from the goodness of his heart. I had to work hard and earn my keep. He was training me to be a medium. To be a charlatan," she corrected herself, "and I decided to be the best charlatan in the business. I've let him command me. I've been his creature. If he'd been honest with me from the start about his plan…"

She stopped, appalled at where her thoughts had taken her. If he'd been honest from the start, she might not even be here. Would she still be helping him?

No, she had only to look at Harcastle to set her mind at rest. She would have ended up at exactly this place because this man drew her like a magnet. Their lives could not have been more different, yet she understood him on a fundamental level. Like her, he distrusted. Like her, he played in shadows. Even if Captain had been honest, she would have ended up in this room unable to hurt Harcastle, whatever it cost her.

"None of that matters," she said. "I *am* here. That's the important thing. You don't trust me and really who could blame you? Don't trust me then. Watch me like a hawk, I won't mind. But I'm here because I want to help and because I'm tired of being Captain's creature. I want to be myself."

She fell silent, surprised by the truth of her own words. Yes, that was what she wanted. To be herself.

Even if she didn't know precisely *who* that was.

• • •

I want to be myself, she said, and strangely, improbably, Alex believed her.

Oh, he fully intended to follow her suggestion and watch her closely. That was a precaution he *had* to take, but he didn't expect her to betray him. And that was strange too, since he almost always expected the worst from people and rarely found himself disappointed in that expectation.

Nightingale's hold over her bothered him for a multitude of reasons. When he'd first met the man, Alex had dismissed him as a mere accomplice. A gross error in judgment. If anything, Evie was the accomplice. And that notion infuriated him, though not for reasons that made any logical sense. She was too formidable a woman to allow one such as Nightingale to use her. She ought to value herself more highly. Alex needed a better understanding of what bound her to this man she called 'Captain.'

"Is Evangeline Jones even your real name?" Though he'd investigated this question, he'd been unable to find a definitive answer.

"No, but it's as good as any other."

He burned to know what name she'd been born with. She seemed to take a "rose by any other name would smell as sweet" stance, but he'd never found that to be true. His entire life so far had been defined by his name. Once he'd been the Marquess of Somerton and that had been a very different affair from being Harcastle. Though Evie held no grand title, what she chose to call herself, be it her original name or something else, mattered. At least, it mattered to Alex. And he couldn't help believing it ought to matter to her too.

"Did Nightingale choose it?"

She hesitated. "We chose it together, but he doesn't like the short form. He wants people to hear 'Evangeline' and think of evangelism and other good, protestant sounding things. Evie's a bit too...garden of Eden."

Silently, Alex vowed never to call her Evangeline again. It would be Evie from now on. "How did you meet him? It might be important," he added when she stiffened.

"I doubt it's relevant."

He heaved an exaggerated sigh. "Humor me, you elusive thing."

"If you must know, he found me at Miss Rose's House of Introduction."

A brothel? He managed to suppress any outward sign of shock, but it was difficult. He'd never mistaken her for a saint or a debutante. He'd assumed she'd had lovers, but...

Something she'd said earlier derailed this line of thought completely.

"You said you were twelve when Captain found you." It was too late to soften the horror in his voice. He doubted he was capable of it. Twelve? The age of consent had been raised to sixteen more than a decade ago.

"I wasn't a prostitute, Harcastle. Though I would have been in a few short weeks or months if Captain hadn't rescued me. I was a skivvy, that's all."

Even so, the things she must have seen when she was only a child. No wonder her feelings for Nightingale were confused. Whatever else he'd done, the man had saved her then.

"How long did you live there?"

"Miss Rose took me in off the street when I was... I'm not sure of my true age, but I suppose I was four or five. Very small. I was grateful to have a roof over my head."

"Fuck."

She smiled as if he'd said something kind. "Thank you."

"For what?"

"I'm not sure… It's the worst part of my story and you don't seem to be throwing me out now that you've heard it. I suppose I'm relieved."

Throw her out? My God, he was in awe of her. That she'd survived at all was remarkable but that she'd become the woman in front of him… "I think you're extraordinary," he said, and he allowed every ounce of his admiration to fill his voice.

Her cheeks turned pink and, to his astonishment, she quickly looked away as if his compliment embarrassed her. "Anyway, you can see why I stayed with Captain so long."

Alex did see but he didn't like it. "You must have researched my private life before that first séance. What did you uncover?" They needed to focus on the here and now. On Nightingale and whatever he was plotting.

"Not true. I personally never researched anyone. That was Captain's domain. He fed me the information I needed."

"So? What information did he feed you?"

"No one knew very much of you before you reached your majority. You studied at home with private tutors. The old duke kept you close. Your sister didn't live with you." She hesitated and Alex suspected that she knew more of Helen. "When you came of age, there were some youthful indiscretions. Nothing very serious, though after what you let slip that day we visited Captain's studio, there were things he failed to discover or at least that he neglected to pass on to me."

She meant his drunkenness. His claim that he preferred water to spirits hadn't fooled her for a moment.

His father had managed to threaten and bully into silence most of the witnesses from those years of petty dissipation. Nightingale might not know about that particular skeleton in Alex's cupboard but perhaps it didn't matter since Alex didn't mind overmuch if people found out. Many men of his class had a wild past and few people cared.

"What else?"

The specter of the séance, and the message he'd received from beyond the grave, loomed between them. Faint resentment stirred when he'd thought he'd long forgiven her. Perhaps she sensed this because she clasped her hands in her lap and kept her gaze fixed on them as she spoke. "Your interest in spiritualism began in those years. You joined the Spiritualist Association and, a few years later, you uncovered your first fraud. You hardly saw your father even though you both continued to live in London year round. That alone suggested an estrangement but then..."

"Go on."

"In 1882, you had him declared of unsound mind. There were no rumors of erratic behavior prior to that time, but you somehow seized control of his affairs and installed a doctor, one with a reputation for incompetence, at Harcastle House. Your father was never seen in public again."

Nightingale had been thorough. The bare recitation of his past acts was sobering.

"Monstrous," he murmured, and he meant the man she described, not Nightingale.

At last, she raised her head and returned his gaze. "I suppose it would be. If it were true."

"Oh, I assure you, every word is true."

She leaned back in her seat. Not, he suspected, for comfort, but out of an unconscious desire to put more distance between them. For several seconds, her mouth hung open. "Why?"

"You tell me. What do you know of my sister's past?"

He saw the moment she made the connection. "No one knew where she was for the first sixteen years of her life but after that she lived in Yorkshire. In an insane asylum. Did...

did your father put her there?"

"He put her there and kept her there for ten years. I never even knew she existed. I only found out because Dr. Carter, who you met earlier, threatened to raise a scandal and my father needed me to quash it for him."

"But you didn't."

"No. He was my father. He helped give me life. I even loved him after a fashion. But, no, I did not help him imprison a perfectly sane woman for the sake of his reputation. I would never do that no matter what I felt I owed him."

His words hit their target. "Oh."

"And just so there are no misunderstandings, you are more, *far more*, than Nightingale's creation."

"Oh." She looked down again but not before he caught the sheen in her eyes. Her rigid spine, the clench of her jaw, the very fact that she refused to look at him, told him she was struggling to keep her emotions in check. He clenched his hands into fists to keep from reaching for her. "You don't really know me—" she began and her voice trembled.

To hell with this. He yanked her across the sofa and into his arms. She stiffened for a moment until she realized he meant only to comfort her, then she settled awkwardly beside him.

"I know you well enough," he said, his tone terse. "I know you lie for a living, but I also know you to be kind."

"Kind?" She shook her head. "I think you're confused."

"When you thought I meant to attack you through Miss Carmichael, you defended her to the hilt. You even broke character to do it."

"She's my friend."

"To whom should you be kind if not a friend?"

"That's loyalty."

He smiled. "So you admit you're loyal?"

"Not to Captain, it would seem."

He'd felt similar guilt when he'd taken Helen's side over his father's, but he'd make the same choice a thousand times over before he allowed his sister to suffer. "Perhaps it's a matter of deciding where your loyalties lie then."

"I made that decision before I came to you."

The tension in his shoulders eased. Talk all he liked about logic and his sense of self-preservation, he couldn't deny the effect her words had on him.

"You're protecting me." He heard the wonder in his own voice. No one protected him. No one thought he needed it.

"Don't sound so smug," she said, misreading him. "I still won't be your mistress."

He laughed softly into her hair. "You and I were doomed from the start."

"Star-crossed," she murmured.

As she sank a little deeper against his side, he realized she could be a comfortable companion despite her prickles. This woman was a person he could have loved if circumstances allowed. He had never loved anyone before, unless he counted his nurse from when he was a child and now Helen.

When he'd first met his sister, he'd doubted he was capable of actually loving her. The most he'd hoped for was the quiet fondness he felt for his few friends. Strong emotion was beyond him. Years of living with his father had taught him to distance himself from his own feelings until he'd almost believed coldness was in his blood. Ice in his veins like the duke.

And, like his sire, he was destined to atrophy as he aged. So he'd thought until Helen, but though their warm relationship had taken him by surprise, it was nothing compared to the shock he experienced now.

The lust he'd felt for the woman in his arms had shaken him. More unexpected still was this creeping tenderness stealing past his innate distrust.

"Is it true you plan to marry?" Her words had begun to slur with tiredness. He ought to leave and let her sleep.

The meaning of her words penetrated. "Where did you hear that?"

"Your cousin, Mr. Ellis, has been conducting discreet inquiries."

"Obviously not discreet enough."

"Is it true?"

He almost denied it. All week, he'd refused to think about the mess his affairs were in beyond selling off a painting or two. He and Ellis had discussed possible solutions, but really there had been only one long-term answer to his problem. He needed to marry a fortune.

"Yes, it's true. I need to choose a bride soon."

"You don't sound very happy about it. Too busy propositioning your social inferiors?"

"Only the one."

"You said 'need'?"

"Yes, I did. If part of Mr. Nightingale's plan is to bleed me for money, he'll be disappointed to learn that I'm almost penniless."

That woke her up a bit. "Penniless? Didn't you renew your offer of five hundred pounds earlier this evening?"

"All right, not penniless."

"Your idea of poor is very different from my idea of poor. Captain says you have no less than three estates dotted around the country and numerous houses."

"And all of them cost far more to manage than they bring in. If all my father's creditors suddenly called in his debts, I'd have nothing. Less than nothing, actually."

"But they won't. Call in the debts, I mean."

"Not if it becomes known I'm to marry a rich heiress."

"I suppose transactions like that are made all the time. Like Mags and Mr. Chase."

"I take it I'm Mags in this scenario?"

"It's nothing to be ashamed of. Not if you're honest with the lady without stooping to cruelty, which I think you will be."

"You sound very certain of my honor." Just as she'd been sure earlier that he was not the sort to usurp his father's property. He wasn't sure what he'd done to earn her good opinion. Perhaps he wasn't the only one who trusted in the face of common sense.

"Very certain," she murmured.

The seconds ticked by but he couldn't make himself move. "Evie?"

No answer.

Her head lolled against his chest, her breaths slow and deep. There it was again, that strange fondness he'd only ever felt for her. He knew at once that he wasn't going to wake her. He would stay here on this sagging old sofa covered in cat hair and, even though his back would hurt tomorrow, he also knew he would count every twinge of discomfort as nothing beside the peace he felt in this moment.

None of this made sense, but that was apparently a state of affairs to which he'd have to grow accustomed.

Chapter Eleven

Evie drifted toward wakefulness enveloped in glorious warmth. Tucked out of sight was the uneasy sense that she'd been worrying about something before she went to sleep. She pushed the feeling away and allowed herself to sink a little deeper.

She was safe.

Nothing could hurt her. Calm, she rose and fell with the warmth. His breaths, she realized. His heartbeat against her ear. His scent like cedar and other clean, woodsy things, all around her. His arms were around her too, something she'd never expected to feel again after yesterday's disclosures.

Ah, there. The source of her disquiet: Captain and his schemes. The things she'd had to confess to Harcastle. How exposed she'd felt. Far worse than when he'd called her a fraud because he hadn't known her then. A sensitive man, he had understood her fear and perhaps that was why he'd made disclosures of his own. Once he had done a dishonorable thing to save his sister, but Evie liked him the better for it.

These thoughts brought with them the remembrance of

where she was. Despite this warmth, this almost peace that beckoned her, she needed to rise before someone found them. When she forced her eyes open, the first thing she saw was her own hand resting on the crisp front of his impossibly white shirt, his fingers encircling her wrist, as though he'd placed her hand there against his chest.

Slowly, she tilted her head back, half expecting to find his sardonic gaze on her. She even braced for whatever sarcastic remark he might make. But no, he was asleep. Eyes shuttered by unfairly long lashes. Head leaning sideways in a position that would surely leave him with an awful crick in his neck when he awoke.

She eased back slightly. Enough to see him a little better but not so much that she wasn't still almost flush against him. How different he looked in repose. As inscrutable as he was, she could always see his mind at work. Evaluating, calculating, and, like her, always questioning. For once, he was serene, a crease between his brows the only sign his dreams might be less than sweet. Her fingers itched to smooth that small crinkle away, and with that urge came a surge of affection that made her stomach drop.

She'd always known she desired him, that she was infatuated with him. These things on their own were disaster enough. But she was in much deeper than even she'd realized. Affection? And for a man who strove to unearth every secret merely because it amused him?

Yet, was that his sole motivation? A shrewd question and one she ought to want answered for her own safety. Unfortunately, she wanted the answer for the silliest reason imaginable; because she wanted to know him. Most particularly at this moment, she wanted to know why he wasn't happy. Somehow she could tell he wasn't.

Irritation ought to accompany the thought. After all, why should a rich, powerful, and well-fed aristocrat be discontented? But the expected feeling didn't come. Whatever his troubles were, however trivial they might turn out to be compared with abject poverty or the hard choices faced by every woman alone in the world, she wanted to know them. Besides, his father sounded like a right bastard. A bit like Captain, actually.

Perhaps pain, whether his or anyone else's, didn't need to be weighed before she allowed herself to feel compassion. Did someone need to be starving before she'd stand them a meal? Much to her amazement, she discovered it was possible to sympathize even with a duke. Compassion, it seemed, was limitless. Or, perhaps, in the end, his troubles mattered to her because they were his and she was fond of him.

Fondness. She hoped that was all this was.

A polite cough sounded from across the room.

Oh no.

Reluctant though she was to face the intruder, her gaze flew to the source of the noise. She didn't even need to turn her head. Helen Carter sat at the desk a few feet away, a pair of reading glasses pushed low on her elegant nose, eyes narrowed perceptively. The other woman regarded Evie with precisely the look she'd earlier feared to find on Harcastle's face, knowing and a little amused, and at last Evie saw the family resemblance. They were an infuriating pair.

It was bad enough that Helen had entered the room before Evie awoke and found her stuck to Harcastle like a limpet, but what had she seen on Evie's face in those first moments? Either she'd think Evie a terrible trollop casting lures far above her station or, worse, a besotted fool.

Evie's first impulse should have been to wait a beat, then ease herself away slowly. To control her breathing and thereby her body's response to the searing embarrassment she felt. Unfortunately, for once Captain's training failed her. She wrenched herself away from Harcastle, causing him to mumble in his sleep, immediately realized her mistake, and leaped to her feet, hands on her cheeks in a foolish attempt to hide the unprecedented blush turning her vermillion.

To compound her sense of mortification, she trod on something soft, something that gave an angry yowl in response. A streak of black shot across the room, its flight checked only by the closed door. The cat looked at Evie over its shoulder and delivered what she could only describe as a withering stare. She could see why there had been so much hair on the sofa.

The creature was *all* fur and angry yellow eyes. It would have been adorable had not its flat face exuded such blatant contempt.

"What did you do to my cat?" Harcastle's voice was croaky with sleep. Of course he'd choose this moment to awaken. The dryness of his tone as he asked the question was the absolute cap to her morning.

"I trod on its tail and now it seems to hate me."

"Don't take it to heart," Helen said, removing her glasses. "That cat hates everyone but Alex. And Alex it barely tolerates."

Harcastle straightened, groaning loudly. His hand went to the back of his neck. "Bastard and I understand each other. We respect one another's privacy and we are not demonstrative by nature."

"When you die," Helen said, "if that thing gets to you before we do, it'll happily feast on your corpse. I hope you realize that."

"The moment I hit the ground," he agreed. "And I'd expect nothing less."

"You named your cat Bastard?" Evie asked.

"Bas-*tet,* not bas-*tard.* After the Egyptian goddess of war." He sighed, presumably at her ignorance. "She had the head of a cat."

Evie sighed back at him. "A less godlike beast I never saw." Bastet licked her paws, eyes still judging Evie and clearly finding her wanting. She was a beautiful cat, obviously well fed, nothing like the skinny wretches of the slums. "I shall call her Tubs."

Alex smiled. "She won't thank you."

Helen, who had watched their exchange with a rueful smile, rose from her seat. "Well, I've finished writing my letter. If you'll excuse me, I'll leave you two to your...discussion."

"Don't go on my account," Evie said. "I'm about to leave." She addressed the next to Harcastle. "I must see Captain."

"Wait," he said and drew her aside. "I think I should see him first. He needs to be at the séance, yes? Otherwise he'll suspect you of losing our wager on purpose."

"So I'll tell him you're suspicious of him and that you want him where you can keep an eye on him."

"I can sell it better. Your time would be better spent recruiting Miss Carmichael."

It wouldn't be the first time Mags had helped at a séance but Evie hated to ask when she knew her friend was preparing for the opening of *Twelfth Night*. Since there was no one else she trusted, she didn't have much choice. The sooner she spoke with Mags, the more time they'd have to prepare, but she didn't like the idea of Harcastle speaking to Captain without her. Though she certainly had no desire to face him, she wanted to maintain control of the situation. She didn't like surprises and she couldn't predict how Harcastle would manage the encounter.

Her reluctance wasn't lost on him if the appraising look he gave her was any indication. "You trust me, don't you?" His eyes weren't all hooded and cynical for once. He was in earnest and she remembered that this man *cared* about what happened to her. His concern was genuine. Not only that, but she was starting to suspect, was almost certain in fact, that he wouldn't ask for anything in return for his help. That was more than could be said for most people.

So unexpected was this revelation that she almost took his hand in hers, but that would have revealed far too much about her own tender feelings. She didn't believe in telling people more than they needed to know, particularly when it came to her emotions. Especially when it was pointless. For dozens of reasons, they had no future. Not even in the short-term. Now that her partnership with Captain had become untenable, she wouldn't stay in London. Sense dictated that she go somewhere far away from Captain's influence.

"Evie, do you trust me?"

Since she had no wish to give away more than she already had, she gave him an answer designed to make him laugh and shatter the moment. "Not entirely, no."

But he didn't laugh. His eyes held hers. "Then allow me to prove myself."

• • •

Alex had never needed to use physical threats to inspire fear. It would be a clumsy way to accomplish something his rank and title achieved so effortlessly. All he need do was be Harcastle as his father had been.

As much as he'd despised his sire, he never found it difficult to slip into the role. It was the ease with which he accomplished it that terrified him. Any suspicion that he might resemble his father disturbed him deeply.

Nightingale hadn't been sufficiently awed at their last meeting with Evie there as a buffer. Alex cursed his earlier self who'd been so obsessed with her that he'd barely looked at the man aiding her. He'd dismissed him with uncharacteristic carelessness.

But today's meeting began well.

Alex sent no word of his intention to call at the studio and had the satisfaction of catching the man off guard. Nightingale hadn't troubled to don his jacket before he answered the door and was obliged to receive his ducal visitor in rolled-up shirtsleeves. His green and blue checkered trousers and waistcoat were good quality but decidedly garish. Alex allowed his gaze to dip to the man's meaty forearms with their smattering of graying hair, then regarded their owner with gently raised brows as though he himself were far too exalted a being to sprout hair in such uncouth places.

"I do hope I haven't called at an inconvenient time. I seem to have caught you...unprepared." Though he doubted it would take the man long to recover.

"Not at all, sir. That is..." Nightingale was at a loss, or so it seemed. "Do come in."

The next few minutes were taken up with the pleasantries. Alex waited on the dilapidated sofa while his host disappeared into the adjoining room, returning some minutes later, jacket restored, bearing a tray with tea and a small plate of biscuits.

Nightingale avoided Alex's gaze until he too was seated on a hard-backed chair he dragged in from the other room. The expression on his face then was self-conscious, like a man who gathers his courage before he makes eye contact. All very gratifying for Alex to behold.

Or it would have been if he believed any of it. To say that he distrusted Nightingale's meek demeanor was an understatement. Was it belated instinct or merely the things Evie had told him? He trusted her with no more rationale than he'd dismissed Nightingale. After a lifetime of skepticism, it would seem he'd chosen to place his faith in a woman he knew to be a liar. How typically perverse of him.

"Miss Jones is to perform a séance at my house and I should like you to attend." Alex made the statement as baldly as possible. His meaning would be clear: *You are not worthy of explanation or preamble.*

Nightingale's eyes widened in what might be genuine surprise. Alex couldn't be sure. "I... Well, of course. It would be an honor."

"I should imagine so." Few ordinary mortals received an invitation from a duke and almost no one at all received one delivered in person. "But I'm not inviting you for the pleasure of your company. I want you where I can see you. In fact, bring that velvet-clad street urchin as well."

For the second time, Alex saw something that looked like genuine surprise flicker in Nightingale's expression. "I... Urchin? I don't..." The man was a study of confusion. He scratched his chin in apparent thought. "I'm not sure I know—"

"Oh, come now. Let's speak plainly. I refer, of course, to the little red-haired gentleman who recited the Lord's Prayer during the partial manifestation we both so recently witnessed. The one who delivered your photographs. I enjoyed the one of Miss Jones very much. We both know you sent it, despite your maddeningly avuncular manner toward her in my presence. I want you and the boy where I can see you during that séance. We'll see how your girl does without her accomplices scribbling on slates in the adjoining room."

"My girl, sir?" The hint of a smile played about the man's lips. "Of course I'll attend the séance. The boy too, since you wish it. But you're quite mistaken if you suppose Miss Jones needs help from the likes of us."

Alex rose unhurriedly without acknowledging the remark. "Oh, and Nightingale..." he said, as the other man began to rise. He made a point of dispensing with the honorific, a subtle insult that meant everything in situations like these. "You may stop throwing her at me. I have only one use for a guttersnipe of Miss Jones's sort and one night is all I require, perhaps less. I certainly have no intention of making her my mistress, so do tell her to stop angling for the position. It isn't dignified. I'll take her when I'm ready, as I'm sure many men have before."

He had hoped to startle a reaction from Nightingale with the crude words. A denial. Perhaps even some anger on Evie's behalf. After all, this man was the closest thing to a father she had ever known. The least he'd expected was more apparent indifference.

But Nightingale laughed.

Perhaps Alex ought to have felt triumphant—the laughter amounted to a decided break in character—but he was so angry on Evie's behalf that he failed to stride from the room as he'd originally intended. Even when he'd marshalled the extremes of his emotions, he didn't walk away. He couldn't. He had to see how Nightingale recovered from such a noticeable slip.

"Forgive me, sir, but I must defend Miss Jones from your accusations on that score. She's intact. I saw to that myself. Kept her closer than I would if she'd been my own daughter. I would hardly seek to tempt a gentleman like yourself with a trull, now would I?"

This was plain speaking at last, but Alex couldn't take any pleasure in having elicited it.

It wasn't that he'd believed the things he'd said about Evie but he hadn't thought her a virgin, either. He'd assumed the woman who'd posed for those photographs must be at least as experienced as he was himself. It hadn't bothered him, first because his attentions hadn't been honorable, and now because she was Evie and, whatever her past, he adored the woman it had made her.

No, what Alex felt was the strange detachment of the man who, perhaps without realizing, thought he had a woman sorted neatly into a box only to find that no woman (or man, for that matter) is so easily confined.

But the carriage…

Surely that made Nightingale's claim unlikely.

"I don't mean that she's entirely ignorant. I assume you know by now I found her at Miss Rose's. Rose is a respectable sort. She doesn't start them as young as some and I got Evie away. But she's an observant girl. She saw a thing or two, I'd wager. The girls in those places talk so frankly as well. Imagine the things she learned from listening. All that knowledge, yet she's untouched. That's a rare thing."

A rare thing indeed. The idea had a predictable effect on Alex's body. The effect it was meant to have. The frisson of lust was quickly swamped by nausea. He was furious with Nightingale who somehow knew the dark twists that would appeal to Alex's baser self, but even more so with himself for being the sort of man who could listen to those words and feel the ache of desire.

And he still didn't believe any of it. Alex had deliberately given Nightingale the impression his interest in Evie was trifling, so now the man was trying to hook him by dripping salacious ideas into Alex's ear like poison. Thank God Nightingale didn't know how truly obsessed Alex had been since the first moment he'd seen Evie or how the longing for her continued to grow.

Her virginity, even if it existed, was nothing.

"Eight o'clock tomorrow evening," he snapped. "Make sure the boy attends."

Alex walked away but he wished he'd done so before Nightingale told his blatant lie. No matter how often he told himself it didn't matter, he could think of little else.

Consequently, he was subdued on the brief carriage ride to Brewer Street, chilled by the calculating light in Nightingale's eyes. The man reminded Alex of a miser gloating over a long-hoarded store of gold. Virginity as valuable commodity. Perhaps not so very different from all those fathers who'd angled their daughters Alex's way over the years. *One virginity, carefully preserved, in return for one dukedom, slightly tarnished.* But unlike them, Nightingale wasn't after a dukedom, which begged the question: what did he want?

Try though he might, Alex couldn't keep his mind on this important question. Instead, he found himself wondering, *is it true?* And he was fascinated by his own preoccupation with the matter. Evie was not a prospective wife, though he didn't give a damn that she would be socially unacceptable in that role. No, the reason he would never consider proposing to Evie was that he couldn't afford her.

Floored by this realization, he let his head drop heavily against the squabs.

Did he want to *marry* Evie? A less restful companion with whom to spend his life he could hardly imagine. Virgin or no, she was a woman with a past. A dark past as alien from his own as it was possible to compass. She was complicated. She told lies and withheld truth. Yet the idea of marrying her didn't fill his heart with panic the way thoughts of the shadowy debutante he was destined for did. Quite the opposite. It felt right.

He forced his head up and mentally shook himself. He couldn't have Evie, so the point was moot. Her alleged virginity, then, ought to have no bearing on him. She was not possible as a wife and, even if she were, why should her lack of sexual partners mean anything? Virginity before marriage did not presuppose faithfulness afterward. He only had to glance at the upper echelons to discern a number of examples where this had not been the case. As a logical being, he therefore doubted that lack of virginity equated to an inability to remain faithful.

He had to admit, however, that he found the idea of Evie's alleged virginity, coupled with her obvious knowledge, titillating.

As the carriage drew to a halt in Brewer Street, Alex could have wept with relief. At last he was obliged to think of something else. He could address the problem of tomorrow's séance and leave these circular and rather alarming thoughts behind.

As he climbed down, he saw Evie walking along the pavement toward her lodgings, a black umbrella angled against the rain. *His* black umbrella presumably taken from the elephant's foot in the hallway of his old lodgings.

She hesitated when she saw him and, for a moment, she was the unknowable woman from the first séance, shrewd eyes taking him in from head to toe. "Well?"

He merely nodded. The deed was done. The plan had been set in motion.

"I won't be long." She strode toward the building, apparently under the impression that he would wait by the carriage, but sod that. If she was aware of him at her heels, she didn't comment. Her hips swayed delightfully as she ascended the stairs ahead of him. At the top, she opened the door.

"Mags!" Her startled cry told him instantly that something was wrong.

He bounded up the last few steps and pushed past her into the room, intent on getting between her and the threat, whatever it was. Later he would reflect that his nerves must have been compromised by the meeting with Nightingale since he fully expected to find that man towering over Miss Carmichael's murdered body, bloody dagger in hand, like a villain in a penny dreadful. He was not usually given to melodrama and this seemed a particularly egregious example given that he'd left Nightingale minutes ago and the man could hardly have beaten him here in a hansom.

Miss Carmichael was on the floor, her white nightgown

plastered to her body with sweat. Evie darted past him and knelt beside her friend before he had a chance to urge caution, then gathered her into her arms.

"Evie?" Her voice was weak. An angry rash covered her face.

"Measles," he said. "Have you had them?"

"Yes," Evie said, and he sighed with relief. So had he. "Pull back the bedcovers," he said, as he knelt to gather Miss Carmichael into his arms. "I'll send for Dr. Carter," he added, once he'd placed the woman on the bed as gently as possible.

"Can't," Miss Carmichael mumbled. "Can't pay."

He looked at Evie. "It's fine," was all he said, but inside shame uncoiled in his belly. He remembered how he'd stood almost exactly where he stood now and demanded to know why Evie didn't get a job as a seamstress or the like instead of conning people. Yes, he'd reasoned, the money was less but at least it was honest work. Now Miss Carmichael, though employed somewhat honestly as an actress, couldn't call for a doctor when she needed one. It was the first time he'd truly begun to understand what Evie had been trying to tell him that day.

Evie nodded her understanding of at least some of everything that was going on behind his '*fine*'. She even rewarded him with a faint smile but he withdrew feeling like a veritable monster, old biblical saws about rich men, camels, and needles flitting through his mind.

Chapter Twelve

Thank God for Alex. Having a rich — or comparatively rich — duke around certainly smoothed away life's difficulties.

The look on his face as he turned away… She longed to know what he'd been thinking.

Poor Mags. She'd been complaining of a cold for the last few days but it hadn't seemed like anything to worry about. People died from the measles. Not every time. Usually it turned out all right, but things went wrong often enough that Evie was glad Alex had gone for Dr. Carter. The spots looked angry. She dimly remembered having measles herself and how itchy and sore the rash had been.

Mags looked at her with eyes wet with tears and Evie remembered about *Twelfth Night*. "Oh, I'm so sorry. Do you need me to get word to the Dovecote?"

Mags nodded, then groaned with pain.

"I'll get some water."

The carriage was long gone by the time Evie got downstairs. It took less than ten minutes to get water from the pump on Broad Street. The water was safe now, so she didn't need to worry about boiling it. She was only going to use it to bathe the rash in any case.

Mags was still awake when she returned. "You're a wonderful actress," Evie said, as she soaked a cloth in the bowl she'd filled. "You'll get another chance."

"I'll have to marry Mr. Chase." Mags sobbed so hard that the words were hard to understand. Evie took several seconds to parse them and make sure she hadn't misunderstood, and when she decided that she'd heard right, she thought Mags might be delirious.

"Marry Mr. Chase? Has he asked you?" Surely not. Chase wasn't an aristocrat like Alex but he was still landed gentry. Gentry didn't marry actresses.

To her astonishment, Mags nodded.

"My God." If this was true, surprised didn't begin to describe her feelings. Evie was plain shocked. "But that's wonderful, isn't it?"

"No." The word had a bitter lilt to it, even through more tears. "Silly boy..." More sobbing. "...proposed to at least four..." Still more sobbing. "...unsuitable girls before me. He'll tire of me before the ink on the registry dries." Even more sobbing. "And I'll have to sleep with him for the rest of my life." In fact, the sobs were approaching a full bout of hysterics. "And I don't want to sleep with him."

Evie couldn't help but smile even though she knew this wasn't funny. Most girls in Mags's place would be thrilled, but her friend's disgust was true and genuine. Ordinarily, Mags would swallow these feelings and do what needed to be done, but her shrewd and practical nature had been entirely consumed by her illness. It was the uncharacteristic outpouring that made Evie smile, not the situation itself. Too many women were forced by poverty to marry where they had no inclination. She could only hope that, when Mags recovered, the material gains in such a marriage would outweigh the price she'd be required to pay.

She opened the door as soon as she heard footsteps on the stairs. Dr. Carter had been a mostly silent foil to his wife yesterday. A tall, plain-faced bear of a man. She'd learned to be cautious of men of his size and strength but she was happy to see how gentle he was with Mags. Doctors could be such pompous pricks, but he spoke to soothe, his gentlemanlike accent so much softer than Alex's clipped, aristocratic voice. A gentle giant, she realized. He and Helen seemed an unlikely pair in some ways, but they appeared to get on together well enough.

She and Alex waited in the dingy hallway while Dr. Carter examined his new patient.

"Are you well?" Alex asked her, and she realized she wasn't. Not entirely.

"She's my only friend now."

"Not true."

He held her hand, and she almost wept. How had they got here, she and the cold, dead-eyed aristocrat who was supposed to be her enemy? He looked at her now with undeniable warmth and she wanted nothing more than to creep into his arms and let him be strong for her.

Naturally, she did no such thing.

"This complicates matters," she said. "Obviously Mags can't help us tomorrow now."

If he thought her unfeeling to talk of their plan while her friend lay ill in the next room, he gave no sign. She sensed no judgment. "A postponement, then?"

"She won't be better for weeks. I don't want to leave things that long."

He nodded. "You know other actresses and such. Can't you ask one of them?"

"No one I know will go against Captain. He might not seem like much to you, but here in Soho, people fear him. Or they're loyal to him. There's no one I would trust to take our side over his."

The door opened and Dr. Carter joined them. "It's definitely measles. It's not often I come across an adult case. Most people catch it in infancy. Still, she's strong. If she's properly taken care of, I don't foresee any problems. I assume you work for a living, Miss Jones, but someone will need to stay with her."

"I can get someone," Alex said, before she could respond. "If you wish, that is."

"We can't afford—"

"Don't be ridiculous," he snapped. "There's no question of that and you know it. You're my..." He stopped, clearly flummoxed. "Well, whatever you are, you're under my protection. There's no question of payment between us. There never could be." He shook his head. "God, this is awkward. Don't make me *emote* in this unspeakable fashion."

He descended the stairs with all the appearance of a terribly important person who had somewhere else to be. If Evie didn't know better, she'd swear he was embarrassed. She'd thought him above such human failings.

Dr. Carter smiled and shook his head. "Never thought I'd see the day," was all he said.

• • •

Although she didn't say so, Evie seemed a little disturbed by the notion of leaving Miss Carmichael with a complete stranger.

Alex couldn't have said precisely how he knew this. Some minute change in her expression, some almost imperceptible glance, must have told him. He reassured her that the woman he'd found—actually Ellis had done the finding—came highly recommended. By the time the woman had been got and brought to Brewer Street, and Carter had finished instructing her to his satisfaction, the light was already fading. It was dark by the time the three of them arrived back at Curzon Street.

Helen had ordered dinner from one of the nearby chop houses. While she bustled about setting the table, Evie stood by the desk, gazing out the window at the lamp lit street. Was she worrying about her friend or formulating a new plan? That he couldn't tell. He could discern her moods well enough but never the workings of her mind. She was a curious person, his Evie. He'd woken this morning to find her nestled beside him like a languid cat. He'd pretended to sleep on just to prolong the sensation of her close and so accessible.

In those few moments, before she'd woken and realized they were not alone, he'd possessed a little piece of her. He'd never felt that way before, even when he'd spent on her naked breasts. He marveled now at the startling intimacy of lying in the embrace of a woman without making love to her.

What Nightingale had said didn't matter. It wasn't the first time he'd told himself that but this time he believed it. Now that he'd seen her again, now in the presence of her sharp edges and surprising soft spots, Nightingale and his poison were nothing. Whoever she was, whatever she turned out to be, she was all that mattered.

"What about Helen?" she said. She'd crossed the room while he was lost in thought and said the words low so that only he could hear. That calculating light he'd come to adore was back in her eyes.

"Which Helen? Wait, not *my* Helen? I think not."

"You told me she's an actress. Surely she could do it."

"Amateur theatricals, not séances."

"My séances *are* amateur theatricals. She'd be perfect."

She'd been thinking about this. Who was he trying to fool? She'd probably decided on this course before the carriage had even departed Soho. Because *of course* she had.

"There's nothing amateurish about you," he said. "No. No, I don't want her involved. It's too dangerous. Something might go wrong."

Immediately he realized his error. Her eyebrows rose almost into her hairline. "So it's perfectly fine for Mags, my dearest friend, to take the risk, alone and friendless though she is, but your sister cannot?"

"Can't what?" Helen asked. She stood by the table, now laid with steaming plates of meat pie and vegetables drenched in gravy. "What can't I do?"

Alex groaned and drew a chair for Evie.

"We should at least ask her," she said.

• • •

Of course Helen said yes.

In fact, her eyes lit with excitement when she understood what was required of her. Since the role of fully materialized spirit required knowledge of a particular type of stagecraft, the two women retired to the bedroom so that Evie could share some of the tricks of her trade. The irony of Helen as first recipient of knowledge he'd been trying to coax from Evie since the moment they'd met was not lost on Alex.

Helen paid no mind to his objections. Her face would be veiled so that Nightingale wouldn't see it, or not much of it at any rate, and if he did chance to see beneath the layers of lace, no one knew what the Duke of Harcastle's bastard sister looked like anyway. All very logical, but he had a bad feeling.

He and Carter were lounging on the sofa in front of the fire. Bastet hogged the only armchair and was purring in her sleep. Alex lit a cigar and offered another to his brother-in-law. "You can't approve of this madness."

Carter shook his head at the proffered cigar. "No, can't say I do."

"Well? Can't you do something?"

Carter shook his head. "You know where Helen's been and what she's suffered. If I start forbidding things, telling her what to do, I might as well have left her at Blackwell."

Alex shuddered. He'd visited Blackwell, the asylum where Helen had been incarcerated for the best part of a decade. He remembered the hard-eyed and desperate woman he'd met there. Contentment had transformed her into the warm if headstrong sister he'd come to love. He'd hate to cause her even a moment's unhappiness but he wanted her safe.

"I can't do it to her," Carter said, as if he'd been considering the matter. "No, I can't. I trust her. We trust each other." He leaned forward and poured himself another helping of brandy. A large one. "But I want to be there tomorrow. Actually in the room."

From the look in Carter's eyes, Alex knew there'd be no gainsaying him. And that was fine. Will Carter was exactly the sort of man he needed on his side.

Chapter Thirteen

Harcastle House was the perfect venue for a séance. As servants bustled in and out of the Blue Room moving furniture and positioning oil lamps and candles, Evie tried to imagine what the finished effect would be.

As awed as she'd been on her first visit by the scale and faded magnificence of this place, she had still recognized that it was not a home. It was a mystery to her how the long line of Harcastles before hers—she winced at the possessive thought but otherwise chose to ignore it—had managed to build a veritable palace, fill it with expensive art and furnishings, yet the effect was still utterly bleak. The perfect playground for a few chain-rattling ghosts.

The Blue Room itself was a case in point. High ceilings, massive windows draped in royal blue velvet, an enormous fireplace flanked by leather armchairs. A long brocade sofa dominated the space, and an elegant writing desk stood by the window. The room might have been charming had it not also been paneled with the darkest wood she had ever seen. The shining black ebony was covered with grotesque ram's heads, a Harcastle emblem, leering like gargoyles.

The floor was uncarpeted and made of the same wood. Her feet echoed eerily as she walked but that was no good for a séance where she needed to move without being observed. When she'd mentioned this to Alex—that is, to *Harcastle*— he'd responded by sending an enormous Persian rug. Somehow its cheerful reds, greens, and tarnished golds were swallowed up by the general dreariness.

She knelt and opened the massive carpetbag she'd brought with her from her most recent visit to Brewer Street. Inside was her "spirit cabinet," in actuality a heavy pair of black velvet curtains. They would reach from floor to ceiling, and once hung in the appropriate place, would obscure a door that led into an adjoining room. They would also provide a small alcove where she could conceal herself or another.

The plan was simple. She was to pull out all the stops and perform the best full-manifestation she could muster, so that Captain couldn't say she hadn't tried. The spirit— Helen in disguise—was to manifest while Evie, bound and concealed beyond the curtain as was the custom at events such as this, provided the usual accompaniment of moaning, rattling, knocking and, inexplicably to her mind, even a few notes from a flute or trumpet. Harcastle would then break with every standard of conduct permissible at a séance and pull back the curtain to reveal Evie in the midst of this absurd behavior. Helen would flee the room before anyone could apprehend her.

Dr. Carter, along with Mr. Ellis, Harcastle's cousin, would be present as witnesses, rendering Evie's exposure lamentably public. Captain too would witness the calamity firsthand and would surely agree that she could not have prevented it. Having lost her wager, she would be forced to make whatever public admissions of guilt Harcastle required, in return for which she would receive five hundred pounds.

Once she'd given Captain his share, she would leave for the continent.

Now, as she watched the servants hang the curtains according to her specifications, she wished she could take more pleasure in the thought that next week she might be taking her ease in the south of France. Actually, she felt nothing.

A fresh start meant leaving the few friends she had. She would miss Mags and Jack. Worst of all, she would miss *him*, and she was furious with herself. Stupid, stupid girl, she had no one but herself to blame. It was one thing to miss him—*of course* she would miss him—but to allow these feelings to poison her joy in escaping Captain's ever-tightening grip? No, that was madness. This was why she shouldn't have permitted herself to soften toward Alex—closing her eyes, she sighed deeply—*Harcastle*. This was why she shouldn't have permitted herself to soften toward Harcastle. But it didn't matter anymore, did it? Falling asleep in his arms last night had been the last in a long line of fatal errors. What she called him was the least of it.

Swiping at a cobweb that clung to her skirt, she strode from the room and down the hall to the study which she entered without knocking.

Alex didn't rise but smiled faintly on seeing her. He was wearing his reading glasses, and words that oughtn't to apply to him, words like *sweet* and *adorable*, invaded her mind. If he was short-sighted, he was human after all, but then she'd known that for a long time. Since the carriage. Or perhaps since the night they'd met when she'd played him such a nasty trick. Tenderness welled in her and the urge to make it all up to him. To drown him in affection.

No. No more of that, she told herself sternly.

He hadn't stayed with her last night. Once Helen and Dr. Carter had retired, Bastet had been her only company. They'd spent the evening maintaining a respectful distance from each other, the cat purring softly on the chair while Evie lay on the saggy couch. This had proved strangely companionable, yet she'd rather have spent the night in Alex's arms.

No, she must treat him as Bastet treated her. With coolness. That was why she didn't greet him beyond a slight inclination of her head.

Another smaller bag awaited her near the fire. She sat down and rummaged through the contents. Inside, among other things, were camphor gum and storax. "Might I trouble you for a glass of whisky?" she asked him.

The decanter was right there on the sideboard. He must keep it for guests since she knew he never indulged. A polite host, he rose and poured the whisky for her.

"And some quicksilver?" she said, when he held the cut-glass tumbler out to her.

His expression darkened. "What are you up to now? Whatever this is for, it had better not be flammable."

"Quite the reverse, I assure you."

He gazed at her for several seconds, searching for a lie. Considering their history, she didn't blame him. Whether or not he was satisfied with what he saw, he went to the mantle and depressed the head of a small golden lion that crouched there. This, she gathered, was how he rang for a servant. Presumably he was going to send out for quicksilver. Mercury wasn't the type of thing most people had on hand, unless they suffered from syphilis.

He didn't speak to her again until after the servant had been and gone. "I'd like your word you won't be using oil of phosphorous at any point this evening," he said then.

It was on the tip of her tongue to tell him to mind his own business. After all, she didn't tell him how to duke. Then again, she was utilizing his house, not to mention his sister, for this séance. And he was right about the danger. She'd never liked using phosphorous in her act. Really it was Captain she needed to tell to bugger off, not Alex.

"I do so swear," she said, holding her hand high.

He smiled and shook his head before returning to whatever he was doing at his desk. It went straight to her heart, that smile. Her foolish, impossible-to-reason-with heart. What a flagellant it had turned out to be.

When the servant returned with the quicksilver a scant quarter of an hour later, she finished mixing her ingredients. Painted onto her hand and left to dry, this paste would come in very useful this evening.

That done, she reached further into the depths of her bag and produced several lengths of rope. Alex's head was down as he concentrated on whatever he was doing, apparently oblivious to her continued presence. She longed for the same insouciance but she was always, always aware of him, so close, yet completely untouchable.

"Hold out your hands, please," she said, crossing to his side.

He glanced up and stilled when he saw the rope. Oh, she had his full attention now all right. Dangerously so. His eyes took on a glazed expression, heavy-lidded yet somehow expectant.

Wasn't that what she wanted deep down? For him to look at her again the way he had when he'd begged her to reconsider her decision about becoming his mistress? Through simple honest lust, she could have his fixed attention without all the feelings and tenderness, the impossible longing and insurmountable obstacles. Through his lust, unobtainable though he was, she held him.

It got to her, the way he didn't say anything. The way he simply turned sideways in his chair and held his hands out. He trusted her in this though she'd done nothing to earn it. He would let her do anything she wanted.

"Place your hands palm down on the arms of the chair."
And he did.

She stepped closer. Close enough to detect the faint cedar scent of his cologne. "Tonight, I will be bound and you will have to bind me, since you are the person I'm supposed to be hoodwinking." She tried to keep her voice businesslike, looping the rope around first one wrist, then the other. "Can you get free?"

He relaxed his arms in response. That was good; she hadn't even been conscious that he'd tensed them. With relatively little difficulty and only a brief expression of discomfort, he used the slack he'd created with that slight resistance against the rope to wriggle free. The backs of his hands were a little scraped up but it had taken him only moments to escape.

"When Captain ties someone, assuming he doesn't wish them to escape, he pushes down to try and reduce the amount of slack. Do you think you can make it look like I'm tightly bound without actually constricting my movement too much?"

"Of course."

"It needs to look believable." She almost asked him to show her, but no. He might enjoy that a little too much and so might she. And then where would they be? "I'll carry a knife in case." She spoke with determined nonchalance, yet still his breaths were shallow, his gaze intent. A tremor went through her in response. "You mustn't look at me that way."

"What way?" But he knew. She could tell.

Despite herself she stepped even closer. It was like stepping into the light. "It's only our bodies, Harcastle." But her voice wasn't as brusque as she'd meant it to be. "Soon I'll be gone and you'll move on to the next obsession. You and I, we're from different worlds. One day, you'll look back on this and wonder what you were thinking."

His hand whipped out and grabbed her wrist. When

he smiled, she wanted to kiss it right off his face. Instead she made herself utterly still. He must never know how he affected her.

"Yes, we're from different worlds," he said. "Our lives couldn't be more different. But you and I..." He released her wrist and interlaced their fingers so they were palm to palm, holding hands like sweethearts. "You and I are the same. Devious and distrustful, we expect everyone to lie to us. Perhaps that's why your moods, your silences, everything you say and do, make perfect sense to me. When I'm with you, *only* when I'm with you, I'm not Harcastle. I'm not acting a part. And I think it's the same for you because you feel it too. That despite what's on the surface, you and I are made of the same stuff."

Oh, he was *ruining* her.

His palm rested warm against hers. As messy, sticky emotion rose within her, her heart seemed to swell until it must surely burst with the strength of her feelings. For the first time, she understood what it was to have a full heart.

"Alex," she whispered, a reproach and a plea. She could bear this so much better if all he wanted was to bed her, if she believed that the true attachment was one-sided. Why must he speak of the bond between them? Didn't he know that, by acknowledging it, he gave it life? "There's no point."

"Because you're leaving," he said. "Because I have all this." He waved his hand, the gesture encompassing not only the room or even the vast, gloomy entirety of Harcastle House, but everything—title, land, duties, dependents.

She shouldn't pity him for being bound to so much privilege, yet seeing the look on his face, she almost did.

"I have to marry an heiress." His grip on her hand tightened almost painfully. "If I don't, I might lose all of it, or at least so much that the title will become a joke. You see, the actual duke himself is nothing. Each one, each generation, is merely a link in the chain. None of this is truly mine. I'm its guardian, and so I must marry a suitable and suitably rich woman and make a little lord who will grow up and become another link in the chain."

"I don't understand." Who was it all for if not the duke?

"I'm not surprised." He laughed bitterly. "It may seem strange but that is how it's always been. I cannot be the man who breaks the chain and so I am bound by it." He eased her hand open and kissed the palm, his lips brushing her skin, barely touching. It was a curiously chivalrous gesture and one that was completely alien to her. "But you see, whatever the unspoken rules may be, I *am* still a man and, from the moment I first saw your face, I recognized something in you."

He rose from his seat and released her hand. He was about to leave the room and she must allow it. If she didn't let him go now, she would want to keep him forever. But he had more to say before he went and, whatever it turned out to be, she sensed it would devastate her.

Sure enough, he stopped before he reached the door, though he didn't turn to face her. "So, no, I won't forget you when you leave, I will never wonder what I was thinking, and I will always, always be sorry that we were not to be."

It was both a declaration and a renunciation. She closed her eyes against the pain of both. When she opened them again, he was gone.

. . .

That night, Alex watched from across the séance room as his cousin and Nightingale made what was undoubtedly polite conversation.

With Ellis, one rarely achieved anything else. The man was scrupulous in his social dealings, unlike Alex who usually couldn't be bothered. Since giving up the demon drink, his focus on his work had been such that he'd allowed his social commitments to fall by the wayside. Ellis wasn't in on tonight's plan. As fond as Alex was of him, in many ways he remained an enigma. Alex doubted he could carry off a scene like this convincingly.

As Nightingale nodded at something Ellis had said, Alex couldn't help marveling a little that he'd actually invited his enemy into his home and given him claret. If this were a few hundred years ago, there might be poison lurking in its depths. He couldn't muster the same animosity for the boy hovering at Nightingale's side. With his faded velvet suit, closely cropped bright red hair, and pale, prematurely wise elfin face, his presence as Nightingale's shadow saddened Alex. What chance did the boy have and what must his life have been?

Carter inclined his head in acknowledgment from his station by the fire. Like Alex, he was steering clear. He was perhaps the only man Alex knew who was incapable of polite dissembling. Raw honesty, that was Carter's way, and Alex had always admired him for it. Helen had chosen well.

At last, Evie stepped from behind the drapes of her spirit cabinet. Her black hair, drawn severely back and neatly parted in the middle as always, shone in the candlelight. She wore the same black gown she'd worn the night of their first meeting. If he only had time, he would buy her dresses. Ruby red, emerald green, and sapphire blue. He wanted to see her hair unbound once before he lost her.

"Good evening, gentlemen," she said. "My preparations are almost complete." Without raising her voice, she commanded the room. She was what they'd all been waiting for. Especially Alex.

All of my life.

He pushed the thought away. "Next to me, Mr. Nightingale, if you please," he said, taking one of the seats that formed a semi-circle in front of the curtains. "And the boy on my other side."

"You heard His Grace, Jack," Nightingale muttered.

Carter and Ellis took the chairs on each end.

"Before I re-enter the cabinet, I will ask one of you to bind me so that everyone may feel confident no chicanery is possible. I will allow His Grace and Mr. Nightingale to decide between them who is to do the honors."

Alex allowed his amusement to show as he turned to the other man. "Any thoughts, Nightingale?"

"I am content for His Grace to secure your bonds. And to supply the rope if he prefers."

The gall of the man when he must know she kept a blade on her person.

"Would you consent to be searched, madam?" Alex asked.

"Not by you, sir," was Evie's tart rejoinder.

Alex laughed outright. "By Mr. Ellis then? Or perhaps Dr. Carter is more to your taste?"

Ellis looked absolutely mortified, Carter impassive.

She heaved an exasperated sigh. "Have you no trusted female retainer? I am a respectable girl, no matter what you think."

"No one doubts that, Miss Jones," Ellis said, because someone had to.

Another sigh. "Very well. Come and search me then, Your Grace. I see you won't be satisfied with anything less. His Grace only, though, if you please." She fixed Alex with a steely glare. "You are, after all, the skeptic I'm here to enlighten."

He rose and followed her into the cabinet. Carter was to keep an eye on Nightingale and his boy while they were gone. No one waited behind the curtain. Helen was still in the adjoining room.

"Well?" Evie said loudly and not for his benefit.

"Extend your arms to the side, please," he said at a similar volume, and waited to see what she would do.

Her arms came up, palms parallel to the floor. Her eyes were lit with challenge.

He felt along each sleeve. The outline of a small blade was plain through the fabric of both forearms. He shook his head but naturally said nothing.

"Is that all?" she said and smiled. Rare as diamonds, those smiles.

He couldn't help himself. "Not quite."

Her eyebrows rose in amusement as he sank down onto his knees before her. First he ran his hands up and down her bodice, pressing lightly. His touch was nothing or almost nothing.

Now it was her turn to shake her head. "Where else, sir?" she whispered.

He stopped smiling as the moment hung between them.

They were safe.

Nothing could happen with four people on the other side of the curtain. He gazed steadily into her eyes as he gathered her skirts together in one hand. Still fixated on her face, he took hold of her ankle. Her breath hitched as he trailed his fingers up and up. He didn't allow himself to dwell on her faltering breaths, on the smooth glide of his hand against her stockings or the sudden shocking feel of soft bare thigh.

The dazed look in her eyes shattered his good intentions. He leaned in as he clasped the other ankle. The sweet lavender smell of her was more than he could bear. His fingers traced circles on her calves as he leaned in for a kiss. She was wet and warm and tasted like claret.

But as always there was no possibility of more. No time and nowhere to go.

He pulled free. "I'm satisfied," he announced.

He was anything but.

As he stepped back into the main room, he was grateful for the flickering gaslights. A steadier light source would not have hidden the signs of arousal that were surely otherwise evident in his face and person. At least if Nightingale noticed anything he would think she'd been following his orders, trying to hook a duke.

She emerged a moment later, looking entirely untouched. Inviolable as ever. His will-o'-the-wisp, always drawing him from the safe path. Always vanishing before he could reach her. He wanted her pinned beneath him, her responses undeniable. It was the only way he would ever be sure of her.

"I'm going to turn down the lights." She moved from lamp to lamp, turning them off completely. By the time she'd finished, the fire was their only source of light.

"Is this not a little much?" he said, because it would seem strange if he didn't.

"My apologies." Her shadowy form—she was the only person not seated—moved to the fire. Kneeling, she plucked a glowing coal direct from the grate and held it up between two fingers.

"Christ," Carter muttered.

Now Alex understood the purpose of that potion she'd been brewing earlier; she'd made at least one of her hands heat-resistant. She carried the coal across the room to a small table that stood to one side of the curtain and used it to light a single candle. It was a good trick and Carter at least was suitably impressed.

"The tongs were right beside you," Alex said drily.

"We have no need of tongs." Her voice was a strange, high stage-whisper. It did indeed sound almost like two people speaking at once. A clever bit of ventriloquism.

"Your Grace." Nightingale sounded oddly hesitant. If Alex hadn't known better, he would have thought he was scared. The man knew how to work a room. "Have you any rope? I think the time may have come to restrain Miss Jones."

Oh, very good. The subtle implication of danger. Alex had to hand it to him; it was an admirable performance. He rose and fetched the cord set aside for this moment from the writing desk drawer. No mean feat given how dark it was. It was good, strong rope but not so thick that she wouldn't be able to cut through it if she had to. She wouldn't even need to retie herself since he intended to "expose" her before they reached that stage.

He led her into the spirit cabinet, and without closing the curtain behind them, he sat her on the chair he found there. First he tied her wrists to the arms, then her ankles to the legs. All this in near total darkness. Only a single candle burned on this side of the curtain and that a stub. He was fairly certain she was going to need a knife, so allowing the curtain to obscure them again, he withdrew the blade from her sleeve and eased it into her fingers.

"Cheating," she whispered.

He placed a quick kiss on her forehead and withdrew.

Only when he was back in his seat waiting—it could take as long as twenty minutes for the "materialization" to begin— did he realize how natural that last casual, affectionate gesture had felt, and this despite what a prickly cactus of a woman she was. Actually, he rather enjoyed her spikes.

Nightingale hadn't requested that Alex be bound too, something Alex had half expected. He wouldn't be the first skeptic to sweep aside the curtain in an attempt to expose a spiritualist. It was always claimed that interrupting the trance endangered the medium's life. He had never needed to stoop to such desperate measures before. And it *was* a stoop. Perhaps that was why Nightingale hadn't bothered. He credited Alex with better taste. Or perhaps he was confident he could simply restrain him.

It was a shame it had come to this, but a curtain dive was the most dramatic way to expose Evie. Carter would spread the news far and wide.

They waited in silence, the only sounds coals shifting and logs crackling. Even the clock on the mantle had been allowed to run silent, its pendulum halted for lack of a winding. It had been ticking his whole life. His father would have dismissed the servant who failed to keep it going. When this was over, Alex would sell it as he would sell every stick of furniture the duke had so much as brushed past. In Harcastle House, that meant everything that wasn't nailed down and some things that were if it could be managed.

A moan sounded from beyond the curtain and set his skin prickling. Ah, the spirits stirred. A short silence followed, then as the tension was fading, another low keening, the sound undoubtedly eerie but undeniably arousing. The moaning continued, slow and measured but so like those pleasure-pain sounds a woman made in bed.

Ellis shifted uncomfortably. Embarrassed, no doubt.

Carter remained absolutely motionless, probably for the same reason. Only the boy looked bored, the only person here too inexperienced to think what Alex was thinking.

Nightingale gave nothing away. Like Alex, he managed to appear at ease, neither unnaturally still nor restive. Both watched with sober, professional interest. They might have been attending a simple tea party.

Inside, Alex was burning, his mind teeming with thoughts of what had almost happened behind the curtain, of her slim, shapely legs and how badly he'd wanted to trail his fingers higher, how sure he'd been that she'd be wet and aching for him. As perhaps she still was.

He wanted to kneel between her delicately parted thighs and kiss and suck. Make love to her with his fingers and his tongue. He'd never done such a thing to a woman in all his well-mannered affairs. There was nothing polite about his feelings for Evie or the things he longed to do to and with her. His arousal grew painful as he listened to the sounds she made. Did she know? Was she doing this to him on purpose?

So distracted was he that he might not have seen the glimmer of light there on the floor if not for Carter and Ellis's simultaneous gasps. A tiny spot on the floor in front of the cabinet, but growing, growing all the time.

Abruptly, Evie's moans ceased. Throttled mid-cry. The silence seemed loud in their absence as the pool of light slowly expanded outward and upward. Not bright and clean like daylight. This emanation possessed a sickly green tinge, unwholesome and disquieting. A tinny, not quite musical sound started up, discordant and jangling. For several moments he remained disoriented, unable to pinpoint precisely what he was seeing.

It looked almost like… Was that a face?

Yes, a face on the floor but obscured by gauze. Or lace? And glowing steadily, its light rising and expanding until it was the width of a woman's shoulders. Before his eyes he was witnessing a woman rising through the floor. Yet he knew there were no trapdoors in this room. Evie had hung curtains and ordered carpet installed, but had called for no carpenter, no plasterer. The ceiling downstairs remained intact. How then?

The answer would be simple. They always were. The tricks were minor. The cracking of an ankle joint could be mistaken for ghostly communication. The observer's imagination did the real work. But now, with this ghostly apparition forming before his eyes, he couldn't think how it was done.

"Is that fabric?" Carter sounded equally fascinated, his physician's mind groping for sense in the madness.

Yes, Alex saw it too. The movement of gently swaying fabric. Something light, like a nightgown. Or a shroud. Up, up the thing came until she stood as tall as he. As tall as

Helen. Soon he must rise and pull back the curtain. There he would find Evie, her bonds cut through, playing with wind chimes or a xylophone. But he almost didn't want to. There was magic in this performance. Not magic as the world understood it and not the magic he'd been searching for, but magic nonetheless. Artistry. For the first time in his life, he hesitated to shatter an illusion.

Nightingale muttered an oath. He was fiddling with something on the floor. A gas lamp, Alex realized, as the other man held the now lit lamp aloft. He must have taken it from the mantelshelf before sitting down.

What was he about?

With the extra light, the vague outline of Helen's facial features showed more clearly through the layers of her veil. Alex tensed but she was not so visible that he would have been able to identify her, his own sister, if he hadn't *known* it was her.

Nightingale cried out and stumbled backward, overturning his chair. "You!" he cried, his voice filled with pain and horror. He dropped the lamp and sprang forward, clearly intending to grab Helen, perhaps rip away her veil.

Fortunately, Carter was there. He lunged, and before Nightingale could take more than a step, pulled the man's left arm back so sharply it was a wonder it didn't break. He kept it there, pulled at that unnatural angle. He didn't speak, didn't say anything to give Helen away. He was simply a gentleman defending a lady.

"How?" Nightingale gasped. "How did you know?"

Alex had wanted to ask the same thing after his father's words had appeared on the slate at that first séance.

Nightingale's reaction was equally anguished and a great deal angrier. "Evie, you little bitch, get out here now!"

Evie appeared, a shadowy figure in the weak light. Small. Vulnerable in a way Alex hadn't thought possible. "What's the matter?" The voice of someone who'd admitted defeat.

Helen, apparently the only person with enough presence of mind to adhere to the original plan, fled the room. Carter watched her go, clearly wanting to follow, but he kept his head, not to mention his tight grip on Nightingale's arm.

"You can let him go now, Dr. Carter," Evie said, once Helen had gone.

But the moment he was free, Nightingale flew at Evie. Alex stepped between them without a thought. Without regard to logic or the plan. Nightingale's gaze darted to Alex's face and his eyes were sharp. God knows what he saw. Too much, judging by his sneer. "I will gut her like a fish while you watch," he snarled.

It was too late for Alex to pretend he didn't care. His enemy had seen everything.

Nightingale smiled and that was the most chilling thing of all. "Come on," he said to the boy, who'd watched the entire debacle, his mouth round with shock. "Jack!" Nightingale snapped when the boy didn't move.

"You don't have to go with him, Jack," Evie said.

"The boy is loyal," Nightingale said, pulling Jack close. The two moved toward the door.

"Alex, don't," Evie whispered, when Alex took a step toward them. "Please."

He nodded because this wasn't the middle ages and he couldn't throw the man in a dungeon. "I will be speaking with the police about this," he said. "No doubt you will receive a visit from them tomorrow."

Nightingale didn't answer, and Alex watched them leave with a sense of unreality. After what had taken place, he ought to dash Nightingale's brains against the wall. Evie placed a hand on his shoulder, soothing and restraining.

Even as he allowed himself to be swayed, he knew he would live to regret it.

Chapter Fourteen

While Dr. Carter went in search of Helen, Evie huddled in one of the fireside chairs, listening only intermittently as Alex explained the situation to his cousin.

A strange one, this Mr. Ellis. She focused on his strangeness because she couldn't bring herself to think about what had happened. The most disturbing part was not knowing what had gone wrong.

Why had Captain reacted as he had? What hidden vulnerability had she stumbled upon? She wanted to be free of him. Instead she had made him her enemy. The thought both terrified her and filled her with a peculiar guilt.

So, Mr. Ellis then... What to make of *him*. Adjectives like *bland* and *gentlemanly* sprang to mind. The sort of man of whom nobody ever said a bad word, but probably because no one remembered him once he was out of their sight. Evie knew that trick. The person able to move about without drawing notice could get away with virtually anything. So, what was Mr. Ellis getting away with?

Alex had mentioned a wife, another distant Harcastle

relation, but where was she? Why did she choose to live apart from her husband? Something about the man bothered her, as though, like her, he played a role. He happened to glance past Alex to where she sat, and in the moment their eyes met, she glimpsed recognition. *I see you*, her look said. *I have your measure*, and though he made no acknowledgment—neither would she in his place—he understood her.

The door opened to readmit Helen and Dr. Carter. The first thing they'd done after Captain's departure had been to relight all the gas lamps, and the luminous paint coating Helen's white gown looked ridiculous in the brighter light. She had removed the veil and her face looked pale and pinched.

"Are you well?" Alex asked her, abandoning his conversation with Ellis mid-sentence.

"Of course I am. He didn't even touch me." Helen reached for her husband's hand. He took it and squeezed. The tiny exchange made Evie's heart hurt. "I do have something to say that might shed light on this evening's events."

"Nightingale looked as if he knew you," Alex said.

"Yes and we *have* met, though I don't think he recognized me."

"I don't understand," Evie started to say but Alex spoke over her.

"You've met him? Christ, Helen, why didn't you say something?"

Helen spoke calmly. "I had no idea until now. Remember that tonight is the first time I laid eyes on your Mr. Nightingale. The man I met was called Higgins. I had no way of knowing they were the same man and I didn't recognize him until he made a fuss." She sank onto one of the chairs left over from the séance. "As most of you know, my mother was an actress. She was...wonderful." Helen smiled wistfully. "And, like many in her profession, she had many friends over the years, most notably my and Alex's father, the duke.

"Another friend, though I think not in this case a lover, was Mr. Higgins. He was a great deal younger then which is why I didn't immediately recognize him. I was only a child but I remember that he was…possessive of her, even controlling at times. He spoke in disparaging terms of my father, though I don't think they'd met or that he even knew his identity. The duke didn't acknowledge me, you see," she explained, directing the words at Evie.

Things began to make sense. Captain had been an actor once but he'd never spoken to Evie about the people he'd known in those days. "Do you think it was your mother he took you for?" she asked.

Helen nodded. "People say I resemble her. He was wild with grief when she died and so furious when the duke came to fetch me away. I think he felt that, as my mother's true friend, he ought to have the raising of me, though he'd barely looked at me before that day."

"So he'll have no trouble deducing who was really under that veil," Alex said, his expression grim.

He was right of course. Captain must have taken Helen's appearance as a deliberate attempt to frighten him with a dead woman's ghost. No wonder he'd been furious.

"You need to get her away from London." Alex spoke directly to Carter.

Helen bristled at his tone and the fact that he addressed her husband instead of her, but she said nothing. She was a judge granting latitude to a lawyer, but Evie could tell Alex was on thin ice.

"Don't go back to Hertfordshire," he went on. "Go to the estate in North Yorkshire. Take the sleeper train."

Carter looked at Helen. "I think it's a good idea."

She nodded. "And what about you, Alex? And Evie? Aren't you coming with us?"

"We'll follow tomorrow."

"But—"

"Evie will be leaving England soon. She may never see London again and she… She'll need to say her goodbyes." He turned to Evie. "To Miss Carmichael and the boy."

His thoughtfulness touched her. She didn't even mind his highhandedness since he'd chosen precisely the plan she'd have settled on herself.

"Thank you," she whispered.

"Ellis, will you accompany Dr. and Mrs. Carter? I may have need of you in the next few days and I'd like an extra man with them."

Mr. Ellis nodded. Evie made a mental note to talk to Alex about his cousin. She didn't think there was anything truly sinister hidden beneath the reserve, but it felt wrong to stay silent. The three of them made plans to meet at the train station within the hour. In the meantime, they all needed to pack. Helen hugged her brother tightly before she left. Evie was glad. He looked exhausted and in dire need of comfort.

The room was too quiet when they'd gone. Poor Alex. He was in need of solace and all he had was her. Unused to sympathy or even tenderness herself, she was at a loss and gazed into the fire instead of at him. "Alone at last."

"Yes," he said, from across the room.

"I understand you want to protect your sister but I wonder if it's occurred to you that she might not be Captain's intended target."

"Of course it's occurred to me. Do you think I liked hearing him threaten you?"

"I don't mean me, either."

"You speak as if Nightingale's motives made any kind of sense. None of us has hurt him."

And suddenly, without knowing why, she was angry. "That's a child's logic." She rose and crossed the room to where he stood near the door. "Captain taught me to read, you know. From Shakespeare. From spiritualist periodicals. And from the Bible. His favorite Bible passage, the one he quoted endlessly, was Numbers 14:18. 'The Lord is slow to anger and abounding in steadfast love, forgiving iniquity and transgression, but he will by no means clear the guilty, visiting—'"

"'Visiting the iniquity of the fathers on the children, to the third and the fourth generation,'" he finished.

"There are numerous passages that say precisely the opposite, but needless to say he didn't bother much with those."

He regarded her with no expression.

"Are you beginning to see? It sounds like he was obsessed with Helen's mother. Come to think of it, in all the time I've known him he's had no woman except a whore now and again at Miss Rose's. Each and every one of them had long red hair like Helen's. You are being punished for your father's sins."

He smiled, a joyless curve that didn't light his eyes. "Someone ought to be."

His anger matched hers, a tangible presence. If there were real ghosts, and unlike Alex she hadn't ruled them out, perhaps they were caused by extremes of emotion. By people's pain and trauma. She didn't know what had transpired between him and his father but she'd begun to understand that a parent who failed to love and nurture their child was as good as an enemy. The love between Alex and Helen was plain to see. What must he have felt when he found her in that asylum?

Her voice trembled. "What he did to Helen was—"

"Unforgivable."

"Yes. Yes, it was. But you didn't do anything wrong. Not to Helen and not to Captain. You don't deserve this."

"But, as you said, that's child's logic."

"And what about what your father did to you?"

"Nothing," he snapped. "It was nothing compared with the nightmare he put Helen through."

He always pretended his pain was unimportant. Perhaps she was partly to blame. She had once lectured him about how little he had to complain of here in his palace. But being raised by the man who had incarcerated his own daughter in a lunatic asylum? She couldn't begin to image what that had been like.

"Let's concede then that other people have it worse. Let's set that aside. Now, tell me what happened to you."

"I barely saw him. There was little enough time for him to abuse me. It was nothing."

"It was *not* nothing."

"He never had a kind word to say. He destroyed the things I loved, dismissed the servants of whom I grew too fond, and when I displeased him…" He hesitated, looking shocked that he was actually saying these things out loud.

"Yes?"

"When I displeased him, he locked me in a dark cupboard. That's all. He didn't beat me. It was—"

"Don't say it was nothing. You were a *child*. He sounds like a monster. I—"

He seized hold of her forearms and kissed her, his lips harsh and punishing, his beard scraping her cheek. If he meant to frighten her, he would be disappointed because she kissed him back with equal violence, telling him without words that she was right. That what he'd been through mattered. That *he* mattered.

The kiss wasn't perfect. Rough hands in each other's hair, they were clumsy and unsteady on their feet. There was pain as well as pleasure but it was real. Elemental and necessary, like breathing.

"Come to bed with me," he said, his breaths ragged.

"Because I need it. Because you're leaving and we both need this before you go." He kissed her again before she could answer and it was different, slow and sensual. Persuasive though she didn't need persuading.

She couldn't remember why she'd resisted for so long. She had to leave him, but first they had this chance. One chance to be together and she couldn't turn her back on it.

"Take me to bed," she whispered.

• • •

They should have stayed in the Blue Room but instead Alex summoned a servant to show Evie to a bedroom while he made arrangements for tomorrow. The way his demeanor altered, apparently desperate for her one moment, all business the next, disturbed her. Where had all that passion gone?

She shivered, hugging herself as she stared at the monstrous four-poster bed with its ancient-looking red hangings. The mahogany headboard boasted the Harcastle coat of arms, a ram on a field of silver beneath a ducal coronet. The bed, more than anything else she'd seen in the house, made her feel small and unwelcome. This was the bed in which the dukes of Harcastle had been born and died. This was a bed for a duchess to lie down in. Alex had probably been conceived on it. By rights, Evie shouldn't be anywhere near it. Impossible to imagine spending even a single night here.

Alex was somewhere downstairs, giving orders, making things safe. He was right to do so of course but it meant he wasn't here to calm her fears.

She turned her back on the bed and found herself looking at a huge mirror. It too had ram's heads carved into its frame. Like the ones in the Blue Room, they leered, somehow sexual and contemptuous at the same time. She transferred her attention to her reflection and examined herself critically. A pale, thin-lipped creature stared back at her. She couldn't imagine what Alex found so compelling, but she didn't doubt that he wanted her. He spoke of deeper feeling and she believed him sincere, though he was probably wrong that he would never forget her. Or if he did remember, he would think how strange it was that he had felt so strongly. In old age, he would dismiss it as youthful folly.

Something inside her rebelled at the thought. She would never be able to forget him. Every man she met would pale in comparison. She didn't want Alex to suffer forever when she left, but she didn't want forgetting her to be easy.

She removed her prim black dress, her shoes, everything but her final layer of undergarments. Her combination was simple, fairly new, and almost pretty. She unbuttoned the front until she'd revealed a hint of bosom, and left her stockings on. Men liked stockings. The lights needed turning down, so she experimented until she had them the way she wanted—dim enough that they deepened the shadows but bright enough that her exposed flesh showed to best advantage.

Almost, she thought, assessing her reflection again. But her hair was far too severe. She removed some of the pins, so that loose waves hung about her shoulders. Yes, almost the same. Sally Harper, the girl who had posed for a naughty picture before she knew her true purpose in this world, gazed back at Evie, her eyes filled with new knowledge. As worldly as she had been back then, she'd gained decades worth of experience in the few short years since.

The doorknob rattled a moment before it turned. She was as ready as she'd ever be as Alex entered, his mouth opening as if he'd been about to speak. Perhaps he'd intended to tell her about the arrangements he'd made for tomorrow, but the sight of her robbed him of speech.

His gaze immediately dipped to her breasts.

"I…" His voice was little more than a croak, so he stopped and simply stared, roaming every inch of her with his eyes.

His obvious admiration made her feel powerful. "Is this what you want?"

"Yes. God, yes." He had a voice like velvet when he was aroused, and her body responded as though he'd caressed her.

"What else? What else do you want?"

His eyes locked with hers. "You."

"How?" She kept any trace of uncertainty out of her voice. Sally Harper knew what she was doing. She was an experienced woman asking a new lover for direction, that was all. If he knew how very far from the truth that was, he would change. He would become far too tender, and Evie would break.

"You," he repeated. "On my bed. On your knees."

He'd taken her cue. He sounded more like her now, cold and uncompromising. Her skin tingled as she took a step toward him.

"Wait. Take the combination off."

Yes, she liked this. He was remote and difficult. A little dangerous.

Slowly, defiantly, she undid the remaining buttons of the combination and let the garment slide down her body. It clung to her breasts a moment before making its final descent to the floor. His hand clenched at his side, but he remained where he was, his gaze on her rapidly hardening nipples, then drifting lower to that place he'd almost touched when he searched her. His desire then had been undeniable. Just as it was now.

When he spoke, she heard the rasp of lust in his voice. "On the bed."

She felt the words in the pulse beating between her legs. Obedient, she knelt on the mattress, facing him across its width.

He shook his head. "With your back to me."

She didn't like that; she wanted to see him. But she did as he asked. It seemed a fair exchange for what he'd given her in the carriage. He had done everything she asked that day. Now they were evening the score. She curled forward until her forehead touched the counterpane.

"You have the roundest arse I've ever seen."

She smiled, closed her eyes, and listened to the rustle of fabric as he undressed. Cool air tickled her back. She inhaled the faint scent of wood smoke from the fire. Anticipation built within her as he fell silent. Where was he? Then the bed dipped as he knelt behind her. She waited, her heartbeat fast in her ears. She was afraid but in a shivery, excited way.

At long last, she felt the gentle pressure of his hand between her shoulder blades. She whimpered a little as his other arm encircled her and he pulled her up against his chest. They were both on their knees, her back pressing against his warmth. Reflected in the huge mirror, she watched mesmerized as his left hand, the light brown skin dark against her too pale flesh, slid across her body to cup her right breast.

He stroked and fondled, all his considerable attention focused on her small, dark nipple. The sensation was pleasant but she remained curiously detached from it. What quickened her breathing was the sight of him doing it, his dark head bent over her shoulder, those clever fingers twisting and pinching in a way that should have been painful, yet somehow wasn't. He was so much bigger than her. With his arm across her body, his other large hand covering her belly, she was surrounded by heat and strength.

Then his fingers began to drift down from her abdomen, down, down until they found that place at last. The one the girls at Rose's claimed the men could hardly ever find. He followed his hand's progress in the mirror as he stroked first gently, then as she began to pant and push against his hand, with increasing firmness. She arched against him, breasts jutting up and forward, her head falling back against him.

Before she could finish, he shoved her facedown on the bed. His grip turned hard and brutal as he positioned her beneath him. Desperate for release, she parted her legs in instinctive welcome.

He hesitated. She felt the question forming in the air over her head, but she didn't want to answer.

"Don't you dare be gentle," she told him.

His grip on her shoulder tightened deliciously. He used his other arm to steady himself and his knee to push her legs further apart. She was soft and wet from her near-climax, so she felt only mild discomfort as he thrust into her. He was deep and he groaned as she pushed back against him.

She expected him to move. This was it, wasn't it? The part men fixated on. But instead he rested his forehead on her shoulder and breathed. It was the strangest thing, to lie locked together but not move.

"Look," he said. And she knew he meant the mirror.

She started to shake her head, but he had already begun to lift. To pull away, she thought, but he brought her with him, pulling her upright against his chest, his cock still buried deep inside her.

"Look," he said again. "I want you to watch me fuck you."

With one hand, he cupped her breast. With the other, he spread her open so that she could see every detail. It was depraved. It was more than she could bear. But she looked, and the moment she did, he began to move. Together they watched each thrust, and when he knew she wouldn't look away, his hand fell away from her breast and found her clitoris again. She gasped, her hands grappling with his, urging him on, harder, faster.

"Look at you," he whispered. "Where did you go,

Evangeline Jones? There's nothing left of you."

It was true. She didn't recognize the woman writhing in his arms. She cried out, the tremors taking her so violently that she couldn't think, only feel as her body shuddered with pleasure. For that one moment, he'd defeated her.

He held her tight, tender until the shaking stopped, and then he began again. He thrust wildly with relentless selfishness until he cried out in turn.

And she knew she'd defeated him, too.

Chapter Fifteen

Alex woke from dreams filled with loss, though the details faded before he'd even opened his eyes. He rolled over in the dark and knew something was wrong.

Evie. Where was Evie? Her side of the bed was cold.

His first thought was that she had left him. That she didn't trust him to keep her safe and so she'd struck out on her own. He sat up, expecting an empty room. Someone was standing by the window. A dark figure in top hat and tails. In that moment, confronted with an unknown intruder and with no way of knowing where Evie was or if she was well, he was truly afraid.

Something about the figure struck him as odd. The coat hung far too low.

His racing heart began to slow as he understood what he was seeing; Evie stood in quarter-profile, gazing out into the night. A whimsical figure. What he'd taken for a gentleman's tailcoat was actually his own discarded evening coat. The top hat was his too, one of several he kept in the adjoining dressing room. She'd been restless while he slept. As always, he wondered what she was thinking. Still fascinated, even though he'd finally had her. Somehow he'd known it would be so.

Being with Evie had been different from all his other sexual encounters. He hadn't felt his usual constraint, had asked for things he hadn't even known he'd wanted, done things he couldn't quite believe. In his mind's eye, he could still see how they'd looked in the mirror. It had been the most exciting encounter of his life by far, yet he wanted more. Not simply to bed her again, though he wanted that too, but *more*. Somehow, the woman standing by the window was as distant as ever.

If Evangeline Jones had disappeared last night, Evie had still been playacting. That had been Sally Harper pinned beneath him and, much as he'd enjoyed the fulfillment of that particular fantasy, it was only a fantasy. People pretended in bed, he knew that. But last night, Alex hadn't, and he wanted to feel the bond between them in bed as well as out of it. He wanted to know her true name.

The air was cold on his naked skin as he rose. She must have heard him moving, but she didn't turn. He paused when he was about a foot from her, taking in the incongruous sight of her wearing his things. The top hat in particular he found adorable, but it was in his way. Without a word, he removed it and set it atop the mirror.

She stiffened as he placed his hands on her shoulders but all he did was ease her back against his chest. Rigid as she was, he half expected her to pull away, so it was an unforeseen pleasure when she relaxed against him.

"Cold?" he asked, his lips brushing her cheek as he spoke. She nodded.

He'd always known what to say with previous lovers in the aftermath of lovemaking, not because he'd felt any affinity with them but because he hadn't cared. Like any type of social discourse, there was an etiquette that kept things civilized and prevented things from becoming sentimental. None of those polite nothings would suffice here when his feelings transcended sentiment. And when last night had broken all his rules.

He'd been crude with Evie, even rough at times, behavior she'd certainly enjoyed, but what if she was hurt by it now in retrospect? He wanted to ask her, but though he'd found the acts themselves occurred naturally at the time, he found them impossible to speak of now. Defeated by his own inconsistency, he rested his chin on top of her head and joined her in staring into the dark.

The horizon began to take on the grayish tint of earliest dawn. Other than that, there wasn't much to see. One didn't stargaze in London. The air wasn't clear enough for that. He was glad he was taking her to Yorkshire. He found the city suffocating if he stayed too long.

They remained that way, each lost in their separate thoughts, for nearly half an hour. They might have stayed there until morning if he hadn't grown cold and slid his arms around her waist for warmth. She turned in the circle of his arms and looked up at him with her fathomless brown eyes, and he realized he hadn't kissed her last night. Not since the Blue Room.

She had the most extraordinary mouth. Though her lips were thin and showed displeasure more readily than anything, whenever she smiled, her entire being seemed transformed. He'd seen it only once or twice and each instance felt like a gift.

He wanted a kiss, nothing more, so he touched his lips to hers almost chastely. Her mouth was soft, feather-light on his. Such a sweet kiss would have been impossible last night with so much turmoil in the air. When she didn't pull away, he kissed her again, tasting her this time. Her arms slid around his shoulders, then up until her fingers tangled in his hair. Something sparked between them, then caught light.

He wasn't surprised when she broke the kiss and stepped back. He couldn't help his body's reaction and it hadn't occurred to him to conceal it. Her gaze shot unerringly to his erection and her eyes widened. Last night he'd stayed behind her and she had seen more of her own body than his, so now he stayed where he was and let her look. Even half an hour ago, he couldn't have imagined he would stand this way, allowing her response to fire his. She seemed almost shocked by the sight of his cockstand.

Her confidence last night, her insistence that he refrain from being gentle, had made him think his original assessment of her past experience accurate after all, but now he wondered. He might have asked her but he sensed she wouldn't appreciate the question. Perhaps, when all was said and done, it was none of his business. If she wished to confide in him, she would. The same was true of her real name.

More pertinent was the glazed look in her eyes. The rapid rise and fall of her bosom, its shadowy curves partially visible beneath the coat. His lips curled with satisfaction. "Again?"

"Yes," she said. No orders this morning. She seemed different. Tentative.

He gathered her into his arms and carried her back to the bed. The coat fell from her shoulders as they crossed the room, so she was entirely nude when he settled on the bed with her on his lap. When she straddled him, her wet cunt nudged his cock until he groaned. Unable to resist the pert breasts mere inches from his face, he leaned forward and tasted one nipple. She moaned and arched her back, thrusting her chest at him—an invitation he was eager to accept. He sucked, the little bud hard on his tongue, until she cried out. Her hands fluttered at his shoulders as he transferred his ministrations to the other nipple, biting and nibbling.

"Touch me," he urged. He lifted her slightly, until his cock sprang up between them. Slowly she reached for him. The timid glide of her hand was torture but then she squeezed. "Yes," he groaned. "Like that. Yes."

She bent her head, intent on her task, as she stroked him the way he liked, the way he'd shown her that day in the carriage. Firm but gentle, then tighter and faster until he almost spent in her hands.

He pulled away. "Tell me what you want."

She seemed surprised. "I don't…"

"You had no difficulty once. Tell me how to please you."

When she didn't speak, he tilted her head back and trailed kisses across her neck and shoulder. "Do you like that?"

"I… Yes."

"I want to be inside you. Do you want that?"

In answer, she rose on her knees and watched as he positioned himself at her entrance.

"Is this what you want?" he asked again.

Their eyes met and held as she sank down onto him.

"Slow," he said when she winced. "Let yourself adjust."

He caught a fleeting glimpse of her elusive smile before she buried her face in his chest. As she breathed slowly in and out, he stroked her back, soothing and cajoling. A moment of calm before the storm. He could have stayed there with her wrapped in his arms. This moment. This closeness. This was what he had missed last night.

He could have stayed like that forever but her hips rocked.

"Easy," he whispered. "Take your time, angel."

She raised her head and smiled again, the sweetest smile he'd ever seen, though the playful tilt at one corner boded ill for his restraint. She rocked again, drawing a groan from somewhere deep in his chest. Then again and again.

She reached past him, grasping the headboard with both hands. The slight change in position embedded him still deeper. Her small but perfect tits hung temptingly, just within reach. He palmed them both, kneading and pinching.

"Oh, please, Alex."

He couldn't hold still any longer. He bucked against her in clumsy counterpoint. "Evie, I can't…"

"Fuck me," she said. "Please, please, please fuck me."

He clutched a great handful of her hair, twisting and pulling it aside. She cried out but not in pain. "You like that," he said, half in wonder. He pulled harder, controlling her movements as if her hair were a chain, kissing her neck as she rose and fell above him. As he lost control completely, she stiffened against him. Their mutual climax left him stunned and laughing. The laughter was definitely another first.

He sobered quickly. Evie was drenched in sweat and shivering like someone in shock.

"All right?"

She nodded, her eyes swimming with tears. His heart was in his mouth when, thank God, she began to laugh. "I'm going to need some time to recover."

The sound of her laughter loosened something in him. "My God, Evie, I thought I'd broken you." He slid down into the bed with her still cradled against his chest. By the time he'd finished pulling the covers up, she was already asleep.

• • •

Evie woke to a grayish dawn and feather-light kisses against her ribs.

She kept her eyes closed and luxuriated in the warmth of his mouth and the faint tickle of his beard. He could be so gentle, this forbidding man with the relentless mind. He'd bedded her with single-minded focus. The experience was exactly what the girls at Rose's had described, and at the same time, nothing like it.

Last night's passion had been sweaty, messy, obscene, and even rough at times. She hadn't minded, had enjoyed every moment. Then, in the early hours of the morning, he'd overturned everything when he'd come to her at the window, eased her back against his chest and simply held her. Consideration like that usually came *before* a man had a woman, not afterward, or so she'd been led to expect. A man courted a woman with kindness because how else was he to get what he wanted? Once he'd had her, what was the point? She'd been feeling rather maudlin that the seduction was now over when he'd taken her into his arms.

They'd stood there a long time before the second bedding and that had been as different from the first as day from night. Whether he'd been tired or whether he experienced the same languorous contentment she'd been feeling, he'd taken such care with her. She hadn't expected that of him and certainly hadn't known herself capable of reciprocating. He'd gazed into her eyes as he moved inside her. Why was that so devastating?

"We need to get up," he murmured now, his breath hot on her skin. He kissed her again and again, his tongue tracing little circles. She groaned and tried to sit up, but he pressed her hips into the mattress. "Don't take me so literally."

"I'll fall asleep," she warned.

"To think I took you for an early riser."

"Well, perhaps if I'd been permitted to sleep for more than a few hours…"

"You didn't complain at the time."

"That's funny." In fact, she couldn't hold back a smile. "You're a funny duke."

"It's what I'm known for."

She gave herself up to the sensation of his lips and hands. It would be so easy to stay here with him. Even this awful bed had taken on a friendly aspect now they'd spent the night curled up in it together.

You could stay. Be his mistress. No one need ever know.

Treacherous little voice.

Yes, she could stay, allow Alex to cage her up somewhere Captain couldn't hurt her. They didn't need the approval of church and state. If he tired of her, that was no worse than tearing herself away now would be.

But what about his heiress? He needed to marry if he wanted to keep the dukedom intact. What was she to do then? Share him? Steal his time and affection from his wife, and one day, his children? The thought made her ill.

Yet she didn't want anyone else to have him. He was hers. Or she was his. The latter was perhaps the problem. Giving yourself to someone, really truly letting yourself belong to another, was always a foolhardy act, no matter how well-intentioned both parties might be.

"Where did you go?" He watched her face with genuine concern.

She shrugged. "You're right. We need to rise."

After all, she needed to say her goodbyes.

• • •

Poor Mags looked much the same, if better cared for. The bedding had been changed and her hair was neat. She even managed a smile when she woke and saw Evie sitting by the bed, though the glad look quickly faded into one of concern.

"Are you all right?" was the first thing she said.

"I think I'm supposed to ask you that," Evie said, trying for a smile of her own.

She must have failed abysmally because Mags frowned. "Tell me."

"Talking wears Miss Carmichael out," Mrs. Radcliffe, the nurse, had cautioned before she'd left to fetch more water from the pump. Evie needed to come to the point and not make poor Mags fish for information.

She took her friend's hand and squeezed it gently. "I've had a bit of a falling out with Captain," she said with deliberate understatement. "I need to leave."

Mags seemed to understand instinctively that Evie didn't mean for a short while. Her eyes filled with tears but she didn't seem shocked or even surprised. "Where will you go?"

"France at first because it's close, but I won't linger long. After that, wherever I can find a home, I suppose. Captain is very angry. He'll say I owe him money on his investment, probably come here looking for me. I don't know when or if I'll be coming back or even if I'll be able to write."

"Is it…" Mags swallowed painfully. "Is it something to do with the duke?"

"It's complicated." In a way, everything came back to Alex. If it wasn't for Captain's obsession, he'd never have rescued Evie from Miss Rose's. She'd be a completely different person now. Their destinies had been entwined long before they'd ever met. "I'm worried about Jack. He worships Captain and sooner or later…" Sooner or later he would be hurt. Perhaps badly. "Watch out for him. If he comes to you, help him if you can."

"You don't need to ask. I'll find him something at the theater. He can carry scenery or run errands."

"You won't be there for long. Not if you marry Mr. Chase."

Mags smiled again, and for a moment, she looked almost like her old self. "I'm not going to marry him. His father paid me a visit. Offered to buy me off."

Evie experienced a moment's outrage on her friend's behalf before relief flooded in. This was good news. The best news she'd heard in a long time. "I hope you got a good price."

"I got the best price." Mags struggled into a sitting

position. "Evie, he bought me a share of the Dovecote. I'm a partner now."

"Oh!" Evie threw her arms around Mags. "Oh, Mags, I'm so happy for you." This would mean financial security and her pick of roles.

"You must thank the duke for me."

Evie stilled. "Harcastle? What does he have to do with this?"

Mags shrugged. "You'll have to ask him that."

It was time to say goodbye but tears built in Evie's chest until she couldn't speak. She'd never had to leave someone she cared about before and it was harder than she'd imagined.

Mags seemed to understand. "Love you," she whispered.

Evie kissed her hand. "You too."

• • •

By the time Evie descended the stairs, she'd managed to subdue any sign of threatening tears. She took several deep breaths before opening the door onto the street where Alex waited in his carriage.

"All right?" He said the words carelessly, without even looking at her, but she knew him well enough now to detect the compassion beneath the nonchalance. She loved that he wasn't always demonstrative in his sympathy. He never swamped her with unwanted sentiment, always allowing her to be herself even if that self was contained to the point of coldness.

"Of course," she said, equally careless.

They sat in silence for several minutes as the carriage rumbled through Soho. The traffic was dreadful as always and it would only get worse. Mist, damp and oppressive, hung in the air, the beginnings of what promised to be a truly dreadful fog.

"Harcastle?"

His brows rose and when he said, "Yes, Miss Jones," she knew he was amused by her sudden return to formality.

"It would seem Mr. Chase's father has bought Mags off with half a theat. Are you in any way responsible for her sudden good fortune?"

He sighed. "All I did was commiserate with him about his son's foolishness and suggest that Miss Carmichael, as a woman of sense, might be persuaded to accept an interest in the theater in lieu of a betrothal ring."

"Is that all? Well, then I will only thank you the little you deserve for saving a woman from an unwanted marriage and *changing her life immeasurably for the better.*"

He frowned, his irritation plain to see. "I do indeed deserve all the accolades for saving Miss Carmichael from a life of ease as a rich fool's wife." He looked directly at her for the first time since she'd entered the carriage. "I admit they'd have been social pariahs, but don't you think she might have grown fond of him?"

"Perhaps." It was an oddly romantic notion coming from Alex, and Evie felt a pang at the thought that he might grow fond of his heiress. She wanted that for him, or at least her better self did. "But Mags isn't... She doesn't actually like men. Not in a romantic way."

He took several moments to process this. "Do you mean that she prefers women?"

She didn't answer unless her amused stare counted.

"But didn't you and she...share a bed?"

"Yes." She couldn't decipher his expression. "I said she prefers women, Harcastle. That doesn't mean she's indiscriminate. I assure you, she behaved like a perfect lady the entire time. We both did. We're more like sisters, really."

His face didn't change but somehow she knew she'd shocked him.

"What does that look mean?" she asked, unable to keep the laughter out of her voice. "Are you relieved or disappointed to hear that I did not engage in a torrid affair with another woman?"

"I'm not sure," he said. "I'm striving not to have an emotion either way."

That sounded about right. "Is that something you do often? Strive not to have feelings, I mean." Although perhaps that was a bit rich coming from her.

Before he could answer, she caught sight of something through the window. A streak of red and gray. "Stop the carriage!" she shrieked.

The carriage shuddered to a halt and she slipped out before Alex could stop her. She hurried forward, pushing past pedestrians until she got to the corner where she'd seen that familiar flash. Yes, there he was, a little way down the street.

"Jack!"

He turned, caught sight of her, and glanced behind him as if he might run. Then he lifted his chin and waited for her approach.

"Jack, I'm sorry about last night," she said when she reached him.

He regarded her warily. "Why'd you do it, Evie? Why turn against Captain?"

The words affected her like a slap to the face. No, it was less violent than that. More permanent. His obvious hurt and disappointment settled on her shoulders like a heavy load, though she'd expected this from him. His devotion to Captain ran too deep.

"He turned against me first." That sounded petty but it also happened to be true.

He shook his head, a denial of her words and of her. "Stay away from me."

"I will, Jack. I don't have a choice in the matter. I'm leaving."

"What? When?" He couldn't hide his distress, despite the rigid set of his jaw. Being forced to choose like this must hurt him a great deal, and she tried to focus on that and not the pain she felt at losing him to Captain.

"Today. *Now*, really. I only wanted to say goodbye."

"Well, now you've said it."

His eyes sparkled with tears she knew he would never allow to fall. So like her. She wished she were the sort of woman who could throw her arms around him and overwhelm him with warmth. He might not like it but at least then he'd have the memory of her affection.

"Well." Straightening his spine, he turned away. "Bye then, Evie."

"If you ever need help," she called after him, "go to Mags at the Dovecote. She'll help you. Promise me, Jack!"

But he didn't answer. He had nothing more to say to her.

She turned and saw Alex standing in the shadows. She didn't know how long he'd been there watching them, but it was too late to conceal her feelings. He didn't say anything. He didn't need to.

"Get me out of here," she said as she allowed him to pull her into the comfort of his arms.

Chapter Sixteen

By the time they reached Stoney Hey Hall near the tiny fishing village of Stoneman's Bay, it was already so dark that Evie couldn't discern much about the surrounding country, not even the craggy face in the hill from which, so Alex informed her, the village took its name.

She'd been expecting another Harcastle House, so she was relieved to find a simple country manor built on a much smaller scale. As the carriage drew to a halt at the end of a circular drive, she gained only a vague impression of a square frontage, its many downstairs windows illuminated with a cheerful yellow glow.

The front door opened and Helen and Dr. Carter appeared, silhouetted in the light. As a footman lowered the carriage steps, Alex leaped down to embrace his sister. Evie turned away to give them privacy. She didn't know how he had the energy to leap anywhere. Her entire body ached with weariness after the long train ride from London to Whitby, then Stoneman's Bay. This last little sprint in the carriage had finished her. After the turmoil of her farewells, her resilience to the rigors of a long day had been at a low ebb.

The footman stood ready to hand her down, but as she went to take his proffered hand, Alex intercepted her. She smiled inwardly at the proprietary gesture even as she rolled her eyes. He had been rather wonderful today. Saying goodbye to Mags and Jack had been more painful than she'd expected. As much as she loved them, she'd always thought of herself as someone remote with little need for companionship. If anything, friendship was dangerous. Hadn't her relationship with Captain proven that? As did the grief she experienced now at parting from them all. Despite everything, she missed Captain. He'd been her closest companion for years before she met Mags. Though she never wanted to see him again, she still grieved his loss. And the way Jack had looked at her... Like she was Judas.

Alex had managed to exude quiet sympathy without obliging her to talk about her feelings. She suspected he too preferred to lick his wounds in peace. When he'd said they were the same, she'd almost dismissed the idea out of hand, but she understood now. And how strange to find a kindred spirit in Mayfair of all places.

She leaned on his arm, allowing him to guide her up the few steps and into the entry hall. He talked over her head with Helen and Dr. Carter, but tired as she was, the words were noise, the buzzing of insects, until Helen put a hand on her arm, drawing her attention.

"Evie, you look done in. If you like, we can send dinner to your room."

"Thank you, no. I want to hear how you've been." Only partially true. Really, she didn't want to go upstairs without Alex. They had so little time left.

"The servants are setting everything out in the dining room. Alex, I wanted to ask you..."

Evie allowed her attention to drift again. The entry hall

was large—quite a bit bigger than the room she'd shared with Mags—and the floor was tiled in shades of green and gray. A huge wooden staircase rose before her, the oak banister, carved with sheaves of wheat, polished to a gleam. An enormous stone fireplace took up most of one wall, its flames casting flickering orange light across the tiles.

Something moved in the shadow of the stairs. A man stood there, his face gaunt and unsmiling. His dark clothes all but disappeared into the darkness, so that he looked like a disembodied head. Her heartbeat quickened in sudden alarm, but as her eyes adjusted, she recognized his butler's garb. If he was a butler, why on earth wasn't he employed at Harcastle House? He'd be perfect there. He was out of place here in this otherwise cheery manor.

"Dinner awaits, Your Grace," he said in a voice like a rusted gate. He spoke with apparent deference while subtly conveying something else. There was nothing wrong with the words or his tone, yet he didn't approve of Alex. An answering dislike rose in her breast.

Alex regarded him soberly but there was a twinkle in his eye, as if he knew his servant's opinion of him only too well and found the whole thing entertaining. "Thank you, Pendle."

Helen opened a door and led the way into the dining room.

Alex seated Evie at a long oak table. "Where's Ellis?" he asked when all four of them were seated.

Dr. Carter answered. "Working. He said he'd eat at his desk."

"Poor Jude," Helen murmured.

The others nodded, and Evie wondered what she was missing. What was so sad about Mr. Ellis working? Most people she knew spent the lion's share of their waking hours working and usually at jobs more physically demanding than

Mr. Ellis's. From things that Helen had said in London, it was obvious Dr. Carter worked hard too. As well as his duty to his patients, he was an expert in lunacy reform, always writing papers and giving lectures.

"Did you see or hear anything more of Nightingale?" Dr. Carter asked.

Before anyone could respond, a female servant arrived with a soup terrine.

"Not a peep," Alex said, when they were alone again. "I trust Ellis has men on the watch?"

"On all sides of the house," Dr. Carter said. "He also sent two men to the village—one at the train station, the other at the inn."

Alex nodded. "It's possible I'm being overly cautious. While we must take Nightingale's vendetta against me and our family seriously, he hasn't been particularly swift about executing it. There's no reason to suppose he'll act immediately."

"But don't you see?" Evie said. "It's precisely because the vendetta, as you call it, is of such long standing that you should be cautious. Imagine you're Captain. You've spent years, more than a decade, plotting. You've invested time and money training an accomplice, and now, when the time for revenge is finally at hand, that accomplice switches sides. How would you react?"

Dr. Carter sighed. "Miss Jones is right. A monomaniac like Nightingale, if thwarted, might very well become violent."

"So, in your professional opinion—"

"You are right to do as you have."

Perhaps because of his status, Alex had a tendency to underestimate threats to his person. If it had been his safety alone in question, Evie suspected they'd still be in London. She was very grateful to Dr. Carter for stating things so plainly.

"What will you do now, Evie?" Helen asked.

"I'm to leave, but…" She glanced at Alex.

"I owe her money."

"That's not strictly true. I haven't fulfilled my side of the bargain." She was supposed to admit her fraud publicly.

"You did all you could. Neither one of us had any idea he knew Helen's mother. We couldn't have foreseen this. After the risk you took with Nightingale, you've earned every penny."

Debatable, though Evie had every intention of taking the money. She wasn't a fool. Pride of that silly sort was for the wealthy.

"*In any case*," she said, emphasizing each word so that he would know she didn't want to continue that particular discussion in front of others, "I'll have to get a train to Southampton where I can board a ship and go…wherever it's going. It doesn't matter where I end up, though I'd prefer somewhere where they speak English since it's the only language I know. I can decide what to do next once I'm clear of Captain."

Helen frowned but said nothing. While the next course— roast pheasant—was served, they all went quiet. Even when the servants withdrew again, conversation was sporadic, each person distracted by their own thoughts. Evie ought to have enjoyed this rare glimpse into how the other half lived. Three-course meals in huge private dining rooms were not something she usually experienced, but instead she kept thinking about Mags. With no stove in their lodgings, they'd always eaten together in chop houses. Noisy and smoky as those places were, they'd had some jolly times.

She sighed. If she didn't stop feeling sorry for herself, she was going to waste these last days with Alex. She refused to do that. If this was all the time they had, she wanted to make the most of it.

• • •

The bedroom Alex took her to after dinner seemed far too good for a guest room, yet it wasn't at the front of the house as master bedchambers usually were. Its greens and golds had a soothing effect. She particularly admired the four-post tester festooned with a silk canopy and purple hangings.

Evie turned to Alex who was loosening his tie. "Is this your room?"

"Yes, it's mine." He stopped, the loose ends of the tie still draped over his shoulders. "Is that all right?"

He didn't seem worried that she might say no, but perhaps it occurred to him that his presumption might offend. Maybe he *should* have asked but she wasn't going to quibble. "Of course." To prove it, she began unbuttoning the front of her dress, her movements unhurried, like a wife undressing in front of her husband after a long life together. "Why did Helen say 'poor Jude'?"

He smiled as he removed his jacket. "She thinks he works too hard. Which he does."

"You told me he's married. Where is Mrs. Ellis?" She let her bodice fall to the floor and began unhooking her skirt.

"There's no great mystery. Like many couples who marry for practical reasons rather than affection, they choose to live apart much of the time." His carelessness seemed genuine but the arrangement struck her as strange.

"Interesting. What were the practical reasons? Money?"

"My father arranged the match as a favor of sorts to her father."

"Why would Mr. Ellis agree to such a thing?"

"I suppose he wanted to please my father. He was unlikely to inherit the dukedom and, with no other prospects, he needed to keep the old duke on side."

Very practical but there was a fine line between practical

and mercenary. Evie wasn't sure where Mr. Ellis's conduct fell. "And Mrs. Ellis? Was she happy with the husband her father arranged?"

"I don't think she had much choice. Something happened, some youthful indiscretion on her part, and her reputation was in jeopardy."

"You don't know what it was?"

"No, I was never in my father's confidence. He was not lenient when it came to other people's frailties, so ordinarily he would have left her to her fate or perhaps married her off to someone outside the family, someone of comparatively low status. Since he chose Ellis for her, in all likelihood it was something he feared would reflect badly on the family. Knowing him, it was a minor transgression. Small sins loomed large in my father's eyes."

"Do you know her well? What's she like?" Wearing only her combination by now, she stood with her hands on her hips.

"Fairly well. She's another distant cousin. An artist. A free-thinker." He finished unbuttoning his waistcoat and allowed the garment to gape open. "Not attributes of which my father approved. He probably expected Ellis to have a moderating effect on her."

She walked toward him and placed her palm on his crisp, white shirtfront, over his heart. "A free-thinking artist?" Difficult to imagine the staid Mr. Ellis with a woman like that. But what about the man she suspected lurked beneath? She tried to imagine marrying someone while maintaining the pretense that she was Evangeline Jones, prudish spiritualist. Impossible. Was that why Ellis didn't live with his wife? Or perhaps it wasn't by choice. Perhaps his wife, amid the terrible intimacy of marriage, had discovered the real man and fled.

No, too melodramatic. Ellis might well be shifty—it took one to know one—but she had no reason to believe him anything worse. "Do you ever think there might be more to him than meets the eye?"

Alex seemed amused. "Ellis? I suppose that's true of anyone. We all have hidden depths."

He didn't seem convinced, and it was almost enough to make her doubt herself. Almost.

"Tired?" he asked.

"So tired." She gave a theatrical yawn.

His lips twitched. "Very well. Quick and perfunctory lovemaking it is."

She squealed as he threw her back onto the bed.

• • •

She made the most extraordinary squawking noise as he pinned her beneath him. He only intended to tease her a little before letting her sleep—it *had* been a long day—but her cheeks turned a becoming shade of pink. Blushing was fatal in a medium and not a flaw she was prone to but he'd seen her cheeks this way at least once before, when he'd made her climax. And she was laughing. Miracle of miracles. Skin glowing, eyes shining, whole body shaking. With a besotted ache in his chest, he watched as she struggled for mastery of herself.

"You are so beautiful when you laugh," he said when she'd caught her breath.

She smiled up at him. "Beautiful? If you like. But you..." Her blush intensified. "Of all the faces I've ever seen, yours is my favorite."

"Because I'm beautiful?"

"No, though you are. I suppose it's because I'm fond of you."

Fond? From any other woman, he'd call that tepid, but from Evie? The admission went to his head like Irish whisky.

He was drunk on this woman, but unlike when he was drinking, his control wasn't slipping. He knew exactly what he was doing. If he were free to make his own choice, he'd ask Evie to marry him right now, sure in the knowledge that he'd never regret it.

But he wasn't free.

"It's been a difficult day. I should let you sleep." He didn't mean it. Hated having to be a gentleman.

She reached up and cupped his cheek, her face soft with the aforementioned fondness. "That may be the stupidest thing you've ever said."

"Thank God," he said a moment before she kissed him.

She tasted of the apple tart that they'd eaten at dinner, her lips warm and soft. As he sank into the kiss, he'd never felt more hers. Oh, he'd *been* hers almost since the beginning, but now she claimed him. She wanted him, and he suspected, not for a little while. If he could somehow deal with Nightingale, she could stay. He couldn't have everything he wanted. He couldn't marry her, but they could be together. They didn't have to lose each other completely. He just needed to convince her. If he could.

Doubt caused a hollow ache in his chest, so he deepened the kiss, his tongue stroking her lower lip. He groaned as she opened for him. *Mine*, his kiss said. Primitive and perhaps delusional. No man could own this woman. She was solitary by nature. Sufficient unto herself.

Mine, his body insisted.

Evie answered in kind, arching her back, pressing into him. *Mine*.

She tugged at his shirt. "I want this off."

Happy to obey, he shrugged free of it and let the garment flutter to the floor beside the bed. Her combination gaped open. He pulled her close and tongued one hard nipple through the linen. They undressed each other, greedy for skin against skin. For touch and taste.

At last, they were both bare and she lay warm and pliant against him. He wanted to make the moment last, to stretch it out into eternity if he could, but when her hand found his cock and squeezed, when he saw how desperate she was, how needy, further delay became impossible. Her legs parted in invitation, her hand positioning him, urging him on.

He entered her in one deep thrust. "Fuck," he groaned.

She laughed and arched her back again. This woman was going to be the death of him.

"Touch yourself." He spoke low, his mouth at her ear.

And she did, clever fingers circling her clitoris.

He began to move and it was everything. No better feeling existed that this, the woman he adored pinned beneath him, her heels digging into his arse, urging him on as he fucked and fucked her. He didn't want it to end, but as she cried out her release, he couldn't prevent it.

"Evie." *I love you. I love you. I will always love you.*

But the words stayed trapped inside his heart.

• • •

It was much easier to sleep at Stoney Hey than in the oppressive grandeur of Harcastle House, but Evie still woke before dawn. In those first moments, she couldn't think what had disturbed her. Through the mist of early morning vagueness, she slowly became aware of the empty space beside her. The absence of warmth.

She rolled out of bed and groped on the floor for her discarded clothes and, as luck would have it, found the combination first. The fire was out, which meant it was so early that the servant hadn't been in to see to it. Where on earth was Alex?

The adjoining room seemed the obvious place to start

looking, so once she'd hooked her petticoat on over the combination, she felt her way to the interior door she'd noticed last night. Yes, the handle turned; it wasn't locked.

The room was some sort of sitting room. Alex sat with his back to her, in an armchair by yet another fire. Presumably he'd lit this one himself. He gave no sign that he noticed her, but somehow she thought he had.

By the faint glow of the gaslights in their sconces, she made out the details of the room—it was small, three of the walls taken up by shelves. Instead of books or ornaments, the shelves held contraptions made of wood and leather. Magic lanterns. She'd noticed several in his bachelor quarters in London too.

"You're quite the collector," she said as she reached his side.

He smiled and took her hand. As she'd suspected, he wasn't a bit surprised by her sudden appearance. "Would you like to hear a sad story?"

"About magic lanterns?"

"Yes. And about me, or rather me as a child."

"About Little Alex, then? Yes. Yes, I would." Actually, she felt pathetically eager for anything that had to do with him. She wanted to drink up all the details of his past and present, and heavy on her heart was the dread that she'd spend the rest of her life yearning for news of him.

There was another chair, but as she glanced around for it, he pulled her down onto his lap. He made a comfortable seat, so she remained where he'd put her despite the indignity.

"When I was nearly six..." He paused, and she saw the conflict in his expression. From past experience of his reluctance to talk about himself, she sensed he was struggling with the urge to remind her that he understood his upbringing had been easy compared with hers. Perhaps remembering what she'd said on this subject the last time they'd discussed his childhood, he suppressed it. "When Little Alex was nearly six, the duke employed a new nanny."

Little Alex. Interesting that he'd taken that up. Was he distancing himself from the events he was about to describe? Did that make talking easier? Regardless, she remained silent, afraid that any interjection would deter him.

"She wasn't the first nanny by any means, but Little Alex was particularly fond of her, and I think, she of him. It was she who gave me my first magic lantern. Birthday presents were forbidden. She knew that, but nevertheless..." He smiled. "She couldn't have hit upon a gift more likely to incur the duke's wrath. Little Alex loved it. I didn't see much of my father in those days. Once a day, for five minutes, I was taken to the study to see him. He would inspect me and question the nanny as to how I'd been spending my time."

It wasn't the crux of his story; she knew from his casual way of speaking. But she was horrified anyway. True, for much of her life she'd had no parent at all, let alone a nanny. But Captain had spent time with her. He'd trained her and even made the lessons fun. Yes, his motives had been selfish. Yes, he'd been looking after his investment. But, as heir to a dukedom, Alex had been an investment too. Why had his father treated him so cavalierly? Why had he barely seen him? Couldn't he have mustered even the semblance of love? Because she knew from experience that a semblance was better than nothing at all.

"Until I was six, I don't remember the duke paying a single visit to the nursery, but one day, a few weeks later, he did." He stopped, eyes distant, remembering.

"He caught you playing with the magic lantern?"

"Naturally." He shook his head. "The Seven Wonders of the World right there in the nursery. That's educational, isn't it? But he called it a frivolous waste of my time and smashed the lantern to pieces with his cane. When I... When Little

Alex cried, he was locked in a cupboard for an entire day."

Captain had never done anything like that. Neither had Miss Rose. Both had planned to use her abominably, but neither had actually done so in the end. Her childhood had been one long series of narrow escapes. She had known hunger and deprivation, and she had been in near constant danger of even worse. But, as she'd recently discovered, pain was particularly searing when inflicted by someone you loved. By someone who was supposed to love you.

"That's appalling," she told him.

"Ah, but you haven't heard the worst part." He seemed amused. She knew what he was going to say. "He dismissed the nanny. By the time I was free of the cupboard, she was already gone."

"He didn't permit you to say goodbye?"

"No, he didn't. He said I'd grown too fond of her, that it wasn't proper to miss a servant."

"Do you know what happened to her?"

His face went like stone. Jaw clenched. Eyes dead and joyless. "He dismissed her without a character. She couldn't find work and she died, alone and penniless."

Evie couldn't remember a time when she'd felt more angry. Frankly, she wanted to dig the old duke up, set fire to his remains, and salt the resulting ashes. How dared he treat an employee that way? How dared he treat a little boy that way? "Bloody aristo," she muttered.

"My sentiments exactly."

"Is that why you want to give me this money? So I don't die alone and penniless?"

She'd been teasing but he answered seriously. "Your situation is nothing like hers. I have no doubt of your ability to survive with or without my money."

"Because I have no scruples, and therefore, no need of a good reference."

This time, he responded with a little more levity. "It's one of the things I admire most about you. Though I would like to make things easier for you if you'll let me."

"Of course I'll let you. I'll take you for every penny if you like."

His fingers traced circles through the linen over her rib cage. "Oh, I'd like."

There was something in his expression. An intensity that eluded her. "How long have you been collecting lanterns?"

"Since I was twelve. That was when I was given an allowance. I hid what I bought. To be honest, by that age, I think I got more satisfaction from defying my father than from the lanterns themselves."

"Do you still buy them?"

"No. I started drinking instead."

"And when you gave that up?"

"I tried a few things. Fencing. Investments. Then spiritualism."

"Why? Why spiritualism?" She'd always wondered.

"I wanted to know if there was anything to it. Like everyone else, I wanted something to believe in."

"But you only found charlatans."

"It turns out I'm rather fond of them. Of two in particular. My sister…" He kept tracing those circles. "And you."

"Helen isn't a charlatan."

He laughed softly, his breath ghosting across her cheek. "You should have met her six years ago."

All at once, the intimacy of this moment—her place on his lap, the casual affection with which he touched her, his breath on her skin—was too much. "Will you show me one?"

Clearly, he'd had other ideas as to where this interlude was headed and it took him a moment to understand what she meant. "A lantern? Now?"

"Yes." She would not acknowledge the hard length of him

pressed against her bottom. He groaned as she slipped free.

It took moments to get a magic lantern working. The one he chose, with its bellows, polished wood, and gleaming brass fittings, resembled Captain's camera. He opened a compartment and lit the kerosene lamp inside, then operated a lever, moving through a series of glass plates. Brightly colored butterflies lit up the wall above the fireplace, then golden sunflowers, a tree laden with cherry blossom. Summer things when it was November and the world seemed to be dying around her. A simple toy shouldn't bring a grown woman so much joy.

She glanced at Alex, but he wasn't watching the images or even the device. His gaze was on her. His hand fell away from the lantern. A forget-me-not, blue and perfect, lit up the wall behind him as he strode toward her. What she saw in his face left her breathless, and she knew he was about to overturn everything.

He only said one word. "Stay."

Chapter Seventeen

Evie responded more or less as Alex had feared. The word *stay*, so small but difficult to utter and spoken so quietly, filled the room. Thunderous silence was her only answer.

"Say something."

Her lips parted infinitesimally a split second before she spun on her heel and marched from the room. He followed, a sense of inevitability weighing his steps.

In the bedroom, she stood with her back to him, struggling into her heavy black skirt.

"Evie."

She turned in the process of hooking the front of her bodice closed, but she didn't look at him. No doubt she told herself she was focusing on the fastenings, but there was something furtive in the way her eyes never even flickered in his direction. "You know I can't."

He knew nothing of the sort. "I'll deal with Nightingale."

"It makes no difference. I won't stay with you."

Not can't; *won't*. The difference between those two small words was vast. His chest tightened painfully. "Why not?"

"What will become of me when it's over?" A simple question asked with no evident emotion.

Alex didn't let that deter him from crossing the room until they stood toe to toe. Slowly, so that she had every chance to turn away or deflect him, he reached out and tilted her chin up so he could see her face. Her eyes flashed defiance. When didn't they? Her lips were thinner than he'd ever seen them, pressed together to suppress whatever she was feeling.

"We've barely begun," he told her. "How can you talk about the end?" If he had his way, they never would. He was hers now.

"I think about it because I must."

"I'm not going to abandon you, Evie."

"No?" She jerked her chin away. "You mean to marry me? Make me your duchess?"

They both knew he couldn't. What she'd never believe was how much he wanted to. God, she'd make a magnificent duchess. She was a chameleon. No role was beyond her. Even if society would never accept her, she'd play the duchess to the hilt. The idea of marrying her, of being with this difficult, bloody-minded enigma for the rest of his days... The very thought made him feel awake. Alive. When he was with her, the rush of life in his veins was almost too much to bear. He saw everything with new eyes. He *felt*.

But the houses would crumble around them. The estates would need to be sold. His dependents would suffer for his selfishness. He would go down in history as the Duke of Harcastle who lost everything. The chain, of which he was but a single link, would be broken, the empty title he passed on little better than a joke.

Evie searched his face. "I didn't think so."

"We both know I can't marry you," he said, "but we can still be together."

"We could. If you promise never to marry anyone else."

Even though they both knew the answer to that too, she allowed the silence to lengthen; he hated her a little for that.

"Do you understand how many people would suffer if my lands and holdings were sold off? There's no way to ensure the livelihoods of my tenants and workers. I can't allow it all to fall into ruin!" He was shouting, he realized. He never shouted. He took a deep breath to steady himself.

"You need money, Alex. I understand that better than anyone. I'm not blaming you. I *admire* you. But I won't be the dirty secret you hide from your wife."

"It needn't be like that. I don't have to be dishonest. There are women who'd willingly exchange a fortune for a title, women who wouldn't expect affection or fidelity."

"And if you find one? Unless you expect this poor woman to live like a nun, you'll need a legitimate heir in the nursery before she can go her own way."

She was right. He wouldn't expect his wife to wait faithfully at home while he lived with Evie, but he couldn't disinherit Ellis with a child he knew wasn't his.

Evie must have read his response in his expression because she asked him, "Could you stand by while I married and *bedded* another man?"

"The thought turns my stomach." He seized hold of her, his hands tightening on her upper arms. "But if it meant you could stay..."

"I'm sorry, Alex. The life you're offering me would make me miserable. I won't do that to myself. Not even for you." There were no tears in her eyes. No tremor in her voice. No uncertainty. She meant this. He saw no way to move her. No weakness to exploit.

Even if he'd seen his way forward, he believed what she said. He *couldn't* make her happy. And if he couldn't do that, he should let her go. Did he love her enough to do that?

"Evie—"

Three raps at the door, then Helen's voice from the other side. "Alex, I'm sorry. It's important."

Evie opened the door. He didn't stop her, even though he was still in his dressing gown.

Helen's face was paper white. "A man matching Nightingale's description arrived in Stoneman's Bay this morning and put up at the Bilge and Barnacle."

His gaze locked with Evie's. For the first time since he'd asked her to stay, he saw a crack in the wall she'd thrown up. *Too soon*, her look said. *We haven't had enough time.*

No, they hadn't. And now they never would.

"Give us a moment," he said to Helen.

"Oh God," Evie whispered when they were alone again.

"I'll make sure Ellis gives you the money today."

"Thank you."

He wanted her to put her arms around him, but he knew she wouldn't. Not once, in all this time, had she been the one to reach for him. But when he pulled her into his arms, she immediately melted against him, fitting snugly against his chest, her head tucked beneath his chin. It was almost enough.

"I'll go to the village with Ellis. Promise me you won't leave before I get back. Remember, it might not even be him."

She nodded, an awkward bobbing against his neck.

"Promise me, Evie."

"I promise."

Was she the sort of woman who kept her vows? He was about to find out.

• • •

Dark clouds glowered overhead as Alex, with Ellis at his side, left the cliff path and took the winding road into Stoneman's Bay.

The tiny fishing village nestled on a steep hill between

two towering cliffs. On the eastern edge, a wide beck flowed down to the harbor. They followed its path toward the shore, passing fishwives sitting on their doorsteps mending nets or heading down to the beach in their double-crowned bonnets and aprons to collect mussels. Later they'd carry home what they'd gathered in baskets balanced on their heads. The menfolk would be out in their cobles—flat-bottomed fishing boats—though judging by that ominous sky, they wouldn't linger long on the water today.

The Bilge and Barnacle was a large brick building overlooking the harbor. It stood so close to the water that, on rough days, the waves crashing over the sea wall forced everyone, commoner or king, to use the tradesman's entrance or risk a soaking.

They were several yards away when Ellis stopped walking. "I still think you should have stayed at the house. I know what Nightingale looks like. You don't need to be here."

"I need to see for myself."

"What should we do now? Walk in and ask for Nightingale by name?"

"Abernathy. The man staying here who matches Nightingale's description is named Abernathy."

"You're hoping it won't be him."

"Naturally." If it wasn't Nightingale, Evie might stay longer.

"Why not get the thing over with?"

"I wouldn't expect *you* to understand." The implication being that Ellis lacked the capacity for deep emotion? It wasn't the sort of remark Alex usually made and he already saw the injustice of it. Ellis never seemed to miss his wife and he never talked about her, but then Alex never asked. They weren't close that way. They didn't talk about their feelings.

"I meant, why not get the confrontation with Nightingale over with. I would never presume to—" Ellis frowned at his feet.

Alex waited for him to continue but whatever he'd been about to say had been caught by that filter of good manners the man hid behind. For the first time, it bothered Alex that he'd never troubled to get to know him properly. They were cousins, after all.

"Have you ever been in love?" he asked.

Ellis didn't deflect the question as Alex half expected. "Of course I—" He shook his head and smiled ruefully. "In the circumstances, you deserve a truthful answer. Yes, I've been in love, and I know what it is to want an unobtainable woman. To burn with the wanting."

Alex didn't even attempt to mask his shock. He'd heard the pain and yearning in Ellis's voice. A depth of feeling of which he hadn't thought him capable. He wanted to ask who she was because it couldn't be Charlotte. Surely "unobtainable" wasn't a word that applied to a man's wife? Unless Charlotte loved someone else. Then the distance, both physical and emotional, between the Ellises began to make sense. All baseless speculation, but even though Alex knew none of the details, he recognized the look on Ellis's face. Evie had been right; there was more to his cousin than met the eye. "I had no idea."

"I wish I could tell you it gets easier as the years pass, but…" Ellis shrugged.

"I wouldn't believe you anyway."

"We should go in." Ellis directed his gaze at the Bilge and Barnacle, clearly embarrassed by his recent disclosure.

Alex was content to let the subject drop for now. He'd left Evie packing her few possessions. Even though she'd promised she'd still be there when he returned, he wouldn't put it past her to bolt. The quicker he got this over with, the quicker he'd be back with her. The sooner he'd know.

"You gave her the money?"

Ellis didn't need to ask who. "Of course."

Naturally, it had occurred to Alex that he could delay giving her the money until he returned. She was too practical to leave with nothing. If she was thinking clearly. After what she'd been through lately, he wasn't sure she was. At least this way she'd be financially secure if she ran. "Come on."

The inn door was never locked at this hour since the guests needed to move freely, so he knocked sharply twice before immediately entering. The innkeeper rushed over the moment he clapped eyes on them. Yes, Mr. Abernathy was staying there. He was eating breakfast. Yes, the innkeeper would be happy to point him out to His Grace.

They followed the proprietor into the public dining room where several people were sitting down with steaming bowls of porridge. "The gentleman by the window, Your Grace."

Alone at a small table sat a man of about forty. Bearded, saturnine, well-favored—he fit the description. But he wasn't Nightingale.

Alex didn't know how to feel.

Evie might stay longer now, but Ellis was right. Alex wanted this thing with Nightingale resolved. When he had reported him to the authorities in London, he'd been fully aware that Nightingale hadn't actually done anything illegal yet. As he'd expected, the police had promised to "*have a word*" with the man. Beyond that, they were powerless. To Alex, Nightingale had been an annoyance. A fly buzzing around, irritating but harmless. Nightingale couldn't hurt him, not really.

Unless it was through the woman he loved.

Alex didn't care about threats to himself, but Nightingale had made a big mistake when he threatened Evie. It was time—long past time—for Alex to take matters into his own hands.

• • •

The grounds of Stoney Hey were beautiful even in this miserable November weather. Evie had spent the time of Alex's absence learning them. A stone path led through the dormant rose garden at the front of the house and wound behind the manor, forking right to more gardens, or straight ahead to the top of steps that took you down to the cliff path. The same way Alex had gone with Mr. Ellis.

Earlier, she'd run along it to the road, all the time afraid that she might meet them coming the other way. Alex would think she was escaping when all she intended was to know the lay of the land. Once she reached the edge of the village and saw the sign pointing to the train station, she ran back again, all the way to the bottom step where she now stood panting.

The wind whipped her skirts as she gazed out to the horizon. The black and purple of a bruised sky bled into the sea—a distant rainstorm, but it would be here soon enough. The North Sea itself was a great, gray wall confining her. She was small, insignificant, but she'd always known that. Everyone was when you got right down to it. Even Alex couldn't change his fate.

"Evie." Alex's voice sounded far away, but when she looked along the path, she saw him coming, closer than she'd expected. The wind was playing tricks. Ellis wasn't with him. He must have stayed behind in the village for some reason.

She waved to show she'd seen him and climbed the steps. When she reached the top, she stopped, waiting for him. His face told her nothing as he climbed the steps, but when he reached her he took her into his arms. His lips tasted of sea salt. Afterward, he leaned his forehead against hers. "It isn't him, Evie."

Reprieve.

She slid her arms around him and melted against his chest. Content to hold each other in the wind and the drizzle, they fit together like puzzle pieces. Though all the things they weren't saying hovered in the air around them, she was happy to leave them there, and for once, so was he.

Thunder rumbled in the distance and finally the heavens opened. Rain lashed down as they ran laughing back to the house. A side door led into a sitting room all painted white. Huge windows looked onto the churning sea, just visible through the driving rain. He led her to the fireplace, an inglenook, all ready to be lit. Once he had the flames roaring nicely, he drew her down onto the floor with him where the heat was fiercest.

She was about to suggest they go upstairs and change out of their soaking wet things when he began unhooking her bodice. "What are you doing?"

"I would have thought that was obvious."

"Someone might come in."

"No one comes here. This is my room. Stand up so I can undo your skirt."

Her outer layers had taken the worst of the downpour. Though her petticoat and combination were both damp, the fire would soon fix that. Alex removed his jacket, waistcoat, and tie, then sat beside her.

"What about your trousers?"

"I didn't want to make you uncomfortable."

"Take them off, for goodness sake."

He did and she saw what nice legs he had. She hadn't particularly noticed before, too busy admiring other physical attributes, but they were long and leanly muscled, dusted with dark hair. His calves looked particularly squeezable. Bitable, even.

"What is it?"

"Nothing." She averted her gaze.

"Come here."

She let him arrange her with her back against his chest, his legs on either side of her, bent at the knee. He tucked her head beneath his chin and wrapped his arms around her. Soon she was deliciously warm and comfortable. Outside the rain hammered on the windows and the thunder rumbled. Inside the fire crackled as she allowed the rise and fall of his breaths to rock her to sleep.

• • •

Alex didn't know how long they stayed that way, Evie curled against him so trustingly. She stroked his chest through his shirt, tracing circles, slower and slower until her hand stilled. She was asleep.

He liked her there in his arms, liked simply being with her even when they didn't talk. Perhaps especially today when there were so many things he couldn't tell her. He couldn't say that he'd left Ellis in the village post office sending multiple telegrams to London because then he'd have to explain that he was having Nightingale's studio turned over in the hope of finding something, *anything*, to incriminate him.

And it wasn't because he thought she'd object. He knew she wouldn't. But he also knew she'd feel guilty about that, as if she were betraying Nightingale. He wouldn't have her suffer over an investigation that might not even bear fruit.

As much as Alex hated those vestiges of a loyalty Nightingale didn't and had never deserved, he couldn't help admiring her steadfastness. She'd been equally loyal to Miss Carmichael.

She shifted in his arms, burrowing closer. Though she'd said little about her feelings toward him, in sleep she sought him out. In sleep, she wanted to be close to him, closer and closer. He *knew* how she felt even if she never said the words out loud, but God, he *longed* to hear her say the words. It wouldn't change anything, but he would always carry with him the precious knowledge that she'd returned his feelings.

He could make her say it. Draw the confession out of her with his words and his body, but he already knew he wouldn't. He wanted nothing from her that was not freely given.

Chapter Eighteen

Alex liked these quiet after-dinner hours when everyone amused themselves.

They all sat in the drawing room, except Ellis who was buried in paperwork as usual. A careless servant had drawn the drapes, leaving a gap in the middle so that an occasional flash of lightning lit the room. Out at sea, the storm raged on, but despite the driving rain and a whistling wind that rattled the sashes, Stoney Hey had been spared thus far.

Alex removed his spectacles and folded *The Whitby Gazette* before setting it on the end table. Despite the gas lamps, it was almost too dark to read. Besides, Evie and Helen's activities proved an irresistible distraction. The two women sat at a small round table, a pewter bowl filled with water on the surface between them.

Carter must have noticed too because he lowered his copy of *The Lancet*. "What are you ladies up to?" *Up to* was a particularly apt phrase.

Alex frowned. "They're scrying, I think."

"Like fortune telling?"

"Nothing so inelegant. Miss Jones will stare into the dark waters until she sees prophetic visions. That's a more rarefied activity than gazing into a cheap glass ball like a carnival worker." Alex shrugged. "But yes, it's the same thing."

Thunder rumbled, followed a moment later by a bright white flash. The water sparkled and reflected light danced across Evie's face as she gazed at its shifting surface.

"How dramatic," Alex drawled.

"But of course," Evie said, as if she'd ordered the weather made to measure.

"Witch."

He received a grin for his pains. Their eyes met briefly but a great deal of communication passed between them. The shared humor of the moment. The affection they felt for each other. The promise of intimacies they would exchange once they were alone together. He would make his witch beg for his cock. Or perhaps he'd do the begging.

Helen rolled her eyes at both of them. "Do be quiet, Alex. Evie's going to show me how to see the future."

"Christ." This from Carter. "As if we don't have enough theatrics in our house."

Helen winked. "You love every moment."

Carter smiled in such a way that it was clear she was right.

Alex had always felt a certain kinship with the other man despite their vastly different circumstances, but that feeling was never stronger than at this moment. Their fates were sealed. Both utterly besotted. Drunk on love. Mated for life with their women like a couple of bloody swans.

But what happened when a swan got separated from his mate?

Evie stared into the water, her expression softening. She looked into the depths as tenderly as she sometimes looked at Alex in the moments after lovemaking. In that state between sleeping and waking. A trance state. "I see…" Her voice was a soft, dreamy whisper. "I see shadows. There is a shadow on your heart. You are afraid…"

Helen gasped and Carter half rose from his chair.

"You're afraid, but you won't allow these fears to hold you long. You will overcome them."

"I…" Helen's face was white. "How did you know?"

Evie looked up from the water, eyes clear, no trace of the apparent trance of moments ago. "Everyone's afraid of something," she said in her normal voice. "It was a sure target. As for the rest, I told you you'd overcome whatever's worrying you, which is exactly what you wanted to hear. See? It's easy."

Helen's sudden smile was radiant. "So simple that it's almost brilliant."

"Even if the sitter remains unconvinced, it's impossible to prove a fraud. There's virtually no risk."

Helen seemed happy, but Alex couldn't help but wonder what she was afraid of. He was incapable of ignoring the situation until she came to him, but taking her aside now would be far too obvious. He forced himself to wait until the end of the evening when everyone was saying good night.

"Helen, a moment." He drew her back into the drawing room.

She stood by the fire, arms crossed over her middle, brows raised. "You're about to ask me what I'm afraid of, aren't you?"

He winced. So much for subtlety. But then subtlety was never a family strength. "And you're probably going to say it's none of my business, but I've always supposed you were fearless, so you'll have to forgive my curiosity."

"As Evie said, no one is fearless." He waited. "Oh, very well. It's not even my fear, really. It's… Have you never wondered why Will and I don't have children?"

Of course he had, but after six years of childless

marriage, he'd naturally assumed they couldn't and that he'd be trespassing on painful territory if he brought the subject up.

"It isn't because we can't. I *assume* we can. But there are ways to prevent conception, and as a doctor, Will knows more about that than most. You see, his first wife died in childbed and he didn't want to risk my health. I was happy enough with that at first. After ten years at Blackwell, I had no desire to rush to motherhood, but now…I'm thirty-two. Now is the time."

"Is Carter being difficult?"

She glared at him. "Don't be ridiculous. Will's practically a saint. He wants me to do what makes me happy. But sometimes, when he doesn't think I'm paying attention, I catch him looking at me and the expression on his face is so… wistful. He's terrified, and even though I'll probably be fine, what if I'm not? I couldn't bear to put him through that loss again."

Alex was completely out of his depth and he must have looked it because Helen burst out laughing. "Don't worry. Will and I are old hands at this marriage business and we're going to be fine. We're going to try for a baby. I only wish life offered guarantees." Her smile faded. "It's you I'm concerned about."

"Me?" It had never occurred to him that Helen would worry about him. "Why on earth are you concerned about me?"

"Ever since I met you, I've known you aren't happy."

"I do all right." But he couldn't quite meet her gaze.

"You seem different when you're with Evie. There's light in your eyes because of her. I see you struggling to rectify our father's mistakes, trying to save the lands and houses. *He's* the one who really lost everything, Alex. You're about to throw away your chance of happiness because of him and that... That infuriates me. He's done enough to both of us, don't you think? We mustn't allow him to go on ruining our lives from beyond the grave."

"You're right. He's the one who ran the estates into the ground. Whether through neglect or malice, this is his fault. But it doesn't matter. I'm Harcastle now. His mistakes are mine. As are his duties. People, innocent people, would suffer if I neglected my responsibilities."

"Perhaps," she said. "But I don't think you've tried hard enough to think your way out. Why is that, do you think?"

"I don't know what you mean." In any case, he had no business "thinking his way out." He was the duke. No one else could take up that burden for him.

"You think you don't deserve to be happy, that's what I mean."

"Bollocks."

"Now you sound like Will." She straightened his tie, a curiously maternal gesture. "I'm tired and I want my husband, but do something for me? At least consider the possibility that you might deserve to spend your life with Evie. Consider also what Evie deserves. The Harcastle chain is heavy and I for one think it's time you cast it off."

Alex lingered in the drawing room after his talk with Helen. The storm waned, though the wind still whistled down the chimney, making the flames dance in the grate. Unlike most gentlemen, he couldn't sit back in an easy chair with a brandy, so he had to content himself with his thoughts and those proved most unsatisfactory company.

His dutiful attempt at fulfilling his role as titular head of the family had resulted, as was so often the case, in a lecture from his younger sister. Helen was adept at seeing to the root of a problem, but she was wrong this time. She said he was throwing happiness away, but she might as well say he was throwing Evie away. And that was balderdash. Evie was the one insisting she had to leave. What could he do that he hadn't done or offered to do?

An answer was not forthcoming, no matter how intently he stared into the flames.

• • •

It was past eleven by the time Alex finally headed upstairs.

He found Evie sitting on a rug in front of the fire in her nightgown, her slim legs tucked to one side. Her hair was loose for once and hung about her shoulders in a dark cloud. A series of cards lay spread out on the floor and she was studying them with a frown.

He closed the door behind him. "What do they say?"

She looked up and stared at him for several seconds. "What do you mean?"

"The cards. What does the future hold?"

She smiled. "I wouldn't know. I'm only playing Patience."

He went a bit nearer and saw that indeed the cards were ordinary playing cards set out in the appropriate formation. "Oh."

With a careless sweep of her hand, she scattered them and rose to her feet. There was something in her expression. An…intent. Her hair was wavy from being pinned so severely, unruly once it escaped its confinement. Much like her. A lock curled over one shoulder and he reached out without thinking. It was soft and silky against his fingers. Cool to the touch.

He remembered when he first saw her, how obsessed he'd been. Such a prim and proper exterior yet he'd known in his bones how wild she'd be when he bedded her. He wanted her again, wanted her every moment he was with her, and he saw that same yearning in her. The air crackled with tension.

He had to force himself to let go of that single lock of

hair. Even that small connection was too much if he wanted to say the things he'd left unsaid this morning. Her refusal had sounded final. He ought to respect it, had intended to, but he couldn't. Not yet.

"We need to talk about—"

She kissed him. Kissed him as she had never kissed him, pulling him down by the lapels of his suit, sliding her arms around him, pressing her body against his. Even as he recognized a deliberate attempt to silence him, her mouth on his, firm and unyielding, hot and demanding, acted like a drug. Silvery mist obscured his thoughts as her tongue stroked his. When she finally broke the kiss, he stood there stunned and blinking.

"Tomorrow," she said. "We'll talk about all that tomorrow, but…"

Her hand was on his chest, over his heart, but now it drifted upward until her fingers touched his lips, still damp from their kiss. She traced the contours of his mouth until he couldn't help but smile. Their eyes met and held and he saw so much emotion in hers. "Tonight I need you."

After that, he was her willing slave.

· · ·

If Alex thought Evie's wishes strange, he never said so.

She stood at the foot of the bed, holding on to one of the posts for support while he devastated her by doing exactly what she wanted. He undressed when she told him to, removing each garment and laying it on a chair. He didn't hurry but was efficient because somehow he knew what she needed. Or perhaps they were so well matched their tastes happened to align. She didn't want to be teased; she only wanted him naked and to witness him getting that way without artifice.

He moved with a fluid grace, his skin bronze in the firelight. He was strong, no doubt from all the usual gentlemanly pursuits. Thighs taut from riding. Shoulders broadened by fencing. The tense and release of his muscles hypnotized her. When he turned to set aside his shirt, she noticed as she never had before the sculpted perfection of his back.

It was not that she hadn't known he was beautiful. Of course she had. But first and foremost he was always Alex. She truly believed he could have the face and physique of a hobgoblin and she would still adore him. But now, as she strove to memorize his every feature, she was undone by him.

He still faced away from her as he removed his trousers and undergarments. She contemplated every inch of his long, lean legs and his glorious backside. Dukes, as far as she knew, were more often than not gout-ridden and decrepit. Alex had no business having an arse that enticing.

When he finally turned toward her, he was almost fully erect. His phallus, amid its patch of dark hair, stood proud against his stomach. Her eyes on him had done that. He was hard simply because she watched him.

He didn't speak, didn't even smile. He simply waited.

"Lie down," she told him.

And he did, flat on his back on the bed. She released her hold on the post and went to his side where she immediately drew the nightgown off over her head. One sweep up and over was all it took, and she caught the abrupt hitch in his breath. Her nipples hardened. Her tiny breasts felt full and heavy. They ached.

She stayed where she was, letting him get his fill. As his dark-eyed gaze traveled over the scant dips and curves of her body, the inside of her thighs grew damp. How could she be so ready when all they'd done was look at each other?

She knelt a moment on the bed, then straddled him. His

hands came to rest on her hips, giving them a gentle squeeze. Her hair curtained them as she leaned in for another kiss. She marveled at the heat of his mouth, then shivered as her breasts grazed his chest. His cock twitched between them, so she reached down to guide him in.

His head rolled back against the pillows as he arched his back, greedy for more of her. His fingers bit into the flesh of her hips as he filled her. It was good but she needed more. She moved one of his hands up to her breast and, as she began to move, rocking her hips in long, slow undulations, he squeezed.

"Harder," she begged, and his hand tightened until it hurt.

He was magnificent. Head back, eyes closed, he gave himself up to her, and she drank in every detail. The turn of his throat. The way sweat dampened his temples. Even the sweep of eyelashes on his cheeks. The bronze cast of his skin against the pale globe of her breast. The strength in him as he twisted beneath her. The angry crease of his brow.

She learned him. She memorized him. Because this was the last time.

As if he'd read her mind, he canted violently to one side, overturning her, reversing their positions so that he loomed over her. His eyes were wide open as he pinned her to the bed and drove into her again and again. Holding his gaze, she met each thrust of his hips, as desperate, as angry, as he.

It was all they needed. This fire, this mutual conflagration. Her entire body— No, her entire self lit up, tiny sparks shivering along every nerve and sinew, as they cried out together.

But it wasn't enough. It would never be enough. And, before the tremors even ended, she knew they would have to begin anew. She would sleep on the train. For now, she needed him again.

• • •

Once Alex was asleep, Evie slipped out of bed and went into the magic lantern room where she had hidden her clothes and carpetbag behind a chair. Sneaking around was beneath her. Such a low, mean way to treat Alex. But she couldn't go on like this.

She knew him. If she told him she was leaving, if she waited to say goodbye like a proper adult, he would try once more to persuade her to stay. If he did that, she didn't trust herself. She was one conversation away from allowing him to seduce her into accepting a life she knew would make her unhappy. Weak as she was, she couldn't face him. If that made her a coward, so be it. At least she was a coward who knew her limits.

Alex was a heavy sleeper and she'd made sure his breaths were slow and deep before she left the bed. Even so, she couldn't take any chances. No last longing look into the bedroom. She hardened her heart, forced herself to think of him as she had that first night when he'd looked at her with cold, dead eyes. He wasn't the man who'd been so tender. He was the aristocrat. The skeptic. The man who'd wanted to destroy her livelihood on a whim. He was the man who would forget her, no matter what he might say in the throes of passion.

She dressed swiftly and crept into the corridor, the carpetbag clutched to her chest, his money sewn into the lining of her bodice. The way was almost entirely free of clutter. The only end table stood at the top of the stairs where she had left an unlit lantern. Despite the powerful urge to rush, she made herself stop and light it. The longer she lingered, the more likely she'd be caught, but if she tripped in the dark, she risked waking everyone or, worse, she might break her neck on the stairs.

The house seemed even larger at night. It wasn't only the darkness. No servants bustled about their work. No butler skulked in the shadows. All was silence. Only the ticking of a clock somewhere and the whine of the wind in the trees disturbed the perfect stillness.

What a pity she couldn't say goodbye to Helen and Dr. Carter. She liked them very much. At least they'd be here to comfort Alex when he realized she was gone.

With the aid of the lantern, she reached the front door without incident. The heavy bolts slid back with more noise than she liked, but she was far enough from the bedrooms and servants quarters that she got away with it. A rush of cold air hit her as she stepped outside. Despite her coat, she shivered.

Thanks to her reconnaissance when Alex had been busy in Stoneman's Bay, she knew the lay of the grounds well enough to find her way unerringly to the cliff path. By the time she stood on it, the horizon was beginning to gray. She still needed her lantern, but dawn approached. Once she reached the village, she wouldn't have too long to wait for the first train. With luck, she would be well on her way when Alex woke, but first she had to get there.

The wind whipped at her skirts until she thought she might take flight. She had to shelter the lantern with her body or risk losing her light. Managing both the lamp and the carpetbag on the long, winding path proved a struggle.

Why are you doing this? a rebellious voice asked. *This is stupid.*

As if to confirm her thoughts, she fell forward. She heard the glass shatter a second before the flame went out.

Oh God, oh God. A terrible dizziness pinned her to the ground. The tide was in and waves crashed far beneath her. Above, the inky black abyss of the sky went on forever. Her hands tore at the grass as if the fragile blades could somehow anchor her and stop her from being sucked into the ether. Why she should fear that and not the fall, she couldn't imagine. Logic was beyond her by then.

She stayed where she was, crouched on the path. A series of deep breaths and she was calm enough to count slowly. When she could bear it, she stared out at the graying horizon. It wasn't even full dark anymore. She could manage without the lantern. She would be fine.

The path stretched ahead. She focused on what she could see of it and forced herself to stand. At least she only had to manage the bag now.

Panic receded and she began to inch forward again. As her confidence increased, she was able to quicken her steps to a more natural walking speed. Farther down, the track curved away from the precipice and the way was easier. She would make the first train. Once it was moving, *then* she would allow herself to remember the warmth in Alex's eyes when he looked at her. She would recall every moment from last night, each image she'd branded into her memory. A self-inflicted wound, a deliberate scar that would never fade. But for now, she suppressed those thoughts.

Soon she would be beyond Captain's reach. He wouldn't be able to use her to hurt Alex. With her gone, Alex could brush him off. Captain would be reduced to an irritant, a pest, a fly. Or perhaps he would try to hurt Helen. If he did, Alex would crush him.

And then what?

Alex would go on as he had before. Eventually he would marry. Perhaps he'd even be happy with his rich bride.

Ahead, she could make out the main road. Once she'd reached it, she'd find the signpost to the train station. Her steps faltered, and she looked back over her shoulder toward Stoney Hey. Even in daylight, she couldn't have seen it from this angle, but she looked back anyway. One last time.

"Goodbye," she whispered.

Straightening her shoulders, she walked away.

Chapter Nineteen

Alex dreamed of drowning. Immense waves crashed over him. Powerful underwater currents dragged him down, down into the depths of the sea. Just as his lungs began to burn, he would kick free and propel himself to the surface, sick with the knowledge that it was all for nothing. Each time he surfaced, he attempted to cry out or to breathe but the current always took him again before he could open his mouth.

Finally, he had his chance. He surfaced and this time managed to shout. Except no sound emerged. And then a towering wave more powerful than any other, stronger than the underwater current, buoyed him up and spat him out onto a sandy beach.

That was the moment he jolted awake, his blood pounding in his ears. He woke all at once. No morning fog. No sleepy stretching. One moment he lay bruised and broken on coarse sand. The next he was wide awake, blinking into the blackness.

Too late.

He knew before he reached across and felt the empty

space. He knew despite the faint warmth lingering on the sheets. Without her nearness to cloud his thinking, he saw last night clearly. It had been Evie's way of saying goodbye.

"Evie?" he called, but he didn't expect an answer.

He lit a lamp and checked the sitting room. When he didn't find her, he looked for her things. She didn't have much to begin with, and he knew a moment's relief when he found one of her carpetbags. A woman with so little couldn't afford to leave so much behind. Of course, if she'd left in the dead of night, she'd almost certainly gone on foot. His relief faded as he realized she would only have taken what she could carry. With a sinking heart he looked in the wardrobe and saw that her few gowns no longer hung there.

He threw on some clothes and banged on the door of Helen's room. Carter emerged, rubbing his eyes. "What's the matter?"

"Evie's gone."

"In this weather? Are you sure?"

"Some of her things are missing." And the weather was bad—the wind howled as if to illustrate the point—but not so terrible that Evie wouldn't chance it if she were desperate. "I kept pushing her to stay. Christ, I'm an idiot. *Of course* she ran." Not once, in her whole life, had she had the freedom to choose the life she wanted. First she'd lived in poverty and then Nightingale had controlled her every move.

Carter glanced over his shoulder, then stepped into the hall, closing the door gently behind him. "Harcastle, you're panicking. You—"

"Don't be absurd! I never panic!" But he was shouting, so he took a breath and spoke more softly. "But it's dark and windy and she doesn't know the path."

"First of all, what makes you so sure she's taken the cliff path? She might have persuaded one of the servants to drive her to the village. Can she ride or drive a cart? She might even still be on the grounds."

"Which is why I don't have time for this. If she's gone or about to go, I need to make sure she's safe. I'm going to follow her to the village."

Carter sighed loudly. "I'll go with you."

"No, stay here. Talk to the servants. Have them search the grounds in case I'm wrong. If she turns up, sit with her. Make sure she stays until I return. Tell her I won't try to persuade her to stay. I only want to say goodbye."

"Will that be true?"

Alex took a deep breath, then exhaled with a shudder. "It will have to be."

He didn't wait for a response. Carter was a good man and he knew what it was to be mad for a woman. Alex trusted him absolutely.

Evie had to be headed to the village—there was nothing else but moorland for miles—and the cliff path was the shortest route. If it turned out she'd gone via the road somehow, she'd still have to wait for the train. If he took the road on horseback, he could intercept her where the path joined the lane or he could head straight to the station and wait for her there.

He grabbed a coat from a hook in the gunroom and took the lamp with him out into the dark.

The stable was at the back of the house, but as he trod the gravel path that led there he began to doubt his chosen course. He imagined himself waiting at the station. Waiting and waiting. The cliff path was long and, in this weather and at night, dangerous. She might stumble and twist an ankle, and that was the least that might happen. Unlike her, he didn't have a bag to manage and she'd be juggling hers with whatever lantern she'd taken. He'd done that walk countless times, knew every stone, every turn of the path. If he followed her on foot, he would almost certainly overtake her.

He hovered in the doorway of the stable momentarily as he made his decision and pivoted. One step was all he'd taken before he heard it: the creak of wood and the anxious whickering of a horse. Far from unusual noises in a stable, yet his heartbeat quickened. He knew he was in trouble a moment before the blow fell. He would register the sharp pain on the back of his head later. It was the force of it that sent him to his knees. He went down face-first in the gravel. The lamp hit the ground but by some fluke it didn't smash. He rolled onto his back, knowing who he would see in the light. He spat dirt onto the ground at Nightingale's feet. Just in time he checked the impulse to sweep his attacker's legs from under him. It would have been a dangerous move, considering the revolver aimed at his heart.

"Easy, Your Grace." Nightingale spoke with no more agitation than would have been evident in a polite chat over tea and biscuits. In every way, he appeared his usual self, from neatly combed hair to excessively dapper suit. But if this—confronting Alex openly this way—was his contingency plan, he must have lost his mind.

Ludicrous as it was, Alex mimicked his polite tone. "I have no intention of making any sudden movements, I assure you."

"A bit late to be out and about, don't you think?"

"Either that or it's unspeakably early."

"Just so, sir. Just so. But Evie was always an early riser. Given you the slip, has she?"

It was too late for Alex to pretend he didn't care about her, though he tried to school his features anyway. Men like this fed on fear. "I take it you saw her."

"And don't think I didn't consider following through on my threat, but I'm a sentimental man. She may be a deceitful bitch but she's like a daughter to me all the same."

The gun was still trained on Alex's chest. He stifled the

urge to shift out of its path. "So you let her go."

"In the circumstances, I call that generous."

"Magnanimous even."

"Still, how do you think she'll feel once she knows her duke is dead? She's a tender-hearted creature deep down. You might say this'll be punishment enough."

Alex forced a smile. "So it's come to this? Years in the planning and this is the way it's going to end, with you shooting me?"

Nightingale shook his head sagely. "A crying shame, isn't it? I'd intended a more elegant revenge. You were going to suffer for the rest of your life, but I can't hurt your sister, not when she has her mother's face. Since I can't bring myself to touch Evie either, I did consider your cousin or your brother-in-law but… Well, it wouldn't be the same, would it?" He eyed Alex coldly. "No, it's a travesty of what I originally intended but I'm going to have to kill you, simple as that."

"Still, a shot to the head? It'll be over in an instant."

"Don't you worry about that, sir. On your feet. Now."

Slowly, Alex rose. He tasted something raw and metallic. Blood, he realized. He must have cut the inside of his lip when he fell.

"Keep your hands where I can see them." Nightingale gestured with the gun in the direction he meant them to take. A quick flick of the wrist, over before Alex had a chance to react. "Walk."

"Where are we going?"

Nightingale didn't answer because it was obvious. They were headed to the cliff.

Halfway across the lawn, Alex chanced a glance back at the house. Some of the windows were lit, so Carter must be organizing the servants as Alex had requested. If someone looked out and saw what was happening… They'd left the lamp behind but the sky was turning from darkest blue to gray, silvery at the horizon. Was there enough light for them to be visible from the house? He wasn't sure.

"Don't look round again," came the gruff warning.

Nightingale was nothing without the gun, but the knowledge that he might snap and shoot at any moment made the back of Alex's neck prickle. Exposed and afraid, he plodded onward. He tried to be logical. If Nightingale truly meant to shoot him, why hadn't he done so at the stable? Why chance this march over the grass? But they'd left the realm of logic behind weeks ago. There was no telling what this man might do.

They reached the top of the long flight of stone steps.

"Go on then," Nightingale said. So nonchalant, like he'd lost interest. His revenge was spoilt. Oh, he'd see things through all right, but the spark was gone. Evie had ruined everything for him when she changed sides; Alex took a certain satisfaction in the thought.

But he was still going to die.

"Keep going," Nightingale said once Alex reached the bottom step. "Keep going straight forward." Alex did as he was told, only stopping when his feet met the edge. "Take a good long look, Your Grace."

Alex did. The tide was in. Waves crashed against jutting rocks. He wasn't afraid of heights but the drop looked vastly different when you knew you were about to go over.

Somewhere along the path, Evie was nearing the road. He hoped so anyway.

Catch that train, he urged silently. *Get as far away from all this as you can. Get away from me and be happy.*

That was all he wanted now. For her to be safe and well. When she heard what had happened to him—*if* she heard— she would be sad for a while. But she was strong and she would recover.

He wished he'd given her more money. He wished he'd

asked her to stay and marry him. The estate would have slowly died around them but it was impossible to care about that with this terrible descent at his feet. Dukes and dukedoms were probably doomed anyway. The world had changed. The new order had no truck with *noblesse oblige*. If he hadn't lost everything, his heirs would have. Perhaps it took staring death in the face to see things clearly.

"What now?" He was shocked by how unafraid he sounded when he was quite sensibly terrified. The effect was almost careless and he was spiteful enough to enjoy squelching Nightingale's pleasure. He struggled to remember why this was happening. Something about his father mistreating Helen's mother. Was that what had made Nightingale angry? Or was he angry because the duke had bedded a woman he regarded as his? For these reasons, whether one or both of them, Nightingale had decided to enact some sort of biblical vengeance, punishing the son for the sins of the father.

"What's so funny?" Until Nightingale asked, Alex hadn't realized he was laughing.

It's all these murky motivations, he wanted to say. Didn't Nightingale realize he was supposed to make these things clear? Where was his sense of literary clarity?

"It all seems so incredibly petty," Alex said, trying to contain his mirth. "I didn't even *like* my father. Hardly anyone did. He hurt Helen and me more than he could ever possibly have hurt you. I'm afraid I find the fact I'm now to die for his sins absolutely hilarious."

Nightingale strode forward and pressed the gun into Alex's temple. "Stop bloody laughing."

Fear was the strangest thing. Having the gun so close and seeing the fury in Nightingale's eyes only made Alex laugh harder.

"Jump," Nightingale ordered.

"Excuse me?"

"Jump over, you arrogant fucker."

Alex sobered abruptly. Nightingale labored under a misapprehension if he thought Alex could be intimidated into a voluntary descent. Clearly he wanted Alex to feel all the terror of his predicament. This was Nightingale's way of drawing things out, of making Alex suffer.

"No," Alex said.

Nightingale dug the steel muzzle harder into the side of Alex's head. "If you don't go over, I'll blow your brains out here and now."

"Then do it."

Nightingale was nearly incandescent with rage. He should have shot Alex. Instead he placed his free hand flat against Alex's back and shoved. Perhaps Alex meant to steady himself or perhaps he intended to take the other man over with him. Either way, he flung an arm around Nightingale's neck. Nightingale struggled, almost dropping the revolver. They both grappled with the gun until it went off with a mighty crack that echoed in the open sky.

Nightingale hit the ground. The last thing Alex heard before he went over was Helen's scream.

Chapter Twenty

The front page of *The Illustrated London News* was torn and crumpled but still legible:

DUKE OF HARCASTLE DECEASED. SISTER WEEPS.

Evie had trodden it underfoot as she navigated the dirty street. She must have glanced down at her feet, reflexively checking for mud and worse as she picked her way along the pavement. And there it had been. Part of a paper dated from the day before. Old news. She didn't remember stooping to gather it up but now she held it in the glow of the streetlamp.

She'd been on her way to catch the packet, which was due to leave at first light. Each step had been an effort because each took her farther from where she truly wanted to be. It was like living life underwater with the current against her. Once she was on the boat, she kept telling herself, this feeling would ease. It had to or she'd spend the rest of her life forcing herself not to return to Alex.

The night she'd left Stoney Hey, the train had seemed a

safe haven. But the moment it began to pull away from the station, she'd felt panic like a bird flapping in her chest. Ever since, she had been at war with herself.

You shouldn't be here. You belong with him.

No, I don't. I can't.

But here and now, holding on to these old scraps of paper with their grainy sketch of Alex beneath that terrible headline, the war was suddenly and dreadfully over. She uncrumpled the pages and tried to read the words through ink that had been smudged by mist and drizzle. An accident, they said. A fall. Helen had witnessed it. The body—

Bile rose in her throat when she got to that part.

The *body* had yet to be recovered from the sea but the fall—hundreds of feet—was not survivable.

It had happened the night she left. He must have been searching for her. Why else would he be out there? Had some genuine accident befallen him or had Captain finally taken his revenge?

Dead. Alex was dead.

The tears wouldn't come. What was wrong with her that she couldn't cry? What a monster she was. She sank onto the ground, her skirts billowing around her. She wasn't fainting, had never felt more awake, but her legs wouldn't hold her upright. She didn't give a damn that she was on her knees where anyone might see her. A detached part of her mind noted the hard pavement, its scrape against her stockings, the wetness and dirt. A weight settled on her chest and in her stomach. A leaden hardness. This couldn't be grief. Grief was an empty, aching thing; she was so full she thought she must suffocate.

Only days ago, he'd held her against his chest and she'd heard his heart beating. He couldn't be dead. It was impossible to imagine a world without Alex even if she never saw him again. And to think she'd left him. Why had she done so when they could have spent every precious last moment together?

Memories flooded in. A rush of *what ifs*, of things she should have done differently. She'd never told him that she loved him. Hadn't even shown him. She'd been too great a coward. She wanted those moments back. She'd given him so little when she should have given everything. Even now she couldn't pay him the meager tribute of her tears.

She had to go back. If she didn't, she might never know what really happened to him. If it was Captain...

If it was Captain, she really thought she might kill him.

A fine mist of rain began to fall as she struggled to her feet. It didn't matter. Her skirts were soaked anyway from sitting on the ground. She turned her face up to the sky and closed her eyes. She couldn't think about what she'd lost or she'd go mad. She needed to be practical.

If she was going back to Yorkshire, she needed her bags, but they were already on the packet. It wasn't far to the docks but the narrow streets wound back on themselves. Dithering about whether to turn left or right proved an effective distraction but she despised herself a little that she could focus on mundane details at a time like this. His death didn't feel real yet. She needed to hear Helen say it was true before she could accept it. Despite this horrible weight pressing in on her, part of her still hoped this might turn out to be some terrible mistake. And that was madness, wasn't it?

The streetlamps were less frequent in this part of town and the alley she'd stopped in was very dark. At the far end, a light shone. If she was where she thought, the harbor should be visible by the time she reached the lamp. She took several deep breaths, and when she was sure she wouldn't stumble, she started forward.

As she stepped into the circle of lamplight, she hesitated, getting her bearings. Strong arms encircled her from behind.

She tried to scream but a hand clamped down over her mouth, smothering the sound. Her assailant yanked her backward into the darkest part of the alley. Spinning her to face him, he pushed her back into the wall.

In that first moment, she almost didn't recognize him. His beard was gone, revealing the square line of his jaw, his hair was shorter, and he was dressed plainly. But even with these changes, even in near total darkness, even terrified half out of her wits, she knew him. The feel of him. His scent. Even the taste of his skin pressed over her mouth.

"Easy, love," Alex whispered.

She stilled completely as his breath tickled her cheek, warm and vital. Alive. Her eyes roved every inch of his face, taking in the faint scrapes and bruises. *Thank God. Thank God.*

Slowly he relaxed his hold. Big mistake.

She slapped him. Awkwardly, ineffectually, but with feeling. Shock at her own actions robbed her of breath. She should apologize. After all, if their roles were reversed… But even as she thought it, she hit him again, on the shoulder this time. And again on the chest. And again and again. Her haphazard blows couldn't have hurt him. After the first, the strength had drained from her so that each new strike was weaker than the last. His efforts to restrain her flailing arms were hampered by his obvious desire not to hurt her. Conversely she couldn't seem to *stop* trying to hurt him.

At last, he pinned her against the wall with the weight of his body. She pushed against him to no avail, and suddenly unable to lash out, she burst into tears. She hadn't sensed it coming, didn't know what to do now that it had happened, but the relief was exquisite as the terrible pressure in her chest eased with each choking sob. Next came a shiver of feeling like the rush of blood into a limb that had been numb.

The only thing that made the surge of pain and joy and

gratitude bearable was his body covering hers and the sound of his voice in her ear. "I'm sorry, Evie. I'm sorry. Please don't."

"I thought you were dead."

"I'm here, love. I'm here with you."

"Please be real. Please, please be real."

"I'm real. I swear."

As tight as he held her, it wasn't enough. She needed it to hurt. She wanted bruises so that later she would know she hadn't imagined this. Her entire body shook.

"You were dead and I never told you. I *should* have told you."

"Yet you still don't." And there was a smile in his voice as if he found her inability to function like a normal woman utterly charming.

"I love you." Her voice broke. "I've loved you for so long."

He rested his forehead against hers and sighed. "Thank you." It could have been funny, that emphatic breath of a thanks, but his voice trembled with gratitude and relief.

Now that she'd finally spoken the words, the worst of her pain lifted and her tears slowed. She felt none of the fear and vulnerability she might have expected to feel after such a declaration. It didn't matter if he didn't say it back. She had spoken the truth and there was unexpected power in that. He held her, their bodies pressed together, and she knew he was almost as relieved to see her again as she was to see him. He must have rushed here unsure if he'd be in time to stop her.

He stroked her hair. "There's so much to say and I don't know where to start."

Evie did. "The paper said you fell. Is that true? Was it Captain? Where is he?"

"We should talk about this somewhere else. This is going to be difficult for you to hear."

He was dead then. No doubt she would be sad later, but

at that moment she had no room in her heart for anyone but Alex. "Tell me now. It won't be worse than what I'm imagining."

And so he told her what had happened. How Captain had wanted to kill him, how they had struggled with the gun which had gone off. How Alex had slipped over the edge of the cliff but how he'd caught hold of an exposed root. He would have died if Helen hadn't been there to help him. While Captain lay bleeding, she and Dr. Carter had saved Alex's life.

"The shot got him in the stomach. By the time they had me safe, he'd fallen unconscious or that was how it seemed."

"Seemed? What do you mean?"

"Helen took me to the gatehouse to look at my wounds while Carter went to fetch his medical bag. By the time he got back, Nightingale had gone. That was the last we saw of him."

"Then he's alive?"

"He looked half dead when we left him. I don't see how he could have survived, but then where is he?"

She didn't know and dozens of other questions clamored for answers. "The paper said you died and that Helen witnessed it. How could they get things so wrong?"

"Ah." He tilted her chin up so that he could see her expression in the feeble dawn light. "The papers didn't make a mistake, not really. They reported what Helen told them. What I asked her to tell them."

The world wobbled on its axis. Or she wobbled. Until now she had been overjoyed at his survival and determined to soak up every moment she had with him until they were forced to part by his inevitable marriage. Now came a trembling hope that he might be about to offer her even more.

He gazed at her expectantly. She had to say something but she didn't want to leap to conclusions. "I don't understand."

"I told you there was only one way for me to save my family's legacy but that isn't true. There's another path

I hadn't considered because it's…well, quite frankly it's immoral and illegal."

She felt a smile tugging at her lips. "Go on."

"Ellis once pointed out that the duchy's finances would be in much better shape if I died. He was joking, of course, but he was also right."

"You're talking about insurance fraud." She eased away from him and began to pace the little stretch of alley nearest them. "You're telling me that everyone thinks you're dead?"

"Not everyone. Helen and Dr. Carter know the truth."

"Dr. Carter? He must be horrified." Even her brief acquaintance with the man had been enough for her to notice his obvious integrity. But he was also besotted with his wife. He would probably do almost anything to make Helen happy.

"Are you?" he asked.

"No, but I'm a terrible person. You shouldn't use me as your moral barometer."

"You are the only woman I've ever loved. The only woman I ever want to marry. I think you are wonderful and extraordinary, but…" He smiled crookedly. "Point taken."

She heard his declaration, but this was too serious. Despite the little skip her heart gave, she was not going to allow him to distract her from the folly of what he proposed. "And the man who apparently prompted this idea? Is he in on it, too?" After all, Mr. Ellis would be the financial beneficiary of this mad scheme.

"Absolutely not. Yes, he joked about this weeks ago, but he would never knowingly participate in anything like this. He's far more suited to be Harcastle than I ever was. What he lacks in presence he makes up for with industriousness and competence. He's thoroughly honorable almost to the point of dullness. Helen and Will have both sworn never to tell him."

Evie wasn't so sure. "You don't think the insurance

money and all the castles might tempt him?"

"If there's one person who wants to be Harcastle even less than I, it's Ellis. The very mention of the possibility always turns him green. It's the part of this that troubles me most. If he knew I even contemplated this, he'd never forgive me."

"Is this why you shaved? It's not much of a disguise even with the clothes and the haircut."

"That's where you come in." He took both her hands in his. "If anyone can help a duke to disappear, it's you."

"This is madness."

"It wouldn't be anything like the life of a duchess or even of a duke's mistress, that's certain. We won't be poor, either. I have money with me and Helen, the sole beneficiary of my personal fortune, will send the rest once the funds are released."

"You know I never cared about any of that." And she had five hundred pounds. As long as neither one of them proved to be a spendthrift, they could manage well enough financially. For her, these were untold riches. "Is this really what *you* want? Do you really think this is a life that can make you happy?"

"I was never happy as Harcastle until I met you. When I'm with you, whoever I am, whatever I'm called, it's like nothing I've ever known. If you don't feel the same—"

"I do. You know I do. There's nothing I want more than to be with you, whatever life you choose." The declaration rolled off her tongue so easily, she wondered why she'd ever been afraid of this. Afraid of him.

A ghost of a smile lit his face as if he understood. "Then let's choose one together."

Oh God, she was going to say yes. Part of her had known that the whole time they'd been talking. Yes to everything. Whatever he wanted.

"Trust me."

The sun was nearly risen, so she did what she had never done before; she let her guard down, discarded that inscrutability Captain had taught her to wear like a mask. She let Alex see everything that was in her heart. Love, fear, her absolute belief in him, in *them*, and the chance they were about to take. "Yes."

"Yes?"

"Yes."

He crushed her to his chest in relief and joy. When he kissed her, it seemed impossible that it was the first time he'd done so since he dragged her into this dank and dirty alley. The surroundings might be less than salubrious but the kiss made such considerations irrelevant. She didn't even miss the beard. The smooth warmth of his skin on hers made up for the loss.

"If we're really going to do this," she said when he let her up for air, "there's something you should know."

He lifted his eyebrows. "More dark secrets?"

"No. It's only..." It was hard to tell him. It had been so long since she'd told anyone. "Hannah. My name—my *original* name—is Hannah. For what it's worth."

His eyes glittered. He swallowed and when he spoke, his voice trembled with emotion. "It's worth a great deal." He offered his hand. "It's an honor to meet you."

She took it and smiled. "I don't know my last name, if I ever had one."

"You can share mine." He shrugged. "Once you've helped me pick one."

"We'll discuss it on the way. Let's hope the boat hasn't gone."

Arm in arm, with the whole world to explore, they emerged from the dark of the alley. The dismal weather didn't matter anymore. For both of them, and for the first time, anything was possible.

Acknowledgments

Thanks first to Mr. Bennet for his unfailing support, technical assistance (all writers should marry software engineers or become one themselves) and marketing savvy. I love you more now than I did the day I married you (and that was a whole lot!)

Thank you to the Bookends team, especially Jessica Alvarez for everything you do, including being the first person besides me to read this one. Your advice made the manuscript stronger and your encouragement helped me through the winter doldrums.

Thank you to everyone at Entangled, especially my amazing editor, Alethea Spiridon. Your enthusiasm for this story has meant so much to me. I'd also like to thank Julia Knapman, my copy editor, for her keen eyes.

Thanks to all the Stannies and Shillies for their words of encouragement, to Jane and Jacquie for their help through a difficult winter, and to my mother for her support, even though she read the sex scenes in my previous book *The Madness of Miss Grey* after I encouraged her not to.

I'd also like to thank the late Houdini. Without "A Magician among the Spirits," I wouldn't have a clue how Victorian spiritualists tricked their clients.

Thank you too to all my readers and reviewers. I honestly appreciate each and every one of you.

About the Author

Julia spent years looking for something to do with her English degree. Insurance underwriting, proofreading academic papers, and waitressing all proved unsatisfying. She spent an alarming amount of time daydreaming at her desk until she decided she might as well put the stories in her head down on paper.

When Julia isn't writing, she enjoys spending time with her two children and her amazing husband/I.T. support.

Also by Julia Bennet...

THE MADNESS OF MISS GREY

Discover more Amara titles...

An Unsuitable Lady for a Lord
a novel by Cathleen Ross

Lord Aaron Lyle has an impossible choice: a bankrupt dukedom, or marriage to some simpering society miss with a huge dowry. Honestly? He'd rather run naked through London. Surely, there must be a third option. Lady Crystal Wilding is a proud bluestocking. Aaron is intrigued...and invites the totally unsuitable lady home, presenting her as a possible match. Imagine their shock when his highly proper family loves her subversive ideas and starts planning the wedding.

The Bewildered Bride
an *Advertisements for Love* novel by Vanessa Riley

Ruth, a Blackamoor heiress, eloped with her true love to Gretna Green. Adam Wilky is a baron—which he never told Ruth. Going back to London, they are nearly beaten to death and he was sold into impressment. Each thought the other dead. Four years later, Adam returns and discovers Ruth alive. But she is furious about all the secrets and it'll take more than remembered passion if he hopes to win his wife back.

THE DUKE'S WICKED WIFE
a *Wicked Secrets* novel by Elizabeth Bright

Sebastian Sinclair, Duke of Wessex, is not in love with Eliza Benton—nor anyone else. But he must marry and produce an heir, and love is not required for either. His future duchess must be of high birth and good nature, a lady unlikely to snipe at him over breakfast. In short, the complete opposite of Eliza. So who better to help him find a suitable bride?

TO TAME A SCANDALOUS LADY
a *Once Upon a Scandal* novel by Liana De la Rosa

Christian Andrews, Marquess of Amstead, notices his assistant trainer has a special way with the horses. But once he realizes *he* is a *she*...and a very beautiful, spirited *she*...he should sack her before scandal breaks. Headstrong Lady Flora Campbell embraces her dream of working with racehorses and disguises herself as a lad to learn as much as she can from premiere expert, Christian Andrews. Although she develops a tendre for the dashing marquess, she can never let on she's not only a woman, but the daughter of a duke...

Printed in Great Britain
by Amazon